A burst of rounds ... e earth, inc...

"Jack, I need a p...

Bolan pivoted to h... sensed the ATV almost on top of him. At the same time he lashed out with his gun hand. The Beretta smashed into the rider's face, knocking him off the vehicle. The ATV continued for several feet before coming to a stop.

The Executioner raced to the vehicle, swung his leg over the seat, holstered his gun and hit the accelerator. The fence loomed a long fifty yards away. More rounds zipped by. The soldier's only saving grace was that the uneven terrain made it difficult for his pursuers to acquire a decent sight.

Suddenly Bolan spotted headlights barreling down the highway. Moments later, the front of an Escalade smashed into the fence with a resounding crunch. The driver's window rolled down and an M-16/M-203 poked through the opening.

Jack Grimaldi had arrived.

Other titles available in this series:

Point of Betrayal	Savage Rule
Ballistic Force	Infiltration
Renegade	Resurgence
Survival Reflex	Kill Shot
Path to War	Stealth Sweep
Blood Dynasty	Grave Mercy
Ultimate Stakes	Treason Play
State of Evil	Assassin's Code
Force Lines	Shadow Strike
Contagion Option	Decision Point
Hellfire Code	Road of Bones
War Drums	Radical Edge
Ripple Effect	Fireburst
Devil's Playground	Oblivion Pact
The Killing Rule	Enemy Arsenal
Patriot Play	State of War
Appointment in Baghdad	Ballistic
Havana Five	Escalation Tactic
The Judas Project	Crisis Diplomacy
Plains of Fire	Apocalypse Ark
Colony of Evil	Lethal Stakes
Hard Passage	Illicit Supply
Interception	Explosive Demand
Cold War Reprise	Ground Zero
Mission: Apocalypse	Jungle Firestorm
Altered State	Terror Ballot
Killing Game	Death Metal
Diplomacy Directive	Justice Run
Betrayed	China White
Sabotage	Payback
Conflict Zone	Chain Reaction
Blood Play	Nightmare Army
Desert Fallout	Critical Exposure
Extraordinary Rendition	Insurrection
Devil's Mark	Armed Response

DON PENDLETON'S MACK BOLAN®

DESERT FALCONS

A GOLD EAGLE BOOK FROM
WORLDWIDE®

TORONTO • NEW YORK • LONDON
AMSTERDAM • PARIS • SYDNEY • HAMBURG
STOCKHOLM • ATHENS • TOKYO • MILAN
MADRID • WARSAW • BUDAPEST • AUCKLAND

Recycling programs
for this product may
not exist in your area.

First edition June 2015

ISBN-13: 978-0-373-61577-3

Special thanks and acknowledgment to
Michael A. Black for his contribution to this work.

Desert Falcons

Printed in U.S.A.

With reasonable men, I will reason; with humane men I will plead; but to tyrants I will give no quarter, nor waste arguments where they will certainly be lost.
—William Lloyd Garrison,
1805–1879

No quarter given. Ever. We must fight back with all our might until the terror threat is contained. Our very freedom is at stake. I will not stand down.
—Mack Bolan

CHAPTER ONE

The Bouncy-Berry Club, Manama, Bahrain

Mahfuj bin Mustapha Rahman watched as the oscillating lights on the ceiling spun, casting variations of color over the gyrating bodies in the center of the room. The flickering beams made his eyes jump, which was disturbing, considering the nature of his mission. What was even more disturbing was the ongoing scene underneath the glow of those blinking, colored bulbs.

Women, albeit Europeans and Westerners, twisted themselves in obscene positions as they flaunted their bodies like the infidel whores they were. At least Rahman hoped the women were infidels. To think of the possibility of a Muslim woman behaving in this manner made the scene even more distasteful. But they were still in a Muslim country, although Bahrain was hardly known for its devout fundamentalism. It was bad enough that Muslim men sneaked to this insignificant island, changed into Western garb, and danced with equally careless abandon. Again, they were mostly Europeans along with a smattering of Americans. U.S. sailors, from the looks of them, bouncing up and down, ogling the females, but Mahfuj was certain that some of them were Saudis. He was certain of one, in particular.

It disgusted him beyond revulsion, and he wished

more than anything that he could step out of this den of iniquity and into the cool night air. But his mission would not allow it, so he filed away the unpleasantness along with all the other sacrifices he had made in the name of God on this jihad, and steeled himself for what he knew was coming. So what if they were all behaving like animals, with the liquor flowing freely from the bar behind them. He had to remain strong. His task demanded it. But what made it more difficult, what disturbed him even more were the stroboscopic glimpses of Prince Amir bin Abdul Sattam Saud, the tall, handsome, well-built man in the tan shirt and blue pants, rotating his hips opposite the infidel whore, the man whose safety Mahfuj had been commanded to ensure.

To think that a member of the house of Saud, the Royal Family, the leaders of his country behaving in such a manner as to disgrace himself….

The prince had changed out of his traditional *thobe* and *ghutra* as soon as his private jet had landed in Bahrain. He'd told his bodyguards to change into Western-style clothing, as well. Many Saudis did that on their trips to Bahrain, to "relax," which was nothing more than a euphemism for their apostate behavior, away from the watchful eyes of the secret police.

Nevertheless, Mahfuj had complied, taking care to wear a loose-fitting shirt due to the bulge created by his sidearm, a Beretta 92 F, so it would not be noticeable strapped in the holster on his belt. The clothes felt foreign to him even though he'd worn them numerous times on these excursions with the prince. They were less confining than his uniform, and this was one time he couldn't afford to let anything interfere with the success of the first phase of the operation.

Mahfuj felt the cell phone in his pants pocket vibrate with an incoming message. He had switched to the silent mode the moment they walked into the place. The blaring music from huge speakers eliminated any chance that he would be able to hear the ring tone, and he couldn't afford to miss the call from his brother Mamum. Taking the phone from his pocket, Mahfuj pressed the button so he could view the text message.

The moment has arrived, God willing.

It was time for the four desert falcons to begin their great jihad.

Mustapha, their father, was the first falcon. Mahfuj, his first born, was the second. Mamum, his younger brother by one year, was the third, and the youngest brother, Masoud, was the fourth. Each had his individual strengths. Mahfuj had always been the strongest, Mamum the most patient, and Masoud the most adaptable. That was why he had been chosen for the foreign assignment. Masoud could blend into any background, like a true *Bedouin*.

Mahfuj replaced the phone in his pocket and moved toward the door, imbuing his movements with as much nonchalance as he could. The dance floor of the nightclub occupied the center of the room, with tables surrounding it and the long, wooden bar running along the rear wall. The entrance had been curtained off by an enclosed corridor, perhaps three meters long, preventing people entering from seeing inside the club. At the doors, a big, muscular security guard stood poised to check and monitor all who sought to enter. Mahfuj glanced at the man, who nodded and smiled, his teeth glowing white among the dark hairs of his beard.

As Mahfuj positioned himself by the interior corner, next to the draped shroud of the canopy obscuring the corridor, he thought of the dream his father had repeatedly told them when they were young boys. How the vision of four falcons sweeping down from the heavens had awakened him, only to allow him a fleeting glimpse of four actual birds of prey diving down upon a cluster unsuspecting rodents. Their father said he knew the dream had been a sign from God.

"At that moment I knew, as I watched the birds' sharp talons sinking into the rodents' flesh, that I would have three sons," his father had said. "We would be four desert falcons, who would be true *Bedouins*, true to our traditions, true to the will of God, who would guide us."

Mahfuj's cell phone vibrated again. He moved closer to the door and then paused to glance back at the gyrating bodies on the dance floor. The prince swung his arms in front of him, looking like a man battling some invisible demon.

At the far end of the corridor the door opened and Mahfuj positioned himself just on the other side of the canopy, out of sight to anyone who entered. Despite the music, he could hear the quick angry shout of the security guard, followed by the piercing pop of a gunshot. Mahfuj's cell phone vibrated again in his pocket, but he did not acknowledge or look at it. Instead he quickly surveyed the dance floor to fix the prince's position. He was on the far right side, still swinging his arms in front of him, dancing with some European whore whose large breasts bounced obscenely under a thin layer of cloth.

Mahfuj waited a few seconds more, not daring to

glance around the corner of the canopy. The flashes from the oscillating lights and the vibrations of the blaring music swept over him like a desert sandstorm, but he steeled himself and remained ready. The man on the other side of the cloth barrier stepped forward, the barrel of his AK-47 rifle preceding him only by inches. Mahfuj reached out and seized the shiny barrel with his right hand just as the man yelled, "*Allahu Akbar*!"

The barrel jerked in Mahfuj's hand. The heat seared his flesh, but his hand was thickly callused, his grip strong, enhanced by the daily exercises he performed immediately after morning prayers. A stream of fire shot outward and Mahfuj was pelted by a stream of hot, ejected shell casings. Still, he held fast to the barrel, allowing the rounds to penetrate the left side of the dance floor. Intermittent screams punctuated the loud music as the dancers twisted and fell under the rain of bullets.

It was essential that his heroism be enhanced by the requisite spilling of blood, like the traditional sacrificing of a lamb. Mahfuj pivoted and cocked his left arm, then whipped the toughened edge of his straightened hand against the assassin's throat, at the juncture of his neck and body. The soft tissue gave way, and Mahfuj felt the popping yield of connecting tissue telling him that he'd succeeded in crushing the man's windpipe. After a few seconds more, the rifle ceased its roar of death, and Mahfuj ripped it from the dying man's hands.

In one smooth motion, he flipped the weapon in such a manner as to bring his hands into a firing position, and sent a 3-round burst into the crumbling figure next to him. As the man dropped to the floor, Mahfuj brought the weapon to his shoulder just as a second man, holding a rifle and three grenades, pushed his way into the door of the club. Mahfuj shot the man in the chest, allowing the rounds to stitch upward to the would-be killer's head. This second man fell.

There would be one more. Mahfuj sidestepped and waited in place, not wanting to advance and thus expose himself in the confines of the corridor. It was, as his military tactics training had taught him, a kill zone. Instead, he forced himself to take a long, deep breath. The acrid smoke from the spent cartridges hung in the air, searing his lungs, burning his eyes; his injured right hand stung with the pain of a thousand needles, but still he did not lower the rifle or relax his guard.

His patience was rewarded seconds later when the third would-be assassin pushed through the door, wild-eyed and holding his AK-47 at port arms.

Foolish move, Mahfuj thought as he leaned around the draping shroud and squeezed off another 3-round burst. The third man dropped to the floor.

Mahfuj stepped forward, kicking the weapons away from the fallen men, pausing to put a round in the back of each of their heads, and then waiting when he got to the door. He glanced through the Plexiglas window and caught a glimpse of the dark van in which the killers had arrived. He kicked open the door, thrust the barrel of the rifle outward and fired off the remaining rounds in the magazine. He was careful to control his aim as the van sped off down the brightly lit street.

He watched it go, still holding the AK-47 in the ready position, its bolt now locked back, indicating an expended magazine.

The taillights of the van receded into the darkness, obscured by the bright dots of the ubiquitous street and building lights. As his hearing slowly returned, Mahfuj thought he could hear the sound of distant police sirens. He let the door swing closed and strode back into the club, holding the rifle in one hand now, so that it looked less threatening. As he rounded the corner, his eyes swept over the dance floor once again. People were huddled in corners and along the bar. Several bodies lay on the floor, some writhing with death throes, others eerily still. Mahfuj kept scanning their faces until he located Prince Amir, crouching in a corner. He strode over to him.

"Your Highness," Mahfuj said, "are you all right?"

The prince's face was awash with the varying colors under the flashing lights. He nodded. The three other members of the prince's bodyguard contingent ran over and flanked them.

"Thanks be to God." Mahfuj extended his hand toward the noble. "Come, my prince. We must leave immediately for a place of safety."

The prince accepted the extended hand and rose on shaky legs. "Mahfuj, you saved my life."

Mahfuj dropped the AK-47 on the floor and led the prince toward the rear exit, directing one of the other bodyguards to get their vehicle. "It was nothing, Your Majesty."

The prince's face jerked into a weak smile as his eyes showed both gratitude and admiration.

And it *was* nothing, Mahfuj thought as he pushed through the people who were slowly rising. After all, stopping a trio of killers was not that hard when you knew how many there would be, what door they'd be using, how they'd be armed, and exactly when they were coming.

Royal Palace, Riyadh, Saudi Arabia

ALHAMDULILLAH, THE MESSAGE SAID. Praise be to God.

Mustapha bin Ahmad Rahman smiled as he read the text on his cell phone, then erased the word. It had come from his eldest son, Mahfuj. Mustapha had overseen the training of his three sons well, and his first born was the strongest and most capable. Yet each of them fit into his overall plan like the fingers of a glove. God willing, all would proceed now that the time had finally come to set things into motion. He glanced at the clock. It was close to midnight, and the elderly king would surely be sleeping. Mustapha knew he would have to wait until the proper notifications came through official channels that the attempt on the life of the king's favorite great grandson, Prince Amir, had been thwarted by his loyal bodyguards, most specifically, Muhfuj.

Mustapha picked up the watch he had disassembled and began working on repairing its intricacies. It had been his hobby since learning the craft from his own grandfather as a small boy. The old man had loved tinkering as a watchmaker, but he was also a secret revolutionary. When his fingers had been blown off building a bomb, he trained Mustapha to take over as the watchmaker. Working with these tiny, intricate, precise parts was his solace of late, a way to relax, like a slow journey through the desert on the back of a camel.

Mustapha was the son of the son of one of the lesser princes fathered by a less-favored son with one of his lesser wives, so his status as a member of the royal family was ensured by his bloodline. Thus, the success of his career as an officer in the military, replete with accomplishments, was a foregone conclusion. Promotions came to him, and soon he'd found himself in the enviable position of full colonel. However, just as the status of his bloodline assured his success, the less than favorable status of his father's father within the house of Saud also relegated him to an inconvenient obscurity. Mustapha worked hard, learning all that he could about the Koran, history and military tactics, which would enable him to become a great leader one day. But eventually the true nature of his position became clear to him. While it ensured comfort and success, he would never attain the coveted favorite, heir-apparent status for which he felt he was destined. He was the offspring of a lesser royal; he was a man who would never be king.

Yet the desire to lead, to achieve greatness burned within Mustapha like a hard, gem-like flame. It fueled his ambition and slowly, cautiously had allowed him to secretly build a base of support among both the enlisted and officer ranks of the military. His physical prowess and other qualities made him a natural leader. Others, even those above him in rank, looked up to him. That he should lead was always obvious, and now, soon, the entire country would see this, would feel the same, but not in a nation vainly named after one family, the House of Saud. No, Saudi Arabia would become simply Arabia. And he would be President Mustapha bin Ahmad Rahman.

He would not make the same mistakes as his predecessors had in 1969 when the air force officers, emboldened by Khaddafi's success in Libya, let hubris and indiscretion overshadow their better judgment. If someone planned to kill the king, he had to be certain the blow was not only fatal, but not anticipated. Word of their plan came to the attention of the United States, and the subsequent intervention of the Americans, who warned King Faisal of the military's plan, had been its ultimate undoing.

This time, however, it would be different. This coup would not be spoiled by indiscreet words or intercepted messages. This time there would be no discovery or intervention by the Americans. No, this desert falcon was wise and learned from the mistakes of others.

Yes, he was the man who would never be king, but he would be president.

It was the will of God, he thought. I will succeed.

Mustapha used the narrow tweezers to clip the last piston into place, then rotated the timepiece and watched as the tiny gears of the Rolex began clicking with a quintessential precision. He replaced its back and set it aside as he removed the second, seemingly identical watch from a pocket in his *thobe*. This one was the same only in superficial appearance. It was not even a true Rolex. Rather, this ersatz version had been given to them by the Russian. It contained the tiny, special tablets designed to induce a fatal cardiac arrhythmia, one of which Mustapha had used to eliminate his predecessor, the minister of defense, leaving the door open for his quick appointment to that esteemed position. It had been the first overt move of his highly complex plan. As a rule, Mustapha knew that it was better to keep a plan simple to ensure success, but when a person wished to eliminate a king, and change a country, an enhanced degree of complexity was requisite. This plan had to be worthy of toppling a king.

It bore a strange similarity to working on a highly sophisticated timepiece: many small intricate parts, all working in conjunction, producing the necessary movements to move the hands of time.

There was a knock on his door, and he quickly pocketed the ersatz Rolex. As he rose, the door opened, and the face of Hamid, the ultra-loyal assistant of the deputy prime minister and the king's bodyguard, appeared in the crack.

"Forgive me, sir, but I saw that your light was on," Hamid said.

Mustapha already knew what this intrusion was about but feigned a benevolent ignorance. He smiled. "Yes, I was up late working on the king's watch."

Hamid's eyes shot to the Rolex. "You have finished it? It is his favorite."

"Not quite yet," Mustapha said. "It is a very complicated timepiece. Many intricate parts that must all function in unison." He lifted an eyebrow. "Is there something you need?"

Hamid nodded and clasped his hands in front of him. "There has been an attempt on the life of Prince Amir."

Mustapha jumped to his feet, continuing his sham. "What? Is he all right?"

Hamid nodded vigorously. "The prince said I was to summon you first, before we awakened the king."

"Of course. We must do so immediately. I will accompany you both."

Hamid straightened his body to its full height. "He also wished me to tell you that your son was the one who saved the prince. He is a hero."

Mustapha nodded. "Thank God. It is well that I named him so aptly—Muhfuj, the protector."

He barely was able to conceal his glee. It was all unfolding as he'd planned.

CHAPTER TWO

Stony Man Farm, Virginia

Mack Bolan jabbed twice and then sent a whistling right cross into the heavy bag with a resounding thump. Jack Grimaldi, who was holding the bag against his body, was propelled back a foot and groaned.

"Man, I bet they felt that one all the way back in South Bend, Indiana," he said.

Bolan chuckled and delivered another rapid series of punches, concluding with a left hook that jolted Grimaldi off balance once again.

"That's it," the Stony Man pilot said, stepping back and letting the bag swing freely. "Round's over."

Bolan glanced at the timer mounted on the wall and shook his head, continuing to punch. "Not for another minute."

"It's over for me." Grimaldi shook his head and wiped his face with his towel. "Besides, it feels like it's raining in here."

They were in the gym at Stony Man Farm. Bolan was sweating profusely due not only to the intensity of his workout, but also the vinyl suit he was wearing. He sent another combination into the bag, sending a spray of perspiration with each blow.

The timer finally rang. Bolan stopped punching and

reached for his towel. He wiped the sweat off his face and neck, and when the timer sounded again, indicating his minute's rest was over, he tossed the towel down and moved to the bag again.

Grimaldi sat on a nearby medicine ball, leaning over with his arms resting on his knees.

"Hey, you have to slow down," he said. "You're making me tired just watching you."

Bolan stepped closer to the inside and began working left and right uppercuts. He caught a flash of movement by the door and whirled.

Barbara Price, the Farm's mission controller, entered the gym and smiled.

"So there you two are." She was dressed in a red sweater and blue jeans that accentuated her curves. Her hand swept her honey-blond hair away from her face as she smiled. "I've been looking for you."

Bolan took a moment to appreciate her beauty and then went back to punching again.

"I'm glad you're here," Grimaldi said. "Now you can hold the bag."

"I would," she said, "but I forgot my raincoat. You're leaving more water on the floor than an autumn thunderstorm."

Bolan delivered a double left hook, low and high.

"Besides," Price said, "Hal's been trying to get hold of you. You haven't been answering your phones."

Grimaldi slapped his sides, then held up his hands. "Not too many pockets in this outfit."

Bolan stopped. "Why? What's up?"

"I'd better let him tell you that. He's in the War Room."

Grimaldi jumped to his feet. "Well, I guess that settles it. Workout's over. Let's hit the showers."

THIRTY MINUTES LATER Bolan and Grimaldi were seated at a conference table across from Hal Brognola, director of the Sensitive Operations Group, based at Stony Man Farm. The big Fed picked up a remote and pressed some buttons that turned on a large flat-screen monitor.

"Nice of you two to drop by," Brognola said. "I've been trying to track you down for over an hour. I should've known you'd either be in the gym or on the range."

"That isn't my fault," Grimaldi said. "Superman here had to get his workout in as soon as we got back."

Brognola got up and poured a cup of coffee from a coffeemaker behind his desk. He took a sip, frowned and shook his head.

"Looks like Aaron made the coffee. As good as ever?" Grimaldi asked.

"It'll put hair on your chest and part it down the middle," Brognola stated. "I had to brief him on a matter. He just left."

Aaron, "the Bear" Kurtzman was renowned for his terrible coffee and his unparalleled computer expertise.

"What's so urgent?" Bolan asked.

Brognola brought the mug to his lips again, started to take another sip, then apparently thought better of it. He set the mug on his desk and pressed another button on the remote. The big screen jumped forward to a frozen-frame depiction of two groups of people facing off on a two-lane asphalt road bisecting a bleak, desertlike landscape. The earth looked brownish-tan and was punctuated with dots of grass, mesquite and mountains in the background. Most of the figures were in tan uniforms, apparently law enforcement of some kind, and at least four of them held back snarling leashed German shepherd dogs. A few extended their arms with various weapons that ranged from handguns to stun guns. Several more of the uniformed men held shotguns.

They faced another group of armed men who stood on the opposite side of the road. They were dressed in desert camouflage BDUs, their black caps low on their foreheads, and carried what appeared to be AR-15 rifles. A gaggle of civilians, both men and women, were interspersed in between the respective uniformed groups. On the right edge of the frozen image a large, dark area partially blocked out the rest of the view.

"You probably saw this on the news last week," Brognola said. "It was out in Nevada."

"Well, we've been a little busy lately," Bolan said. "Remember?"

Brognola nodded and pressed the remote again. The frozen scene jumped to life as the sound of loud voices and barking dogs emanated from the television's speakers. The group of officers moved forward, behind the lurching dogs. One of them apparently sprayed some sort of aerosol irritant toward the agitated civilians. A few of them retreated, coughing and wheezing. The black-hatted camouflaged figures didn't move and kept their rifles at port arms. The darkened section at the right side of the screen jolted forward, and it became apparent that it was actually the rear flank of a horse. The man atop the steed was brandishing an upside-down American flag on a six-foot pole. The horse trotted forward. Both the uniformed officers and the civilians backed up to opposite sides of the road as the animal began snorting. A reporter appeared on the left side of the screen holding a microphone. His anxious expression gave way to a nervous smile as he began to speak in a tremulous voice.

"This ongoing dispute between rancher Rand Autry and the federal authorities has been escalating to a critical confrontation for weeks now over a dispute about open range grazing and water rights and the government's claim that Mr. Autry has repeatedly refused to pay taxes for these activities. In response to a cease-and-desist order along with the forced confiscation of a portion of Mr. Autry's cattle, an armed group calling themselves the People's New Minutemen Militia have announced their support for Mr. Autry and have assembled at the entrance to his property in what they have termed an affront to the pursuit of life, liberty and the pursuit of happiness. Federal authorities—"

Brognola punched the remote and froze the video again. He turned to Bolan and Grimaldi.

"Life, liberty and the pursuit of happiness," Grimaldi said. "That's a catchy phrase. I wonder where they got that one?"

"Don't let the rhetoric fool you," Brognola said as he held up his hand, forming a small space between his index finger and thumb. "They were this close to a full-scale confrontation. That's Rand Autry riding the horse with the flag in distress."

"Who were the uniforms?" Grimaldi asked. "State police?"

Brognola shook his head. "Bureau of Land Management park rangers."

"Interesting," Bolan said. "But hardly something we would get involved in, right?"

Brognola took another sip of coffee and grinned. "It gets better." He pressed the remote and fast-forwarded the video, stopping on a picture of Autry holding the flag on the horse as the animal reared on its hind legs. The picture dissolved, and a new image appeared of the same man, clad in a Stetson hat and a bright, Western-style shirt, standing in front of a lectern with a panoramic painting of picturesque mountains and flowing rivers on a huge panel behind him. The words Land of the Free were stenciled in black letters over the mountains. He appeared to be addressing an audience in a medium-sized auditorium.

"We are all gathered here at Camp Freedom today to celebrate our freedom and our way of life," Autry said, "and to address the most critical and dangerous threat to our existence since the Communists. I'm talking about our current administration in Washington and the secret deals they're making to circumvent the American way of life. They're defiling the very law of the land, denying the very things that made this country great."

The audience applauded.

Autry bowed his head slightly in appreciation and acknowledgment. "As we speak, they've been playing both ends against the middle, coddling the Jews in Israel, while making deals with the Muslims, all to support the welfare state our great country has become supporting urban blacks who've made our city streets free-fire zones. Our cities have regressed a hundred years, back to the times when we worried about the marauding Indian tribes. And it's not enough that the federal government is flaunting these things in front of our faces every day on the five o'clock news, but they continue to tax the common folk, the people who built this great country, to pay for it all. As far as the government's concerned, 'we the people' doesn't apply if you're a white American, despite the fact that the blacks, Indians and Latinos are all supported by our tax dollars that the government continues to take and take and take."

As Autry held up his fist, Brognola froze the image once again.

"Thanks," Bolan said. "A little of that guy goes a long way."

"He's a real equal-opportunity bigot, all right," Grimaldi added. "Is there any ethnic group he hasn't managed to insult?"

Brognola chuckled.

"He mentioned Camp Freedom," Bolan stated. "What's that?"

"His rather sizable ranch just outside of Las Vegas," Brognola said. "In recent years it's been transformed into a veritable fortress, with Autry and his son as the commandants."

"I think we saw his better image in the first recording," Grimaldi said. "The horse's ass. But at least he didn't say anything derogatory about the Italians."

"Give him time," Brognola replied. "He's managed to offend just about everybody."

"As much as I dislike loud-mouthed bigots," Bolan said, "what does this have to do with us?"

Brognola swiveled his chair back to the conference table and placed his crossed forearms on its top. "Autry's got serious money problems. Although he's purported to have sizable assets, he owes the government a lot, to the tune of fifteen million. He's desperate. The word is that there's been some suspicious goings-on in southern Nevada, including dealings with the Mexican cartels and a possible arms deal. The People's New Minutemen Militia, which you got a glimpse of in that news piece, is rumored to be interested in purchasing some pretty serious weaponry at Autry's behest. Russian organized crime is purportedly involved."

"It sounds more like a job for ATF than us," Bolan replied. "This guy may be a loudmouth and a public nuisance, but he's hardly a blip on our radar, is he?"

Brognola shook his head slowly. "There's a bit more than just that going on. Ever hear of Prince Amir bin Abdul Sattam Saud?"

"Prince Amir?" Bolan asked. "As in one of the lesser-knowns in the Royal Family of Saudi Arabia?"

Brognola nodded. "One and the same. While he's one of many royal heirs to the throne, it's rumored he's the king's favorite grandson. He's got the reputation of being something of a playboy."

"Man, I bet women flock to him," Grimaldi said.

"In droves, apparently," Brognola said. "While there's certainly no shortage of heir-apparents, Prince Amir is thought to be a real-deal contender. Like I said, he's the king's favorite grandson.

"There was an attempt on the prince's life last night in Bahrain. It was foiled by his bodyguards."

"Who tried to kill him?" Bolan asked.

"As far as we know," Brognola said, "and the Saudis and Bahrainis are playing this close to their vests, the assassins were Shi'ite Saudis from the Eastern Province."

"Sunnis and Shi'ites," Grimaldi said. "They've been going at it just about forever."

"There's no moderation when it comes to their disputes," Brognola stated.

"Moderation," Grimaldi said. "No such word in their dictionary."

"Have either of you ever hear of Colonel Herbert Francis Coltrain?"

"The publisher of *Mercenary One* magazine?" Grimaldi said. "Yeah, I met him a couple years ago at the Shot Show in Vegas. That guy's been almost as many hot places as we have."

"Well, he founded the Desert Warfare Training Academy some ten years ago. It's a rather prestigious school. They trained a lot of the Private Military Organizations we were using over in Iraq and Afghanistan. His instructors were all ex-military, a lot of them special-ops vets."

"The operative word being 'were'?" Bolan asked.

Brognola nodded. "Colonel Coltrain sold the school about a year or so ago to some foreign company. They made a few changes, including personnel, but it's still considered one of the preeminent nonmilitary training academies around."

"All that's interesting," Bolan said. "But how does that factor into our current situation?"

Brognola sighed. "The prince is scheduled to attend the desert warfare tactics school out in Nevada this coming week. With all of the anti-Muslim stuff this guy Autry's been spewing, and the rumors of his militia boys trying to gear up for something big, the President's a little worried that things could go to hell in a handbasket in a hurry."

"I can't say as I can blame him," Bolan said. "What does he want us to do?"

"Go out there and keep an eye on things. The prince will have some Secret Service guys watching over him, but with this Bureau of Land Management dispute with Autry heating up and all over the news, the potential is there for a real conflagration. You two are both signed up for the desert warfare course, by the way."

"Back to school?" Grimaldi asked. "Wasn't that an old Rodney Dangerfield movie?"

"One of my all-time favorites," Brognola said. He took a quick sip of coffee, then emitted another dissatisfied-sounding grunt. "The Feds are also out and about in the area checking out the rumors of some possible student radicals, too. The NSA has intercepted a bunch of anti-American internet garbage being spewed by some radical cleric out of Yemen named Ibrahim al Shabahb. He may be trying to recruit some impressionable lone wolves here in the States to stir up some trouble."

"You have any more information on that?" Bolan asked.

Brognola handed each of them a briefing folder. "There are some Homeland Security reports in there. They give it a medium to high confidence level."

"Please, tell me we're not going commercial," Grimaldi said. "You know how I hate it when somebody else is flying the plane."

"They're fueling up the Learjet as we speak," Brognola said. "How the hell else would you guys be able to take all your special equipment?"

"Yeah, it might be a little tricky getting it through TSA," Grimaldi said with a grin and a wink.

Brognola smiled. "Any questions?"

Bolan shook his head as he got to his feet.

"Your plane will be ready to roll in two hours."

CHAPTER THREE

Camp Freedom, Nevada

It was early evening but prematurely dark as the head-lights of the Jeep bounced over the rough gravel back road. Fedor Androkovich checked the security strap on the low-slung, tactical holster securing his 9 mm SIG Sauer P223 semi-auto pistol as he braced himself in the passenger seat of the vehicle. He thought about the complexity of the plan. There was a lot that could go wrong, which bothered him. Still, he was used to car-rying out complicated endeavors. He had been raised on them practically since birth.

His entire youth had been spent under the tutelage of the KGB, and later in its successors, the FSB and the SVR, in a special school that trained him and oth-ers to be sleeper agents in the United States. But after twenty years it had grown both tiresome and tedious, like his current, deep cover assignment, which was why he'd begun laying the secret groundwork to walk away from it all. When the Arabs had covertly approached him, the decision had been easy, almost preordained.

As much as he disliked going by his American alias, Frank Andrews, he had to admit the name had served him well. And soon, he would be rich. He could choose another name in a short time. Any one he wanted. Perhaps he would go with one with a little more European flair. He was tired of masquerading as an American.

"There they are," Red Stevens said. His real name was actually Rudolph Strogoff, and he, too, was a product of the highly secret American Assimilation School in Gdansk, only a generation later. As a result, his American accent was as flawless as Androkovich's. His auburn hair had earned him the appropriate nickname, "Red." He was fifteen years younger than Fedor, and consequently less experienced at staying deep within their established cover here in the United States. But just the same, during the past year Strogoff had all but vanished, and the advantage was obvious. He had become Red, but he followed Androkovich's directions without question.

"Do you see them?" Strogoff asked, pointing to two sets of headlights parked about a hundred yards away on the highway.

"I hope their lights didn't attract too much attention," his partner replied. "Stop here and I'll get the gate."

Androkovich jumped out of the Jeep and jogged toward the seven-foot-high chain-link fence that surrounded the perimeter of Camp Freedom and secured the access to the compound via this back road. He unlocked the gate and swung it open, pausing to peer around at the desert terrain. A hot wind blew across the plains, capturing wisps of sand and adding a hint of grit to the air. Nothing seemed to be moving, but the Russian brought the night-vision goggles up to his eyes and did another quick scan. Nothing stirred except for an occasional tumbleweed. The timing couldn't be better. All he had to worry about now was the possibility of some random patrol or the possibility of an over-inquisitive reporter or motorist happening upon them.

Thus, it was best to proceed with all due speed. He turned and motioned for Strogoff to pull forward on to the highway. Androkovich hopped into the open Jeep as it was going by him. They bounced over the juncture between the macadamized road and the asphalt and sped toward the two parked vehicles farther down. As they drove past the two cars, Androkovich perused them. The first was a dark limousine, the second the ambulance that they had purchased from a surplus municipality sale in neighboring Arizona. It was perfect for their purposes.

A limo in the desert, Androkovich thought. Leave it to the Arabs to be stupid as well as ostentatious. He wondered if their Bedouin ancestors were turning over in their sandy graves.

"Pull behind them and wait," he said.

Strogoff slowed down again and then swung the Jeep in a wide circle, dipping on to the shoulder and coming to a stop behind the ambulance.

"Wait here," Androkovich said as he got out. "I'll go talk to them."

His companion nodded, his black baseball cap riding low on his forehead.

Androkovich crossed in front of the Jeep and walked on the right side of the ambulance. He glanced inside as he passed, seeing the waspish face of George Duncan behind the wheel. He nodded as he passed, and Duncan responded with a halfhearted salute. The Russian kept walking and heard the sound of the locks being popped as he got close to the rear door of the limo. He reached for the handle and pulled the door open.

"Good evening," he said as he slid inside.

Two men, both Saudis, stared at him. Androkovich knew the younger of the two well: Masoud, the youngest son of Mustapha Rahman. Masoud was slender and looked quite dapper in his cream-colored suit. His hair was stylishly cut and the hair on his face was trimmed to a neat mustache and goatee.

"You have seen the vehicle," Masoud said. "Is it what you wanted?"

"It is," the Russian replied. "You purchased it in Arizona, as I instructed?"

"Yes."

Androkovich nodded. He waited a few seconds, not wanting to seem too presumptuous so as to upset the Arab, then asked, "Did you initiate the transfer of my money?"

The Arab nodded. "Of course. It was done earlier today, as you instructed."

The Russian smiled. "And as soon as I have verified the deposit, I will proceed with the next phase." He let his smile fade for the moment. "And I assume you brought my expense money tonight?"

Masoud snapped his fingers, and his associate removed a leather bag from the floor area and set it on the seat between them. The associate began unzipping it, but Masoud placed his hand on top of the other man's. His dark eyes stared at Androkovich.

"Do you have the…how do you say it?"

"The English term is scapegoats. And, yes, they have been recruited, as your father instructed."

"Your English is excellent, for a Russian," Masoud said. "They are Saudi Shi'ites?"

"Yes. Also as your father instructed."

Masoud lifted his hand, and the other man finished unzipping the case. Androkovich could see the bundles of currency. "As you requested, in various denominations of U.S. currency." His lips curled back over his teeth in a mirthless grin. "You may count it if you wish."

The Russian shook his head as he closed the case. "There is no need. Our relationship has been built on trust, has it not?"

Masoud uttered a short, harsh-sounding laugh. "Trust. Do you know that two of my father's uncles were killed fighting the Russians with the *Mujahideen* in Afghanistan many years ago?"

"And now their sons fight the Americans."

Masoud was about to speak when the driver lowered the shield behind the front seat and said something in Arabic.

"What did he say?" Androkovich asked.

The other man's eyes flashed. "A vehicle is approaching from the rear."

Androkovich took a small, handheld radio from his pistol belt and brought it to his lips. "Do you see a car approaching?"

"Yes," came the reply. "From our rear." A few seconds went by, then, "It looks like it's pulling up behind me. Red police light on the dashboard."

"Police." Masoud leaned forward and grasped the Russian's forearm. "We must not be discovered. This transaction must not be traced to us."

Androkovich glared into the Arab's dark eyes until the man removed his hand. "It will not be." He slid toward the door. "Stay here until I return."

He jerked the door handle and moved out of the limo with a smooth, fluid grace. He stepped quickly across the dusty shoulder of the road and into the darkened area approximately three yards to the side. The car behind the Jeep appeared to be a black vehicle with no overt police insignias. The passenger door opened and a man in a light-colored uniform got out holding a flashlight. Its bright light shone over the Jeep and then the ambulance. The fingers of Androkovich's right hand closed over the handle of his pistol, drawing it slowly out of the tactical holster. His other hand withdrew the cylindrical sound suppressor from the pouch on his belt. He matched up the threads and screwed it in place on the end of the barrel as he listened.

"Federal agents," the man on the driver's side said in a loud voice.

Feds…FBI? But they didn't wear uniforms or make traffic stops. Most likely these two were BLM bird dogs assigned to patrol the perimeter of the disputed territory, which most likely meant they weren't in radio contact with any of the police dispatch centers.

The guy stood on the passenger side of the Jeep, shining the beam of his flashlight over Strogoff.

"What's the problem, Officer?" Strogoff asked, his voice sounding like a typical American motorist.

"What are you doing out here?" the policeman asked.

"Just meeting some friends. Did I do something wrong?"

"Let me see some identification."

"Don't think I have any with me," Strogoff said, sounding gregarious. "Wallet's back at the ranch. We usually don't drive this vehicle on the road. Just came to see if these folks needed help, is all."

"You're from Camp Freedom, aren't you?" the man

on the passenger side asked. "What are you doing out here this time of night?"

That was the wrong question, Androkovich thought as he ignored the three glowing tritium dots of the sights and switched instead to the laser light snapped on the laser sight. The circular bulk of the suppressor that rose over the end of the barrel rendered the standard night sights of the SIG Sauer useless. He centered the red dot on the back of the closer man's neck. Of course, any question at this point was the wrong one. And the last, as well.

He squeezed the trigger and felt the reduced recoil of the round, and its accompanying ripping sound.

The man on the passenger side of the Jeep emitted a husking groan as his upper body jerked momentarily before he slumped forward.

"Jeff?" the officer on the other side said. "What's wrong?"

Strogoff reached out the window and pushed the other officer, causing the man to take two wobbly steps backward as he began reaching for his weapon. Androkovich moved to the side, his SIG Sauer still held in the firing position. The small, circular red dot danced on the man's face.

The Russian squeezed the trigger a millisecond later, the subdued crack of the round piercing the stillness of the desert night once again. The officer crumpled to the road.

Strogoff jumped out of the Jeep and straddled the man, while his companion ran to the unmarked squad car, finding it empty. A radio was mounted under the dashboard, but it was silent. Had they called in their location? Perhaps not. A mobile data computer sat on a metal shelf. He checked the screen and saw some sort of format for obtaining data, but the cursor blinked over an empty space. He wondered again if they had been in communication with their support base. Better to move quickly. The car and the bodies would have to be disposed of with cautious but immediate expedience. He glanced to his right and saw Strogoff going through the dead man's pockets.

"See if they have handheld radios," Androkovich called. His ears were buzzing slightly from the subdued reverberation of the rounds going off, but he knew this would subside shortly. He retraced his steps to the place from which he'd fired, shone his flashlight on the ground and looked for the expended shell casings. He found one, but the second one eluded him in the dust and darkness, despite the flashlight. The clock was ticking, and he felt like abandoning his search, thinking perhaps that the desert sand would sweep over the casing. But he also knew the devil, as they said, was in the details. Now was not the time to be careless. Shining the light again, sweeping it over the ground, he located and retrieved the second shell casing.

He went to the other dead man and began going through his pockets. The policeman had a Glock 19 in a nylon holster and two extra magazines. A cell phone was clipped to his belt. Androkovich immediately removed it, took out the battery and placed the items in his pants pocket. He found the dead man's ID case and flipped it open. A Bureau of Land Management Park Ranger ID card was under a clear plastic flap opposite a small, gold-colored badge. He pocketed that also.

From the other side of the Jeep, Strogoff stood and

said, "This guy's a BLM park ranger. No radio that I can find."

"Get his cell phone and deactivate it," his companion said, rising. "Take their weapons and wallets and load them into the trunk of their car."

Strogoff nodded and picked up the supine figure.

Androkovich considered their options. "We'll leave them somewhere in the desert. They won't be found for a few days, at least."

Strogoff cocked his head toward the other vehicles. "And them?"

"I'll get our money from the Arab. Duncan can take the ambulance to the barn. I'll drive their car. You follow me in the Jeep."

His partner nodded and began dragging the dead man back toward the unmarked squad car.

Androkovich strode to the side of the ambulance. Duncan had a white-knuckle grip on the steering wheel, and his face was covered with sweat.

"Did you kill them?" he asked.

"I had no choice."

"Shit, I hope it doesn't bring more heat down on us."

"I don't pay you to think. Just follow orders. Take this vehicle to the farthest barn on the compound and lock it up. Then you're done for this evening."

Duncan nodded and shifted the ambulance into Drive. Androkovich watched him ride out and around the limo toward the back road entrance and turn on to it. He glanced over his shoulder and saw Strogoff dragging the second dead BLM ranger toward the vehicle. He exhaled slowly as he walked toward the limousine.

The complicated plan had just become a little bit more complicated.

CHAPTER FOUR

Riyadh, Saudi Arabia

Mustapha Rahman sat on the soft cushions on the floor of his well-appointed apartment and watched as his second son, Mamum, poured some of the sweet mint tea into a cup for their three guests.

Mamum, the trustworthy. It had been he who had driven the three Shi'ites to Bahrain to conduct the attack on the nightclub, which had allowed Mahfuj, the protector, to perform the heroic rescue. That act had, in turn, ensured the trust and confidence of both the prince and the king.

Mustapha's three guests were all high-ranking military men, and each had committed himself to the plan. Mustapha had no doubt as to their loyalty. With the assassination attempt the previous night, and the first part of the plan successfully initiated, they were well beyond the point of no return.

It was like a Bedouin pilgrim crossing the desert on his holy hajj, Mustapha thought. To stop at any point in the seemingly endless sands was to embrace death.

Colonel Tariq Matayyib, the weakest link in the chain, Mustapha knew, was perspiring heavily. He accepted the tea from Mamum and sipped at it.

Mustapha reached out and laid a hand on Matayyib's thigh in reassurance.

"Do not worry, my brother," Mustapha said. "All is well. It will work as I have foretold."

Matayyib nodded, accompanied by a very nervous smile. "I have placed my faith and my life in your hands, but still I see the knife being drawn across my throat in my dreams, should we fail."

Mustapha squeezed Matayyib's leg again in reassurance. "I have just received a message from my youngest son, Masoud. All is going according to plan."

This was not entirely true. Masoud had risked using his satellite phone to inform Mustapha about the near catastrophe of the previous evening. It was already morning here in Arabia.

Yes, Arabia, Mustapha thought. He would no longer use the name of the house of traitors to designate his country, the only one in the modern world named after a specific family. As if it were their personal possession.

He glanced at the chess board that the other two colonels had set up. The pieces were configured piece-meal around the board, without any clear strategy or plan of action on the part of either player. Thinking two or three moves ahead was something Mustapha prided himself in being able to do. Even as a boy he'd had the knack for strategy and planning. Perhaps it was a result of his grandfather's careful instruction in the art of repairing the timepieces. It had taught Mustapha the intricacies of the most complicated series of motions, all seemingly working independent of each other, but collectively accomplishing one purpose.

He leaned over and moved the black queen belonging

to Colonel Arak Hafeez, thus placing the white king of Colonel Kalif Samad in check.

The eyes of Hafeez widened. "You have virtually won the game for me with one move."

He grinned and pointed at Samad. "You will be checkmated in two more moves."

"Did you have so little faith that I could not?" Mustapha said.

Hafeez smiled. "Never for a moment."

Mustapha turned back to Matayyib. "Do you not see? It is a sign from God. All is well."

Matayyib nodded, but his face was still wet, and the perspiration had begun to seep through his tan uniform shirt despite the air conditioning.

"Why do you worry?" Mustapha asked.

"My father…" Matayyib lowered his head. "He told me of the scene of long ago. He was only a boy then, but he saw them lined up in the public square. Their heads rolled on the stones, and he swore he saw the lips of one of them moving in prayer, begging for forgiveness."

Mustapha frowned. He, too, had heard the tales of the failed coup d'état of 1966. A group of air force officers had planned to wrest power from the decadent king, but the Americans had discovered their intentions and warned then-King Faisal. The monarch had immediately arrested them and, after rebuking their treachery, subsequently had all of them beheaded in the city square. Not a pleasant thought, but Mustapha knew this time his plan would succeed. The Americans would not be able to warn the king this time. He shook his head vehemently. This time we shall strike with the swiftness of a falcon…four desert falcons.

"Must I again tell you of my dream?" His voice was loud, steady, unwavering. "My dream of the four falcons? I was told by a holy man that it was a sign, a prophecy from God."

Matayyib compressed his lips.

"Remember," Mustapha said, increasing his grip on the other man's thigh to convey the rectitude of his pronouncement, "that the prophet himself, blessed be his name, was guided by his dreams."

Matayyib's face looked distorted now and Mustapha realized he'd been exerting too much pressure in his fervor. He released the other man's thigh. "You need to spend more time playing football."

Matayyib's expression showed relief now, but his body emanated the smell of encroaching fear.

But perhaps a little fear was good at this point.

"My son Mahfuj is now the most trusted bodyguard of Prince Amir," Mustapha said. He reached down and moved the rook to block the retreat of the white king. "It has been insisted upon that Mahfuj, who saved the prince's life, be placed in charge of the bodyguard contingent." He reached over to make the final move to checkmate the white king. Everything was falling into place in life, just as on the chessboard. "Now, quit worrying and drink your sweet tea. But first, say it."

Matayyib's dark eyes flashed for an instant, as if he were confused…or doubtful.

"Say it, my brother," Mustapha said, knowing he had the full attention of all of them. "Show me you are committed to our plan. Show me your confidence in our course of action."

"Praise be to God," Matayyib said. "We shall succeed."

Yes, indeed, Mustapha thought. He turned and looked at each of them, holding his gaze steady as he searched their eyes.

"Yes, we shall," he said. "Soon, you will each be generals."

The three of them exchanged glances as smiles crept over their faces.

And I, Mustapha thought, shall be the supreme leader of a new Arabia.

Las Vegas, Nevada

"THERE SHE IS," Grimaldi said, pointing through the windshield of their black, Cadillac Escalade as Bolan drove northbound on Las Vegas Boulevard from the car rental place. "My favorite sign."

Bolan glanced back at the huge Welcome to Fabulous Las Vegas, Nevada sign that was set in the middle of the grassy area that separated the north- and south-bound lanes of the boulevard. Groups of people were lining up to get photographed by the sign, which was shaped similarly to a giant cocktail glass.

They'd touched down at McCarran Airport an hour ago, and with the three hours they'd picked up flying west, it was not yet noon. After arranging to secure their Learjet in one of the private hangars, they secured their rental car.

Each man had a suitcase and a black nylon duffel bag that contained their traveling arsenals and equipment: body armor, night-vision goggles, gas masks, flash-bang and CS grenades, knives, pistols, two M-4 rifles, two MP-5 submachine guns, numerous magazines and a copious amount of ammunition. Flying commercial, as Grimaldi had pointed out, would have been more than just a little problematic.

"Well, how about we swing by the Peppermill and get a couple of steaks?" Grimaldi patted his stomach. "I'm starving, and remember, I did all the flying to get us here in a timely fashion."

"I'll buy you a sandwich and an energy drink instead. I want to drop this stuff off and do a recon. Let's go."

AARON "THE BEAR" KURTZMAN had reserved a condominium for them just southeast of the Strip. It was close enough to the entertainment action, yet far enough away to allow for quick departures to the outlying areas, including the site of the desert warfare training seminar. The condo was also equipped with two rather large safes that enabled them to secure their weapons. As soon as they arrived, they carried their duffels into the bedroom and Bolan removed his Beretta 93-R from the bag along with two extra magazines.

"Planning on going to war early?" Grimaldi asked. "I thought that damn class wasn't supposed to start until tomorrow."

"It's better to be prepared," Bolan replied.

"You got that right," Grimaldi said, taking out his SIG Sauer P 223 and one extra mag and setting them on the bed. "But did anybody ever tell you you're the world's oldest Boy Scout?"

"Just you," Bolan said. "Nobody else who did is around to talk about it."

Grimaldi raised his hands, palms outward. "No offense, partner."

Bolan slipped the end of his belt through the loops of his pancake holster and snapped the Beretta into place.

The holster had a special safety guard that gripped the trigger guard to prevent the weapon from falling out of or being ripped from its holster.

He inserted the two magazines into the holder on the left, front side of his belt. He was almost ready to roll. The only thing left to do was to remove his large, folding Espada knife from the duffel bag and clip it inside the right pocket on the leg of his black cargo pants. He then stowed the two duffel bags with their remaining weaponry in the safe and donned a windbreaker to cover his weapons.

"Almost ready?" he asked.

Grimaldi was putting his arms through the loops of a shoulder holster rig. He turned and scrutinized his reflection in the mirror over the dresser. "Almost."

Bolan took out his cell phone. "I'm going to check in with Hal."

Brognola answered on the first ring. "I was hoping you'd call. How are the accommodations?"

"First-rate," Bolan said, putting the phone on speaker so Grimaldi could monitor the situation. "Tell the Bear he did a great job setting us up."

"He'll be glad to hear that. Kind of makes up for all the times we send you to those rat holes all over the place." Brognola cleared his throat. "Bad enough I gotta send you to that damn desert warfare training seminar. Hell, you and Jack could probably teach the instructors how to do it."

"You can always pick up something," Bolan said. "Nobody knows it all."

Brognola laughed. "Yeah, you can take the soldier out of the jungle, but not the jungle out of the man."

"Anything new?"

"As a matter of fact, yeah. The FBI agents are on their way to the area. It seems two BLM park rangers disappeared last night. They didn't report in at the conclusion of their shift."

Bolan considered that. "Where did they disappear?"

"They were assigned to prowl around the disputed area of Autry's place. Camp Freedom."

"Did they report anything suspicious?"

"Just that they noticed some vehicular traffic on the main highway by the back entrance and were going to investigate. Apparently there's a private road that runs from the main compound area. It's gated, and there were no signs of entry there, forced or otherwise."

"Did they call in any license plates on the vehicles?"

"Negative," Brognola said. "They aren't monitored by any dispatching base, although they do have the capacity to get on local law enforcement radio bands to call for help if they need it. They maintain a mobile data terminal computer log of their activities, but there were no entries or transmissions after the one about them noticing the vehicular traffic."

"What about GPS locators?"

"Struck out again. There is a GPS transponder in the vehicle, but it stopped transmitting about an hour after their last report. And it was miles away from Camp Freedom, according to its last recorded location."

"Did you find out anything more about Rand Autry or that militia group we saw on the news?"

"Like I said, the FBI's got some agents en route to investigate the disappearance. They probably plan to interview Autry as a matter of routine investigation. Not that they have anything solid to connect him to it.

"As for the People's New Minutemen Militia, they've

been active for the past year or so, but we don't know much about them. They don't seem to be affiliated with any criminal organization, and the report that they're trying to buy more arms is unsubstantiated at this time. For now, they're just a paramilitary group that sprung up about the same time as this thing with Autry started. They appear to be little more than a group of security guards for this Camp Freedom place of his. I'll send you some aerial surveillance photos. The place is pretty big and looks well-fortified."

"If he's got all that property," Bolan asked, "why is he in dispute with the BLM?"

"Autry's been letting his cattle graze on what he claims is open range, per some proclamation from 1857. All his neighboring ranchers have been paying grazing and water rights to let their cattle use land in the same area. Since Autry refuses to recognize the federal government's authority, he hasn't. He owes a couple of million in back taxes. Now, the government is knocking on his door intending to collect."

"This sounds like something to be decided in the courts."

"It was. Autry lost the first round, but he's appealing. In the meantime he's recruited this small, private army to protect him, and they're well-armed and apparently intend to stay that way. That's where the possibility of the illegal arms deal enters into things. Add that to Autry's recent televised outbursts calling for action against the Muslims, who he's blaming for being in cahoots with the government, and you can see why the President is a bit worried there might be trouble with one of the royal heirs being in the area."

"I think it's time Jack and I got a look at this Camp

Freedom," Bolan said. "In the meantime, email us those surveillance pictures."

"Will do. Anything else?"

"Not for the moment."

"Okay. Keep me posted about Prince Amir," Brognola said, then hung up.

CHAPTER FIVE

Bolan surveyed the scene on the desert highway as they approached in the Escalade. Several police barricades had been placed across the road. About fifty yards farther down, a large group of people was milling about on the road. At the barricades, a pair of uniformed state troopers waved at the line of cars to turn and go in the other direction.

"Looks like we're arriving late for the party," Grimaldi said from the driver's seat. "So much for your recon."

"We can still find out some things," Bolan replied.

"Okie-doke," Grimaldi said, pulling forward as the car in front of them made a U-turn. The trooper, who looked hot and exasperated, waved emphatically for them to turn as well, but Grimaldi slowly crept forward and lowered his window.

"Turn it around, bud," the trooper said. "Road's closed."

Bolan held up his Department of Justice credentials that identified him as Agent Matt Cooper. The trooper strode to the window and scrutinized them. Grimaldi quickly got out his ID and held it up, as well.

"DOJ?" the trooper said. "Just what I need, another couple of Feds." He stepped back and waved them through, calling to his partner to move the barricade.

Grimaldi nodded a "thanks," drove around the barricade and scanned the crowd ahead. Several news vans, antennas erect, were parked on the side of the road. A gaggle of news reporters, some with microphones, stood in front of the camcorders as two groups of people seemed to be engaged in a face-off of some sort. One side appeared to be police, the other some sort of uniformed men wearing camouflaged BDUs, black baseball caps, and bloused pants over desert warfare boots.

Most likely the militia Brognola mentioned, Bolan thought as Grimaldi pulled the Escalade on to the shoulder of the road, shut off the engine and grabbed his ball cap. Bolan did the same. The hats, along with their sunglasses, afforded them a modicum of anonymity as they ran the gauntlet of news cameras.

Grimaldi tapped the brim of his cap, which was black with white letters spelling out Las Vegas. "Maybe I'll wear this at that damn desert warfare class. What do you think?"

"Yeah," Bolan said as they passed by the reporters and showed their IDs to another police officer manning the inner perimeter. "Those white letters make a nice target."

As they got closer, Bolan saw that both groups were armed, but the militia members seemed to have an edge since they held what appeared to be AR-15s with 30-round magazines at port arms. They seemed to be well-disciplined and were lined up across a paved road that had a gate and a seven-foot-high chain-link fence running perpendicular along an expansive perimeter. A large metal sign was posted over the gate, reading Camp Freedom. Below it, lesser signs proclaimed various warnings: Private Property—No Trespassing, Violators Will Be Dealt With Accordingly.

"Looks like the mark of a man who values his privacy," Grimaldi said.

Bolan said nothing. He was too busy assessing the various shades of tan uniforms on what appeared to be the cop side: more state troopers, what appeared to be county sheriff officers, and several he didn't recognize until he and Grimaldi got close enough to see the patches on the men's sleeves: BLM—Bureau of Land Management. A big, barrel-chested man in a county sheriff's uniform stood at the front along with two people in blue polo shirts and dark slacks. One of these was an attractive woman with dark hair pulled back into a ponytail.

"Hey, check out the babe," Grimaldi said. "She's hot."

"She's also FBI," Bolan said, discerning the yellow lettering stenciled on the upper left side of her shirt.

Across from them, two of the militia men stood at rigid attention, saying nothing. In front of these a rather obese, middle-aged man in cowboy garb and a similarly dressed woman gesticulated emphatically. Bolan recognized both of them from the file Brognola had given him: Shane and Eileen, the two children of Randall "Rand" Autry, the owner and master of Camp Freedom. Bolan also knew that while Shane was purported to be more or less a gofer for his autocratic father, Eileen had graduated from Harvard Law School. She was a rather attractive woman with blond hair and a nice figure that filled out her Western shirt and blue jeans. She wore a buckskin vest, and her pants were tucked into highly polished, decorative cowboy boots. Her brother, Bolan knew, was eight years older, placing him in his early forties. His Stetson hat was set low on his forehead, riding over a pair of eyes set deep into a face that looked like an inflated balloon. An expansive gut pulled the bottom of his red shirt tightly over the top of a pair of blue jeans, held in place by a fancy leather belt with a decorative silver buckle.

"Ms. Autry," the female FBI agent said, "all we're asking is a chance to speak with your father regarding this incident. Your cooperation would be greatly appreciated."

"My father will make a statement when he's good and ready," Eileen said, her voice calm but defiant. "And not before."

"When will that be?"

"When he gets here," Shane said. "Now, get your unlawful assembly off our property."

"This is public road," one of the uniformed BLM rangers said. "And two of our personnel disappeared in this area. We have a right to be here."

Shane's face took on a belligerent expression. "You want to talk about rights? What about our rights as citizens? What about you jack-booted government thugs harassing us without authority? What about—"

The uniformed BLM ranger jumped forward, but the big man in the tan uniform raised a massive arm to hold him back. He silenced the man with a mean look.

"Thank you, Sheriff Dundee," Eileen said, "You saved my brother from an unwarranted assault and saved this government thug and his department from a horrendous lawsuit." She smiled and pointed toward the news crews. "Let's not forget that this entire incident is being recorded."

Dundee nodded and held up his hand. "I'm not in any position to forget anything, ma'am. And, please, excuse the exuberance of my fellow law-enforcement officer here, but understandably, he is a bit concerned, as we all are, about those two missing park rangers."

"Park rangers," Shane said in a disgusted tone. "Ain't no parks around here for them to patrol." He spit on the ground between him and the law-enforcement personnel.

"Shane," Dundee said, "I've known you for a long time, but if you do that again I'll take you in."

"Oh, that'll look good in front of all these cameras, won't it?" Shane did a little dance. "Come on, big man. Don't talk about it, do it." He threw his arm back toward the line of stoic militiamen. "I'd like to see you try it."

Eileen turned and put her hand on her brother's shoulder. The situation looked about ready to explode. Bolan stepped closer, but stayed about fifteen feet away from the principal players sizing each one up.

As they stood nose to nose in momentary silence, a rhythmic, clopping sound became noticeable. Bolan looked for the source of it and saw a man wearing a white Stetson hat rapidly approaching on a white horse alongside the paved road inside the gates. He held an American flag on a pole that was hooked into his left stirrup. The flag was upside-down.

"Looks like Rand Autry's here," Bolan said.

Grimaldi nodded. "Damn, just like John Wayne in one of those old Westerns."

"Shane," Rand Autry said loudly as he pulled back on the reins, slowing the horse to a stop. He then urged the animal cautiously forward. Several of the militiamen broke ranks to allow him passage. One of them, obviously the leader, was a big, broad-shouldered guy with light-colored eyes. He issued a command to the militiaman next to him to take over as he accompanied the elder Autry to the front of the standoff. This second militiaman had reddish hair and a wiry build. Although he looked formidable, he appeared a few years younger than the big guy and nowhere near as powerful.

Bolan took note of the big guy's massive forearms as he shouldered his AR-15 and strode beside the horse. The man also wore what appeared to be a 9 mm SIG Sauer P 223 pistol in a low-slung tactical holster. Everything about him exuded military bearing and discipline. Bolan wondered what this guy's game was.

Rand Autry looked less impressive the closer he got. Under the brim of his hat his tanned face looked lined with creases, and his movements were stiff, as if he was fighting off pain with each one. Still, his physique, though a bit bulky and padded with age, gave off an aura of authority. His hands were large and powerful-looking.

"Dundee," he said from his saddle, "as a duly elected public official of the sheriff's department, you are the only member of this lynch mob that I regard with any official law enforcement capacity."

The big sheriff, obviously uncomfortable being forced to look up at Autry, nodded. "Why don't you dismount so we can talk about this, Rand?"

Autry smirked and shook the upside-down flag. "I can hear you fine from up here. Now, what the hell do you want?"

Dundee took a deep breath and was about to speak when the FBI agent spoke first.

"Mr. Autry, I'm Special Agent Dylan, FBI. We'd like to speak with you."

Autry transferred his gaze to her. "FBI? About what?"

"Two Bureau of Land Management Park Rangers disappeared in this vicinity last night," she said. "May we come in and talk with you?"

Autry's large head tilted to the side. "Dylan? That a Jew name?"

The woman flushed, then nodded. "Sir, we do need to speak with you concerning this incident."

Eileen stepped forward. "Do you have a warrant to search our premises?"

"No, but we just—"

"Then this conversation is over," Eileen said, cutting her off. "My father knows nothing about this matter and has nothing more to say."

Bolan detected an edge of trepidation in her tone. A second later he knew why.

"The government sends a Jewess out here to do their bidding, huh?" Autry's voice had lowered to a growl. "Figures. You damn Jews run everything."

Agent Dylan looked up at him. "I beg your pardon?"

"Daddy," Eileen started to say, but there was no shutting up the old man now.

"Thought they'd send some jezebel to try to trick me," he said, shaking the flag. "But this is still a free country, under attack by a corrupt federal government that's in bed with those bastards in the Middle East. I'm standing up for free Americans everywhere—"

"Daddy, please," Eileen shouted. "Turn around and go back to the house."

"Aww, let him talk," Shane said. "All he's doing is telling the truth."

Eileen whirled toward the law-enforcement contingent, her extended index finger shaking like a pistol to emphasize her words. "Sheriff Dundee, I'm advising you in front of these reporters and witnesses that we know nothing about this alleged disappearance of any BLM rangers. We are refusing you access to our land without the proper authorization in the form of a valid warrant, and if you wish to speak to us, obtain a subpoena." She turned and grabbed the bridle of her father's horse and began walking back toward the big gate with a forceful stride.

One of the uniformed BLM rangers started to move forward, but the well-built guy who had accompanied Autry and his horse to the forefront raised an open palm.

"You heard the lady," he said. "We have nothing to say."

Shane, who was standing off to the side smirking, laughed and said, "You tell him, Frank." With that, he, too began walking back toward the gate.

The BLM ranger balled up his fists and took another step forward, but Dundee grabbed him.

"Let's not make the situation any worse," the sheriff said.

The militiaman, Frank, began to walk backward, keeping his eyes on the crowd of police before him. His head turned slightly, and he issued a command for the rest the militiamen to "stand down and return to base."

"That guy's had some extensive training," Bolan said.

"He's got the moves, that's for sure," Grimaldi agreed. "Looks like somebody to step aside from, all right."

Bolan wondered what the guy's story was.

He and Grimaldi started to turn to go back to their Escalade when he heard Special Agent Dylan call, "One moment, please, gentlemen."

Bolan turned. She was rather pretty, with dark eyes and an olive complexion. He estimated her to be about five-seven, 125 pounds, and in excellent shape.

"I'm Special Agent Gila Dylan," she stated. "FBI."

"We know," Grimaldi said, flashing a wide grin. "We heard you introduce yourself."

She swiveled her gaze toward him and let the faint trace of a smile grace her lips. "Who are you guys? I don't remember seeing you before."

"That's because we just got here," Grimaldi said quickly. "Believe me, we're very memorable."

Bolan held up his DOJ identification while she scrutinized it. After a few seconds, Grimaldi held his up, as well. "I didn't get notified that someone else from Justice was involved in this investigation."

"You know our motto," Grimaldi replied. "Justice never sleeps."

"Actually," Bolan said, "we're here on another matter and just stopped by to lend our support."

The second FBI agent stepped forward with an extended palm.

"Special Agent Lon Banks," he said. He looked to be right out of the academy and a few years younger than his distaff partner. They shook.

The barrel-chested sheriff stepped up and offered his hand, too. "I'm Sheriff Wayne Dundee. This has already turned into a multiagency investigation. Glad to have you aboard."

"Exactly what is the nature of your investigation?" Dylan asked.

"Classified," Grimaldi said.

"I'm going to have to call my supervisor about this."

"Let me give you a number that'll verify us," Bolan said, taking out his pad and pen. "In the meantime, why don't we get out of the sun and away from these reporters?"

She looked around and nodded. "Good point."

They began walking back toward their vehicles.

"Any idea where those two rangers disappeared?" Bolan asked.

She shook her head. "Their last known location was on the highway near the back forty of Camp Freedom." Dylan smirked. "What an oxymoron."

"That guy's a moron, all right," Grimaldi said. "Oxy or otherwise."

His quip got a tweak of a smile out of her, but her expression turned serious again. "We were hoping to get permission to check his ranch, or should I say his fortified compound? Fat chance he'd cooperate. The man obviously has some hidden agenda, but what?"

"Do you know anything about those militiamen he's got backing him up?" Bolan asked.

"Not as much as we'd like to," she said. They were still in the inner perimeter and about twenty yards from the gaggle of reporters and news cameras. "So, I've told you my story. Now, what's yours?"

After quickly assessing that they were still far enough away from any probing boom mikes, Bolan raised his hand in front of his lips and said quietly, "We're here attending a desert warfare training seminar."

The crease between Dylan's eyebrows deepened again as she canted her head to look at him. "Oh?"

"Washington has some safety concerns about another of the seminar attendees."

"The Saudi prince?" Dylan whispered.

Bolan nodded.

"I read an informational Bureau memo that he'd be attending," she said. "But I thought the Secret Service had a contingent accompanying him for protection."

"They do," Bolan said. "We're augmenting them."

"Hedging our bets, so to speak," Grimaldi added.

She considered that and nodded. "I can understand that. The Secret Service is already complaining about the last time he was in Vegas. Their code name for him is Royal Dissidence.

"Let's keep in touch," she added. "We should get together and compare notes ASAP." She gave Bolan one of her business cards. "Call me later and we'll set up a meet."

"Hey," Grimaldi said, "can I get one of those, too?"

Turning toward him, she smiled demurely. "Sorry. I just brought one." She and her partner brushed by them going toward their government sedan.

Bolan watched her go, then glanced back over his shoulder at the gate to Camp Freedom. The militiamen were filing back inside the compound with military precision, following Autry on his large white horse toward a group of buildings approximately a hundred yards from the gate. Two men stood by the gate, watching the law enforcement retreat. One of them was the big guy who'd accompanied Autry to the front of the confrontation. The other was the younger version with the red hair.

There was something about that big guy that bothered Bolan, but he couldn't put his finger on it. Had they crossed paths before? Maybe it was more the type than the actual individual.

Whatever or whoever he was, Bolan thought, he looked like he knew his stuff.

"You know," Grimaldi said, slapping Bolan on the shoulder, "I think Agent Dylan digs me."

Bolan held up her card as he headed for the Escalade. "Obviously."

CHAPTER SIX

Fedor Androkovich watched as the contingent of law enforcement agents began to disperse. The news cameras were still on the scene, and they would be moving closer to the gate as soon as the police dispersed, trying for an interview and using their zoom lenses to take long-range shots of the compound. Luckily, they'd stashed the ambulance in one of the barns Autry used as a storage facility. Androkovich doubted the old fool would discover it there, and the younger Autry was too preoccupied with drinking and his other activities to have much curiosity or ambition. Nevertheless, the Russian decided that he'd post a guard just to be sure. They still had to finish the painting.

"I didn't think they'd trace those two missing agents so quickly," Rudolph Strogoff said in Russian. "Do you think we buried the bodies deep enough?"

His partner turned toward him and frowned. "How many times have I told you to speak only in English when we're on a mission?"

Strogoff flushed. "Sorry."

He was back to using his Southern-style drawl. Good. It was imperative that they stayed totally in character during an assignment, and particularly this assignment. With what the Saudi conspirators were paying him, Androkovich knew this would be his last one, too.

In another week or so, he would be living it up on the Riviera with a beautiful woman on each arm.

"How did they know to come here to question Autry about those rangers?" Strogoff asked.

His partner shrugged. "They were grasping at straws. If they had any solid evidence, other than their suspicions, they would have acted."

He was still scanning the departing law enforcement officers. Two, in particular, piqued his interest. They weren't the ones who had been involved in the minor fracas. These two had arrived after the others, but were singled out by the female FBI agent. She'd given the bigger one something. A note or card. Both men had the look of total professionals. He noticed that they wore their sidearms strapped to their belts, with extra magazine pouches on the opposite side for quick reloading during a firefight. The larger of the two looked to be in excellent physical condition and moved with the grace of a jungle cat. He also had some sort of folding knife clipped to the lower pocket of his trousers—another indication that this man was experienced. The way he moved, his calm, yet observant demeanor, all added up to a man who had been there, done that, as the Americans were fond of saying. And even now, as they all were leaving, this man had paused to glance back at the gate.

It was almost as if he was looking directly at me, Androkovich thought. As if he was delivering a message that they were destined to meet again.

"What about their car?" Strogoff asked. "Do you think they will find it?"

"We disabled the GPS devices and destroyed the radio. They have to locate it by air search, but it will probably take them at least a day or two. Besides, it's still far enough away that they will have no crumbs to lead them back here."

"I hope not. You seem awful quiet. Is something wrong?"

"Did you notice anything out of the ordinary about that group of police?"

Strogoff compressed his lips, thought for a moment, and then said, "You mean the two who came later, that you were staring at?"

This one is a quick learner, Androkovich thought. Wise beyond his years, which meant that when the time came for him to jettison his past and start over, Strogoff would become a liability. He didn't want to take the chance of having to look over his shoulder when his new life began. Soon those two BLM rangers would not be alone in their unmarked graves.

Somewhere over the Atlantic Ocean

MAHFUJ RAHMAN FOUND HIMSELF staring out the oval-shaped window at the fluffy layer of clouds several hundred meters below him, set against the blue sky. It was the first time he had been on a jet aircraft for a transatlantic flight. He had repelled and fast-roped from helicopters during his military training, but those crafts had hovered only thirty or forty meters above the ground. And, of course, he had flown in the prince's private Learjet on the royal's frequent trips to Bahrain, but those flights were short in duration. This one, which had left Riyadh about ten hours ago, was not even half completed. The projected time, with the refueling stops, was nineteen hours. With the time zone differences, when they landed, it would only be the early evening of the day they'd left.

It was strange, as if time had slowed to accommodate the prince. He slumbered in the sumptuous bedroom compartment of the plane, claiming that flying long distances disturbed his equilibrium. Never mind that the rest of them had to spend the nineteen hours plus in the discomfort of the standard airline seats. The prince would never be able to survive in the desert. He was not a warrior, not fit to be a leader, not a true *Bedouin*.

When they had left the airport Mahfuj remembered the expression on his father's face as he wrapped a new bandage around Mahfuj's injured hand. His father's face was hard, unsympathetic, yet he knew the concern was there.

"I am sorry that you sustained this injury, my son," his father had said.

Mahfuj had smiled and flexed his fingers. "It will soon be gone. I have lost none of my strength."

They had been standing apart from the others in the terminal, watching as bag after bag of the prince's luggage was loaded into the cargo bay of the jet.

"So many bags for such a short trip," his father had whispered.

"Nor will he need all of them," Mahfuj had added.

They'd said nothing of the intended plan. There was no need. Mustapha and his three sons had long ago committed each part to memory. There would be no discernable trace, no telltale line for the National Guard to pick up and follow. He'd watched as his father reached in his pocket and withdrew the king's wristwatch.

"You still have not completed the repair on that?" Mahfuj had asked.

His father had shaken his head. "It is almost complete. The watch is such that it requires no battery. Only the inertia of someone wearing it to set in motion its tiny gears." He'd smiled a knowing smile once again. "I wish to be certain everything is complete and in its place before I return it to the king."

Mahfuj understood his father's meaning. It was a metaphor for their intricate plan: each part dependent upon the working of the other, all simultaneously acting together in a special synergy of epic proportions.

"Give my regards to your brother Masoud, in the country of the infidels," Mustapha had said.

The crew had signaled it was time to board. Mahfuj had leaned forward and kissed his father's cheek. Mustapha had done the same to him.

"May God be with you, my son."

They both knew this could be the last time they would see each other in this life. Even if their plan succeeded, much could still go wrong, and their every movement was fraught with danger until the final act was completed. But the hourglass had been turned. The sand was draining. It could not be stopped. "And with you, my father."

The pain from his burned hand had almost subsided when Abdullah, the largest of the prince's bodyguard contingent, ambled down the aisle and lowered his enormous frame into the seat next to Mahfuj.

"It is a long flight, my brother," the big man said. "I have been asleep. You would do well to rest."

"Perhaps later," Mahfuj said. "I have a lot on my mind."

Abdullah grunted and nodded. "Does your hand still hurt?"

Mahfuj shook his head. "There is pain, but it is a good pain. A reminder of one's mission."

"To protect the prince," Abdullah said with a nod. "We would all die for him, if necessary, but it was you who saved him at the nightclub. You should wear your wound as a badge of honor."

Mahfuj smiled slightly. If this big fool only knew what was in store, he thought.

"But hopefully," Abdullah continued, "none of us will be hurt or injured again on this trip."

"If it is the will of God," Mahfuj said. He lowered his seat to the incline position and closed his eyes. "Perhaps I will try to rest. As you suggest."

Abdullah grunted again. "I will wake you when we land."

And I will give you a proper burial when the time comes, Mahfuj thought.

Camp Freedom, Unincorporated Clark County, Nevada

IN THE CONFINES of the small, dark room inside the far barracks of Camp Freedom, Fedor Androkovich watched as "radical cleric Ibrahim al Shabahb" typed a message to Hassan, one of the two young Muslim students the Yemeni sheikh had recruited on his website. He put a hand on the man's shoulder and leaned close to him. He was not a radical cleric in Yemen, as the two young Muslim students believed, but an expatriate Iraqi, brought here after being a translator for the army during Operation Iraqi Freedom. Fedor'd had no trouble enticing him to drop off the Americans' radar and resurface as "Pancho," a Mexican member of the Russian's little militia.

For the most part, Shabahb was kept out sight at the Autry ranch, surfacing only occasionally. For the most part he kept to himself, surfing the internet for who knew what when he wasn't trying to recruit impressionable young Saudis to join the jihad. And the two that he had on the line now were the perfect pair. Young, impressionable, radicalized and filled with just enough fervor that they could be easily manipulated. Shabahb sent another instant message to one of them via the computer.

He grinned as the reply came back, glancing up at Androkovich for approval. "He says all is well."

The Arab's penchant for greasy, American food, an uncharacteristic fondness for beer, and an aversion to showering despite the substantial desert heat gave his corpulent body a rather pungent and repulsive odor. Several empty cans of beer sat atop an overflowing wastebasket along with the wrinkled papers from a fast-food joint.

He is not unlike one of the pigs these Muslims so despised, the Russian thought with some amusement. But he had endured far worse. He would make sure that the payoff, down the line, would be laced with the pleasant fragrances of women bathed in French perfume.

"They are set to arrive as planned?" he asked.

"But of course," Shabahb said. "Have I not become a master fisherman?" He laughed. "What do you wish me to tell them?"

"Tell them to take a taxi to this hotel and to wait there until they are contacted." He handed the Arab a card with the name of a cheap hotel on the outskirts of the Strip. "Reservations have already been made."

Shabahb nodded and typed the message and clicked the mouse button to send it.

"Please, get me another can of that cold beer." Shabahb gestured toward the small refrigerator. "All the work on this computer has given me a tremendous thirst. I feel like I've been marching in Baghdad."

Androkovich grinned. He didn't want the man to imbibe just yet. An inebriated cleric would be too prone to make a mistake, and that was something he couldn't afford at this crucial juncture.

"In one minute, my friend. Let's first make sure we have these two fish hooked and on the line."

They sat in silence, the Arab glanced furtively at the refrigerator, and then back to the screen of the computer. "It takes some time, since the message is routed through so many servers."

"I know. I set it up that way, remember?"

Shabahb grunted and licked his lips. "Please, I need a drink. I'll get it myself."

The Russian made a tsking sound and squeezed the Arab's shoulder, increasing the pressure until the man grunted in pain. "Not till we're sure."

Understood. It is the will of God.

"Do you see?" Shabahb asked. "Is it not just as I predicted?"

Androkovich smiled and stepped over to the refrigerator. He pulled open the door and removed one of the frosty cans and set it on the desk next to the computer. As the Arab reached for it, the Russian placed his hand on top of the can and shook his head.

"First, give them the reassurance of the faithful." He

smiled, allowing a trace of malevolence to filter into the expression. "Tell them their service and loyalty will be rewarded in this life and the next."

Shabahb snorted as his fingers danced over the keyboard.

"What did you tell them?"

"I told them that their faith and service would be rewarded with the customary number of virgins in paradise." He laughed. "It will be enough to sway them. But for us, my friend, we know the value of a woman who has had plenty of practice in pleasing a man, do we not?"

Androkovich was not amused by the Arab's attempt at camaraderie. "Make sure they're hooked before you make jokes."

Shabahb sent another message and received a confirmation. He pointed to the screen.

"See? They have replied. Now, may I please have my beer?"

Androkovich caught the Arab's gaze and held it for a long five seconds, and then let a smile creep over his lips as he lifted his hand from the top of the beer can.

"Sure, my friend," he said, deciding to ease up a little on the man. "Quench your thirst. Drink deep from the well."

As he watched, Shabahb popped the tab on the can and guzzled the beer.

"Thanks, boss," Shabahb said, pausing to exhale.

"Have another one, my friend." He opened the door to the refrigerator, grabbed a can and tossed it to the Arab, then took out the burner cell phone he used for communications with Masoud. It was time to work on the newest wrinkle in the plan.

He stepped outside into the early-evening air and admired the majestic sweep of the mountains in the distance. He was going to miss this view. Perhaps, once this was over and the Saudis had paid him in full, he would settle near another mountain range, but definitely not in the desert, or the United States. Just as he was about to call Masoud's number, Androkovich heard a clip-clopping of hooves. He turned and saw Eileen Autry atop her brown-and-white horse. She called out to him.

He slipped the phone back into his pocket and turned as she rode up. Her blond hair was pulled back in a ponytail, and she wore a tan blouse that clung tightly over the swell of her breasts. Her legs looked long and lean in blue jean pants, which were tucked into ornate, leather riding boots.

"I've been wanting to talk with you," she said.

He disliked looking up to anyone, especially a woman, but he anticipated that the conversation would be shorter if she didn't dismount.

"What can I do for you, Ms. Autry?" he asked.

"I know my brother hired you to maintain security," she said, "but we don't want our ranch turned into some armed camp."

Androkovich raised an eyebrow and smiled.

This could be a problem, he thought, depending on what she had seen.

"What do you mean?" he asked.

The horse's head twisted to the side, and the animal snorted. Eileen tugged the reins a bit. "I mean, you and your men didn't have to have all those rifles earlier. The situation was touchy enough."

The Russian nodded, but added, "Your brother wanted a show of force. Perhaps you'd better speak to him."

"Believe me, I will." She adjusted her grip on the reins, and the big animal shifted, causing Androkovich to step back. "And what were your men doing down by the rear gate? It looked like they were planting some kind of mechanical devices."

Shit, he thought. If she'd taken a closer look, would she know what they were?

He gambled she would not, being the spoiled, pampered rich-girl type.

"Those are special devices to alert us if anyone trespasses," he said. "But be careful if you're riding over in that area. There's a lot of lines and wires that could trip your horse."

The woman's expression took on a startled, angry look. "Then, clean up the area immediately. As I said, we don't want our ranch turned into some kind of fortress."

"Perhaps you'd better take the matter up with your brother," he said. "It was all done on his orders."

"Shane told you to do that?"

He knew her male sibling would agree to anything Androkovich said. "That's right. And although I report directly to him, I don't want to get in the middle of a family feud. All I'm trying to do is make sure you're all protected."

Eileen's eyes flashed. "I'll speak with him." She jerked the reins hard, and the horse's head turned away. In a moment she was moving back toward the house at a fast trot.

The Russian took a deep breath and scrolled down to Shane Autry's cell phone number. He'd have to give him a heads-up that Eileen was on the warpath, and then call Masoud. He felt like one of the circus jugglers he had seen once in Moscow in his youth.

So many balls to keep in the air at the same time, he thought.

And sometimes it felt like he was juggling some damn meat cleavers.

FBI Field Office, Las Vegas, Nevada

BOLAN STUDIED THE large map on the wall of Special Agent Gila Dylan's office. As maps went, this one was pretty detailed and covered a substantial amount of the county. Not only had she highlighted in red the location of Camp Freedom and the last known location of the two missing BLM Park Rangers, but she also had the route of the Las Vegas Marathon in yellow and the site of the desert warfare training seminar in orange.

Agent Dylan walked into the office holding a thick file and sat down behind her desk.

"Sorry to keep you two waiting," she said, "but I had to check in with my supervisor on all the latest developments."

"Government bureaucracy at its finest," Grimaldi said with a wide smile. "We're totally familiar with how the system works. And how it doesn't."

She flashed a lips-only semi-smile. "I also verified you two through that phone number you gave me. I was told to cooperate and extend you every courtesy."

"Your map seems pretty comprehensive," Bolan said, pointing at the wall area. "How many cases do you have going?"

Dylan turned her chair so she was facing the map. "The marathon and the desert warfare school are just on there in the way of general events in the area I had to be mindful of. I had Camp Freedom highlighted due to Mr. Autry's penchant for butting heads with the Bureau of Land Management and his little, well-trained militia. Originally, we were interested in how they were getting their equipment." She paged through the sheaf of papers in her file, extracted one and handed it across the desk to Bolan.

He accepted it and saw a computerized graphic of a stretch of highway with an intersecting road perpendicular to a line that was designated Fence Line.

"That is, until those two BLM rangers disappeared last night," she said. "The unexplained disappearance of two federal employees is a Bureau case. That shows their last known location. The highway they were patrolling is in the area of public domain lands that Autry has been arguing about. The road there is the back access road into his little fiefdom."

"Fiefdom?" Grimaldi said, leaning over to glance at the paper. "I'd say it looks more like Fort Knox, West."

"Good analogy," she said, getting up from her chair.

Grimaldi elbowed Bolan and gave a slight nod.

"As you can see," Dylan said as she traced her fingers over the larger map on the wall, "they were in this area here at 7:23 p.m. Their mobile data terminal in their vehicle indicated that they were checking on a cluster of vehicles on the road. There were no further transmissions after that."

"Any information on the other vehicles?" Bolan asked.

Dylan shook her head. "Unfortunately, no. Theirs isn't like regular police procedures where they do traffic stops and call in license numbers. Instead, they have a general area to keep an eye on, in this case, the public land in the Autry dispute. Plus, there's no dispatch service monitoring their activities other than a basic review of their transmitted reports the next day. They're pretty much on their own."

"Is there any way to track the agents or their vehicle?" Bolan asked.

"Ordinarily, there would be," she said. "There were GPS monitors in both of their cell phones, and in the car's MDT, as well. Unfortunately, after they apparently cleared from their vehicular check, they drove off in a northeasterly direction, and, very soon thereafter, all three GPS devices ceased to function."

"Which wouldn't be likely without some sort of help," Bolan said. "You think they might be inside Autry's place?"

"It's possible." She moved her hand over to the red highlighted section. "He does have several large structures on his land. Our surveillance records indicate that the four buildings are used for storage, but of exactly what, we don't know. Any one of them is large enough to hold numerous vehicles."

"Autry's primarily a cattle rancher, right?" Bolan asked.

She nodded.

"Then why does he need so many barns? I could see it if he was into dairy farming, but he's known for letting his cattle graze on the range, right?"

"On government-owned land, mostly." She tapped the map again. "This region here is at the middle of the dispute. It was designated by the BLM back in 1978, to be used as a wild mustang sanctuary. Well, Autry and the other ranchers in the area began letting their cattle graze on the land. Eventually, an agreement was reached that the ranchers would pay a nominal fee for water and grazing rights. They all did, except one." She smiled. "Care to guess who?"

"Our friend Autry," Grimaldi stated.

Dylan nodded. "In the meantime, there's not much we can do as far as getting a warrant to search Camp Freedom until we get something solid linking Autry with the disappearance of those rangers. We're doing flyovers of the area with a special infrared scanning device that shows any recent interruptions in the top soil. We're hoping to locate something."

"We've got a few other things to check out, Agent Dylan," Bolan said, rising from his chair. He handed her a card with his cell phone number on it. "If we can be of any assistance, give me a call."

She accepted the card with thanks and walked them to the door. As they exited the building, the early evening heat embraced them.

Bolan took out the remote and clicked it twice, unlocking the Escalade as he headed for the driver's door. "Hal said the prince's jet was scheduled to land here at 6:45 p.m. I want to size him up."

Riyadh, Saudi Arabia

MUSTAPHA HELD THE king's Rolex watch in his hand and watched as the second hand swept around the bejeweled face of the timepiece with perfect precision. The king had asked him how soon the watch would be ready, and Mustapha had replied with a deferential smile and shrug. "I want to be absolutely certain that all of the intricate mechanisms are functioning properly." The old royal had seemed to accept this explanation.

In reality the Rolex was functioning perfectly. Mustapha would slip it back on the king's wrist only when it was time to tell him that his grandson, the prince, had been killed. Mustapha wanted to watch the light dim in the old man's eyes as he knew the reign of the House of Saud was finished in this land. No longer would the greedy royals force their oppressive ways upon the populace. It would be a new beginning for his country. A new rise to greatness, unencumbered by the yoke of royal oppression.

Mustapha had reset the watch at the precise moment when Mahfuj had informed him that the charade in Bahrain had succeeded. That was, in effect, the official commencement of their plan…the point of no return. Mustapha made a vow that he would keep the watch until the plan had run its full course. It would be a final symbolic act of defiance. It would signify to the old monarch that his time, and that of the royal family, had run out.

His first-born son was with the prince in the U.S., and Mustapha and his second-born son were here in Arabia at his side. Masoud, his youngest son, had emailed him that his negotiations with the Russian were proceeding as planned, except for a minor, unexpected development regarding the exchange of some of the funding. Apparently, the Americans had stepped up their surveillance of Camp Freedom due to some unforeseen incident, so meeting the Russian to give him the front money for the weapons purchase would be a bit more problematic.

This new development worried Mustapha slightly, but he knew Masoud was capable of handling his end of things. He'd assured his father that the Russian had successfully recruited the two Shi'ite scapegoats, who would be initially blamed for the kidnapping and murder of the decadent prince. And the magnitude of another marathon bombing within the continental United States, one in which a member of the Royal Family was involved, would ensure that the Americans would not interfere when the Saudi military moved in to take charge and restore order. In the end, all the Americans really cared about was keeping the spigots of oil open and flowing. And once he was president of the new Arabia, Mustapha would see to that, but at his own price. A price that guaranteed the sovereignty and development of his country.

Mustapha felt a new wave of fatigue sweep over him. He had been unable to sleep since he had seen Mahfuj off at the airport. He remembered the look in the eyes of his first-born. Eagerness, anticipation, but not fear. Mahfuj was ready, as if he'd been training his whole life for this moment. And in a way, he had. They all had. It was preordained, ever since he had seen the four desert falcons in his dream.

Mustapha glanced at his own watch and then to the blank screen on his smartphone. It was almost dawn…time for morning prayers. Mustapha set down the king's Rolex and completed the washing ritual. He then unrolled his prayer rug and placed it on the floor, facing Mecca. The Learjet had been in flight for more than nineteen hours. Barring any complications, they should be landing soon at their destination, half a world away. He would ask God for strength and guidance. He needed to hear from Mahfuj before sleep would come. Then, and only then, would he allow himself some rest.

He had just knelt to begin the prayer when the screen of his smartphone chimed with an incoming message.

God forgive me, he thought as he rose from the prayer rug and quickly checked the message. It was from Mahfuj.

Father, we have landed safely. I will meet Masoud later. All is well.

"Thanks be to God," Mustapha murmured.

All is well, he thought. As time continues to march onward toward victory.

McCarran Airport, Las Vegas, Nevada

BOLAN AND GRIMALDI stood just inside the doorway of the private hangar and watched as suitcase after suitcase was unloaded from the cargo bay of the Learjet. In all, Bolan counted twenty-seven pieces of luggage. He wondered how many were in the prince's entourage, and how many pieces of the luggage belonged to them.

"Looks like this dude doesn't know the definition of traveling light," Grimaldi said.

"Looks like," Bolan replied. He was watching a tall man in a dark suit approaching them, talking into his left wrist as he walked.

"I love it when those guys do that," Grimaldi said. "It's so James Bondish."

"The guy does have Secret Service Agent written all over him," Bolan said.

"This is a restricted area," the agent said. "You'll have to leave."

Bolan flashed his Department of Justice identification.

Grimaldi flashed his ID, as well.

The agent scrutinized both of them, then said, "I'm Special Agent Berquist, Secret Service. What's DOJ doing here?"

The agent's confusion was understandable, but Bolan didn't have the time or the patience for long-winded explanations of their cover story. "Who's the special-agent-in-charge?"

"Special Agent Draper," Berquist stated.

"How about getting hold of him so I don't have to explain myself twice?" Bolan said as affably as he could.

Berquist compressed his lips, obviously thinking it over, and then spoke into his wrist once more. "Looks like they're DOJ. They want to see you." He listened for a moment, then pointed to a room at the far end of the hangar. "Report to that room and wait."

"Hey, buddy," Grimaldi said, "we don't wait for anybody."

Bolan tapped him on the shoulder and shook his head. "Has the prince deplaned yet?"

Berquist stared at him, his eyes showing a touch of obvious surprise. He shook his head and nodded toward the plane. "No, sir. They're in there now with customs. Apparently, they just woke him up, and he's getting dressed."

"Tell your boss we need to speak with him ASAP. We'll be out of sight in the room for now, but we need to see him before you take off for the prince's hotel."

"It's a matter of national security," Grimaldi added.

The agent nodded. "Yes, sir." He took another step back and whispered into his left cuff again.

Bolan guided his partner toward the room about forty feet away at the far end of the hangar. Perhaps it would be better if they retained a bit of anonymity for now, as far as the prince and his entourage were concerned.. It could make it easier to keep tabs on him during the training course.

Bolan opened the door, and he and Grimaldi stepped inside and stood by the large glass window. They watched as more luggage was unloaded. A pair of vehicles, a van and a stretch limo, pulled up. Some airport luggage handlers and two men in traditional Arab dress stood by the van as three other men, whom Bolan assumed to be customs agents, began to inspect the luggage. A broad-shouldered fellow emerged from the door of the plane looking almost like a taller clone of the first Secret Service agent they'd seen. He turned and said something to someone still inside, trotted down the steps and walked briskly toward the room. Bolan continued to watch the entire scene. The man opened the door and stepped inside, extending his hand.

"I'm Special Agent Steven Draper."

As they shook, Bolan sized up the man: late thirties, obviously very fit, neat haircut, sharply dressed. The guy exuded the customary professionalism of the Secret Service.

"My agent said you guys are DOJ," Draper said. "What's Justice doing here?"

"We're here on a parallel investigation," Bolan replied. "I take it you're aware of the most recent developments concerning the elevation of the current threat level?"

Draper nodded. "If you're talking about that flake, Autry, and his anti-Muslim comments, we are. But we've planned for every contingency concerning the prince's safety."

"I'm sure you have. We've been assigned more or less as an augmentation."

"Yeah," Grimaldi added. "We'll be up close and personal with His Highness attending the desert warfare course."

Draper nodded. "We'll be on the sidelines, but it's good to know that someone will be on the inside, as well. I'll need to verify your credentials, of course, and like to remind you that we're the primary agency in charge here."

"No problem," Bolan said. "I have a number you can call to verify our assignment."

Bolan held up his hand to halt Draper's response as he observed a group of men descending from the jet. Four were obviously Secret Service. The others were dressed in traditional *thobes* and *ghutras*. Bolan counted five of them. One of them was huge and looked like a walking refrigerator. A sixth Arab stopped at the top of the stairs and stood arms akimbo.

"Which one's the prince?" he asked.

"He's the one at the top," Draper said. "He just about had us pulling our hair out on his last trip to Vegas."

"We heard he was problematic," Bolan said.

"That's putting it mildly," Draper stated. "They're staying at the Algonquin. The Saudis rented an entire floor of the hotel. It makes it easier for us to restrict the access to the area, but this guy had an endless parade of women, booze and problems the entire time. He claimed he didn't like the crowded atmosphere of the casinos, so he had them move a couple of crap tables up to his room, along with a band so he could dance the night away."

"Sounds like a lot of royal babysitting," Grimaldi said.

Draper flashed a lopsided smile. "You got that right."

Bolan studied the prince, memorizing the man's bearded face and sizing up the royal as best he could at that distance. He knew he'd have more opportunities over the course of the next few days, but his first impression was that of a young man totally used to having everything done for him. It would be interesting to see how he performed under pressure, if he actually intended to partake of any of the desert warfare training.

"Booze?" Grimaldi said. "I thought Muslims didn't drink."

"I guess nobody told the prince that," Draper said. "We had to seize and delete several embarrassing photos from the cell phones of some of those in attendance."

Bolan had been surveying the other members of the prince's entourage. One, in particular, a medium-sized but wiry-looking guy with a bandaged right hand, had piqued the Executioner's interest. Not only did the Arab move with a certain smooth assertiveness, but he was the only member of the entourage who seemed to be taking note of their surroundings. The Arab's head moved around with a predator's piercing gaze, finally stopping at the room and locking eyes with Bolan.

At least one of Humpty Dumpty's men is alert and ready to keep him from falling, Bolan thought. That guy bears watching.

But at the same time, the soldier couldn't help but wonder if the bodyguard was thinking the same thing.

CHAPTER SEVEN

The Algonquin Hotel & Casino, Las Vegas, Nevada

As always, Mahfuj had awakened before dawn for his morning prayers. He and the others in the detail each had their own rooms. Since the prince had rented the entire floor, several of the American Secret Service agents were stationed there, as well. Two of them had been assigned to stand guard in the hallway all night. After he'd risen, Mahfuj had gone to the door of his room and opened it a crack. The two Americans were still there, looking tired but alert. Their presence could be a problem later on, when the time came to take the prince, but Mahfuj knew he could deal with them. The best way was to gain their trust, especially of their leader, Draper.

The lax sentry did not see the knife that slit his throat. Mahfuj remembered his father telling him that when he was just a boy.

I must gain the trust of the infidels, he thought.

He glanced out the large window. It was almost dawn.

After washing himself and placing his prayer rug toward the east, he'd begun his recitation of the two *fardh* and the two *sunnah*. He did not want to miss his prayers and felt a residual anger at the decadent prince, whose flagrant apostasy the evening before at the airport had forced Mahfuj to forgo *maghrib*. Upon completion he rose and did his customary exercises.

He performed push-ups, sit-ups, squats and a dozen of the Tae Kwon Do forms he had mastered for his black belt. His father had seen to it that Mahfuj and his brothers had the very best of the Korean instructors that had been brought in for the special training. Even though the teachers were not Muslims and were segregated in the special camps where the rest of the infidels stayed, Mahfuj had taken to the training well; more so than his two brothers, who completed the very minimum at their father's insistence. By age twelve Mahfuj had become a black belt and could break four pine boards with but a single punch or kick. He continued to condition his hands, soaking them in brine and plunging them into pots of sand to toughen his skin. That had enabled him to seize the hot barrel of the would-be assassin's rifle in Bahrain without recoiling. And now, even though his hand was practically healed, his "heroic act," as the king had put it, was a good diversionary source for his current mission.

He stood in the spacious room now, covered with perspiration despite the air-conditioning that kept it as cool as a desert oasis.

His cell phone chimed with an incoming text.

It was from Masoud: Can you meet?

He replied with a text that he would be at the prescribed place in one hour and forty minutes and then went to shower.

Desert Warfare Training Academy

BOLAN AND GRIMALDI trotted through the last section of the obstacle course in the desert warfare training site.

Perhaps fifty other men and a smattering of women were lumbering through various stages of the course. As obstacle courses went, this one was pretty standard, and Bolan found himself actually enjoying the physicality of the challenge, even in the dry heat. Grimaldi, however, was having a bit more difficulty. The Executioner slowed his pace a bit to allow his partner to keep up.

It's all about staying together, Bolan thought as he watched Grimaldi vault over a horizontal log, his face and neck red with exertion.

"You good to go?" Bolan asked.

"Damn straight," Grimaldi gasped. His head shot to his right where another team of four guys was creeping up on them.

After running through parallel rows of old car tires, scaling a hanging net looped over a thirty-foot wall and fast-roping down the other side, they came to a fifteen-foot wall with four thick ropes hanging about midway down. Bolan put an extra zing in his last two steps and jumped high, seizing the rope. Grimaldi failed to anticipate the height, and his jump fell short, his fingers brushing the end of the suspended rope.

He fell back down, swore and backed up a few feet to run at it again. This had allowed the four-man team to gain a few steps on them. They were almost even now.

Grimaldi's head bobbled to the side as he glanced at them. "Shit."

"Need a hand?" Bolan asked. The Executioner was already halfway up the wall.

"I got it, dammit," Grimaldi said as he took three running steps to make the jump. This time he was successful. "Keep going. Those assholes are gaining on us."

Bolan went up, hand over hand, until he was able

to grab the top edge of the board and then slide over. Instead of dropping down the other side, he straddled the wall momentarily to make sure his partner was able to make it.

Grimaldi's feet slipped several times before he gained enough purchase to scramble up the wall.

They dropped to the soft sand on the other side, but Grimaldi's landing was a bit off balance, and he fell.

"You all right?" Bolan asked.

Grimaldi grunted that he was. "Now quit asking."

To their right, the four-man team in desert camos had just finished scaling their respective barrier. One of them, a short, dark-haired guy in his early twenties, looked over and grinned. "Need some help, ladies?"

From the looks of them, Bolan figured they were ex-military. Probably getting this desert warfare certificate so they could pad their resumes a bit before applying to some private military contractor's outfit for the big bucks.

"Come on, let's smoke those bastards," Grimaldi said, getting to his feet and giving the guy the finger.

Bolan and Grimaldi actually pulled ahead by several yards as they both jumped a four-foot ditch and sprinted toward the last obstacle, a telephone-pole-sized log set on three-foot-high concrete anchors. The object was to race along the log without falling into the gravel-laden pit on the ground underneath. Bolan reached the log first, with Grimaldi right behind him. The four-man team was perhaps twenty-five feet behind them now. If they could cross this last barrier without any problems, the finish line was only a short sprint away.

The log had been treated with creosote, which made it slippery. Bolan's lightweight desert combat boots with the corrugated soles gripped the wood with efficiency. The trick, he knew, was to maintain your balance without sacrificing too much speed. Trying to go too fast increased your chances of slipping. Bolan elevated his arms to his chest, similar to a boxer's stance, for better balance. Behind him he could hear Grimaldi's periodic grunts.

"Looking good so far," Grimaldi yelled.

Bolan didn't look back but estimated his partner was about twenty feet behind him.

He was nearing the end of the log now. Fifteen feet… ten…five…

Jumping off and landing in the sandy earth, Bolan turned to assess the informal race.

Grimaldi was nearing the end of their log. About twenty-five feet to their right the four-man team was doing a credible job of traversing their obstacle. All four of them were moving with a quick, yet cautious stride. The Stony Man pilot was still ahead, though.

"You got it, Jack," Bolan yelled, giving Grimaldi some verbal encouragement. In reality, he knew winning this informal little race meant nothing, but the competition of even an impromptu game was always a good motivator. The Executioner also knew that the place to make your mistakes was in training, rather than in the field. Still, with only about six more feet for Grimaldi to go, this one appeared to be won. The short guy who'd tried to bait them with the catcall glanced over with a worried look.

Bolan kept his face impassive.

Grimaldi had about three feet to go now. Maybe two more steps.

Suddenly, as his right foot came forward, the sole

of his boot landed on the curvature of the log, and he lurched forward. He spread his arms to keep his balance and did a little stutter step with his left foot, causing it to slide around the log, as well. He went straight down, each leg looping around the log, his groin smacking down on to the hard surface.

Grimaldi's face twisted into a cartoonish grimace, but he managed to grab the top of the log with his hands to keep from falling off.

The short guy bringing up the rear of the four-man team grinned and shouted, "Keep going. We got them."

One-by-one the four-man team moved to the end of their log and jumped off.

Grimaldi emitted a low groan as he watched them scampering toward the finish line.

"Damn slick boots," Grimaldi said through clenched teeth. His upper body lolled on the top of the log for a few seconds. "We had them beat, too."

"Don't worry about it," Bolan said.

"Easy for you to say." He managed to sit upright and then swing his right leg up on to the log, walked the last two steps and hopped off. "Oh, man, that hurt."

"Well," Bolan said, "Hal did say this course was a bit of a ball buster, didn't he?"

Grimaldi snorted a half laugh and said, "Fifty thousand comedians out of work and you have to take their jobs?"

Bolan knew that his partner was okay now. He extended his hand outward. "Need a hand?"

Grimaldi snorted again. "Nah, just a new set of balls. Aww, hell, it's not like this is my first time at the rodeo." He straightened and started a slow jog toward the finish line. "Come on. Let's complete this thing."

As they trotted across the finish, one of the instructors clicked a stopwatch and shook his head. "Tough break. You guys had the lead, hands down, until that last little slip."

"Tell me about it," Grimaldi said, still gripping his crotch.

The instructor pointed toward a pair of foam coolers in the shade of a primitive-looking gazebo. "Get yourselves some water."

The four-man team that had beaten them was standing next to the coolers. The short, dark-haired guy who'd teased them at the last barrier reached into the closest one, withdrew a bottle of water and tossed it like a football at Grimaldi.

"Here, put some ice on your family jewels," he said.

Bolan stretched and caught the bottle. The expression on his face told the dark-haired guy to back off. The four of them gave the Executioner and Grimaldi a wide berth as they walked to the coolers. Bolan tossed the water bottle back to the short guy and said, "Thanks, but we'll get our own."

The short guy nodded and flashed a quick smile. "No offense meant."

"None taken," Bolan said. He reached in and withdrew two bottles, giving one to Grimaldi.

One of the other instructors drove up in a Hummer and pointed toward a tan Quonset hut about thirty yards away. "The class will resume over there."

The four-man team left the shade of the gazebo and started a trek toward the building. The team leader nodded to Bolan in a sign of respect. The Executioner nodded back.

"I hope we have a chance to lock horns with those

assholes again," Grimaldi said as he twisted the cap on his water bottle. "I'd like to knock that one little bastard's ass all the way up to his mouth."

"We've got two more days, so I'm sure we will," Bolan said, taking a drink of water. "But let's not forget why we're here. The mission comes first."

"Yeah, yeah, I know," Grimaldi said. He drank some more water. "It's just that I don't like coming in second."

"It's a lot better to come in first when it really counts," Bolan told. "This was just the warm-up."

"Yeah," Grimaldi said, bending over at the waist a few more times. "They say even the great Joe Louis used to get punched in the face during his training camps. But when he stepped into that ring, he was the king."

"Speaking of royalty, I wonder where His Royal Highness is?"

Grimaldi looked around. "Yeah, you're right. If he was out here sweating, you can be sure Draper and the rest of his team would be running interference. I haven't seen hide nor hair of any of them."

"Report to Building A when you're sufficiently recovered," the guy in the Hummer said. His voice had a Missouri twang to it.

"Say," Grimaldi said, walking up to the driver's door in a casual, good-old-boy fashion. "Where you from?"

The guy squinted. "Why you asking?"

Grimaldi shrugged and flashed a grin. "Just thought I detected a Southern accent. I'm from the South myself."

"Oh, you don't sound like it."

"That's because I was just born there. Raised up

north. But I never forgot my roots. You're from Texas, right?"

The guy shook his head. "Missouri."

"Oh, well," Grimaldi said. "I was close." He extended his hand, and the guy shook it. Grimaldi leaned closer. "How about a favor, one Southern boy to another?"

The guy's head cocked to the side, his face quizzical.

"Give us a ride up there. I busted my balls on that last obstacle."

The guy looked around and nodded, hooking his thumb toward the back door. As they got in he said, "I'm supposed to stay down here to shoo people up to Building A, but I guess it'll be all right."

"We appreciate it," Grimaldi said. "Say, I heard that there was some kind of important Arab dude in this class. Where is he?"

Bolan saw the guy's eyes flash in the rearview mirror. He was obviously uncomfortable discussing this subject. "Actually, I'm not supposed to mention him."

"I won't tell if you don't," Grimaldi said.

"He's some kind of Saudi prince or something," the guy replied. "We got briefed by the Secret Service months ago and again last week. We aren't supposed to tell anybody about this, and they've been checking the course out for the past week, guarding things and doing surveillances."

"Oh, yeah?" Grimaldi said. "How'd he do on that obstacle course?"

"He hasn't come in yet today."

"Huh?"

"The prince is having trouble adjusting to the time zone change." The guy pulled up to the side of the Quonset hut.

Bolan pushed the door open and slid out.

"Well, isn't that a kick in the head," Grimaldi said, getting out himself. "I hope the rest of the course doesn't upset his delicate sensibilities."

"Cool it," Bolan ordered.

Grimaldi slammed the door and offered his hand to the guy once again. "Thanks, bud. Say, what's your name?"

"George," the guy said. "George Duncan."

"Okay, see you around, George." Grimaldi waved as the big Hummer took off.

"Well, at least we now know why we haven't seen the prince today. Sounds like the guy's a marshmallow."

"Maybe that's a good thing," Bolan said. "Draper and his crew have enough to worry about."

Grimaldi nodded in agreement. "Draper did seem like a good guy. I guess he deserves the break."

"That's not what I'm talking about," Bolan said. "Did your newfound buddy, George, look familiar?"

Grimaldi considered the question, compressed his lips, then shook his head. "Can't say that he did. Why?"

"He was at the Autry place yesterday," Bolan said. "He's one of the militia."

The Algonquin Hotel and Casino

MAHFUJ NODDED TO the two American Secret Service agents in the hallway as he walked toward the elevators. One of them perked up.

"Are you guys leaving?" the agent asked.

Mahfuj forced his most beatific smile and shook his head emphatically.

"His Royal Highness has not yet…recovered from

his journey," he said in perfect English. "I am afraid the change in the time difference has adversely affected him. He still rests, but plans to rise soon to replenish himself."

The agent nodded.

I must do more to gain their trust and their favor, Mahfuj thought.

He smiled again and held up his bandaged right hand. "I must go to a pharmacy to purchase some medical supplies. I assume there is one close by?"

The agent raised his hand and spoke into the microphone on his wrist. "Team leader, I've got one coming down." He pressed the button for the elevator. "Can you give him directions to the nearest drugstore?"

Mahfuj listened but heard no sound as the agent nodded.

He must have a microphone in his ear, Mahfuj thought. Their communication equipment was excellent.

"One of the team members will meet you in the lobby to show you the way."

"Thank you."

It was now 9:38 a.m., and he was certain there would be enough people in the casino of this place of decadence to obscure him as he proceeded to his meeting with Masoud.

Gain their trust, he thought again.

"You and your associate have been on guard a long time?" Mahfuj asked.

The agent shook his head. "Only a few hours."

"May I bring you back some refreshments, then? Some coffee perhaps?"

The agent politely declined, but smiled as he did so.

The elevator doors opened, and Mahfuj knew the man had interpreted his offer as one of friendship

He stepped inside and pressed the button for the lobby. The door slid closed, and Mahfuj found himself alone in the cubicle, his reflection staring back at him from the mirrored surfaces that composed the ceiling and walls of the box. They were on the top floor, and the elevator paused to stop several times before reaching the bottom level. With each stop more people got on, pathetic-looking men, both young and old, clad in bright shirts and pants that didn't descend past their knees. And the women… Most dressed like whores, in tight-fitting garments that failed to conceal their bodies at all. None of them had the decency to cover their hair, their faces, or their breasts, for that matter. It was a parade of decadence. These people had no shame, much less any sense of devotion. As more and more infidels crowded into the small space around him, Mahfuj retreated into himself, reviewing his morning thus far.

The prince had insisted that they all wear Western-style clothing while attending the desert warfare training seminar.

The course, Mahfuj knew, was a sham…merely another worthless medal that the prince could place on his uniform with all the other false medallions he hadn't really earned. But perhaps this one he would genuinely deserve. He would, if all went according to plan, be learning much about the tactics, and consequences, of real desert warfare.

The elevator finally reached the lobby, and Mahfuj stood near the rear corner and watched as everyone else departed. As he stepped through the doors, he saw the two agents approaching him. One was named Draper, and he was in charge of the others.

"Has the prince changed his mind about attending the course this morning?" Agent Draper asked.

Mahfuj had assessed this man carefully the night before. He seemed capable, for an American, and Mahfuj knew he had to gain this one's trust more so than that of the others. He smiled.

"His Royal Highness has not recovered from the strain of the journey," he said, holding up his bandaged hand again. "But I must attend to my injury."

"Oh, the drugstore, right?" Draper smiled, as well. "I'll have one of my men escort you to the closest one."

Mahfuj shook his head. "That is not necessary. I wish to acquaint myself a bit with our surroundings, especially your famous Las Vegas Strip."

Draper lifted an eyebrow. "So I take it the prince won't be leaving for the seminar anytime soon?"

"No. He will most likely be ready after he dines in one hour."

Draper nodded and pointed to the throngs of people huddled close to the sea of noisy, pinging machines. "The Strip's that way, through the casino. Just follow the yellow brick road."

Mahfuj glanced downward. The carpeting was red and full of lush designs, but a saffron pathway was woven into the surface. He caught the Secret Service agent's meaning and proceeded to walk toward an exit.

He took a look around as he strolled through the sea of infidels. Forlorn devils, all of them, plopping down their currency in futile attempts to achieve some sort of financial victory against this house of Satan. His father had warned him about the decadence of the West, with their disdain for the will of God and their innate hatred of Islam.

He glanced over his shoulder to see if any of the Secret Service agents were following him. Viewing none, he paused and stepped into a small gift shop, pretending to peruse the gaudy clothes and worthless trinkets in the window, while all the time scanning the crowd. No one stood out.

Masoud had emailed him a picture and a map of their meeting place. It was a large fountain adorned with statues in the front courtyard of the hotel. Mahfuj glanced at his watch. It was 9:53 a.m. Masoud would be waiting, but it was imperative that no one followed.

He surveyed the crowd again. The clerk approached and asked if she could help him. She was a typical Western whore, with a painted face, flaunting her exposed body parts. Under Sharia law she would have been whipped a hundred times.

"No, thank you," Mahfuj replied, affecting his most beatific smile once again. "I am on my way to a meeting."

He turned and strode out of the doors, keeping a brisk pace until he reached the main exit, pausing one more time to stop and conduct countersurveillance.

The place was a wasteland of decadence that dwarfed even the most vivid descriptions. He was glad that he was there to view it firsthand. It was good to know the enemy, good to know what he was fighting against.

Outside he stepped into hot, dry air and felt drenched in an accustomed warmth of the sun's rays. At last he felt at home. After all, this was the same sun that shone on the deserts of his homeland.

Desert Warfare Training Academy

BOLAN LEANED IN the shade of the overhanging awning on the front of the Quonset hut as he dialed Stony Man Farm on the cell phone to check in. He told Grimaldi to go inside and cool off in the air-conditioning, but his partner wouldn't hear of it. He leaned against the wall, guzzling water.

Hal Brognola answered on the first ring. "How's Vegas? You guys having any luck at the tables?"

"Yeah, right," Bolan said. "We're at the desert warfare training seminar."

"Oh, yeah? How's that going?"

"So far, it's a real ball-buster," Bolan said, looking at Grimaldi.

Brognola laughed. "I'll have to have you tell me about it when you get back. How are things looking with the prince?"

"So far he's a no-show today. We caught a glimpse of him and his entourage at the airport last night. We met the Secret Service agents guarding him, as well."

Bolan could hear typing on a keyboard.

"Yeah, okay," Brognola said. "Special Agent Steven Draper is the SAC, according to the file Aaron got. Looks to be more than up to the task. He's worked dignitary protection before."

"We met him, too," Bolan said. "Seems like a good man. But I need you to check on something else."

"Name it."

Bolan gave him a quick rundown about the two missing BLM Park Rangers, the confrontation at the Autry ranch and the militia group standing guard at Camp Freedom.

"Yeah, I was just reading up on them," Brognola said.

"One of them is working here at the desert warfare training facility. He's a white guy about twenty-five or six. Goes by the name of George Duncan."

Bolan heard more clicking, then Brognola said, "Hmm, I don't see anything in this file on that connection. I'm sure the Secret Service must've run background checks on the staff there. I'll look into it."

"Okay." He stopped as a group of about twenty sweaty men and women in BDUs began trudging into the Quonset hut. "Our class is about to start. I'll check back later."

"Roger that," Brognola said. "I'll see what else I can find out on George and the Minutemen."

"Look for some guy named Frank, last name unknown. He seemed to be running the show, from what I could tell." Bolan terminated the call and headed for the entrance.

Grimaldi pulled open the door. "Ah," he said, fanning himself. "At least we're getting out of the heat for a while."

"Maybe," Bolan said as he watched the Hummer pull up with George Duncan inside. "Maybe not."

The Grand Marquis Hotel and Casino

MAHFUJ WATCHED THE gurgling water cascading down from a spout between the white statues of two near-naked women. The concrete replica of a huge, muscular man holding some type of long spear was seated between them.

Even their statues are obscene, he thought. No wonder my father was so emphatic in his warnings to me about this place of evil and decadence.

He felt a hand on his shoulder and turned. It was Masoud.

Remembering their father's instructions not to show undue familiarity, Mahfuj resisted the urge to embrace his brother. Instead, he remained impassive.

"Excuse me, but would you be so kind as to take a picture of me by this fountain?" Masoud asked.

He had shaved his once-full beard, leaving only a sparse band around his mouth, and was wearing typical Western clothing, a gray cotton shirt and tan slacks. For all practical purposes, he could pass for a non-Muslim.

"Certainly," Mahfuj said. He accepted the camera from his brother and stepped back, pretending to fumble with it. "How do you work this?"

Masoud stepped closer and whispered, "Inside, there is a small coffee shop. It is called Starbucks. Meet me there."

Mahfuj nodded, and Masoud stepped back and posed next to the fountain.

After he took the picture, Mahfuj handed the camera back and the two men left in different directions.

Mahfuj crossed a rather substantial courtyard and continued through the glass doors of the casino. He was stunned at the immensity of the scene that appeared before him. This room held row after row of flashing, ringing machines set under a high ceiling full of lights that made the interior both illuminated and seductive.

As seductive as Satan's lair, he thought.

He scanned the signs indicating various locations: Casino, Hotel Registration, Restaurants, Shops, etc.

Following the arrow that pointed toward Restaurants, he soon found the small coffee shop and went inside.

More scantily clad women, girls really, pranced and strutted behind a glass counter, flaunting their bodies without shame. One asked him for his order, and Mahfuj was taken aback. Before he could answer, Masoud was at his side saying, "This gentlemen will have—" Masoud rattled off something that Mahfuj did not understand. His brother pointed to a table in the far corner, almost out of sight of the entrance. Mahfuj went there and took a seat, keeping his face to the door. He scanned the crowd of people passing by but did not see anyone he recognized. It was doubtful that any of the Secret Service agents had followed him this far. He allowed himself to relax slightly as his brother sat in the chair opposite him with two paper cups.

"This coffee is fantastic," Masoud said, peeling off the plastic lid from his own cup. "Try some."

Mahfuj watched as the steamy vapor rose from the dark liquid. Suddenly he was worried. Had his own brother been corrupted by the ways of the infidels? "Did you say your prayers this morning?"

Masoud studied Mahfuj's expression for several seconds, and then he smiled. Seeing the white teeth flashing in contrast to his brother's dark face brought back the remembrance of their youthful games and allayed his concern slightly.

"Don't worry," Masoud said. "I have not been affected by my time in the land of the great Satan." He brought the paper cup to his lips and drank with caution, motioning for Mahfuj to do the same. "But do try this coffee. You'll like it."

Mahfuj left his cup untouched. He wanted as little

to do with this corrupt culture as possible. Silently, he thanked God for being the first-born, the strongest, the one his father had chosen for the most difficult part of the plan.

"My brother," Masoud said as a crease formed between his dark eyebrows. "Your hand is bandaged. Are you injured?"

Mahfuj shook his head as he spoke and flicked his pursed lips. "It is nothing. A trifle that I have been using to my advantage. How goes the rest of the plan? Have you heard from Father?"

"I emailed him this morning. All is well. Everything is going accordingly."

Mahfuj listened as he continued to scan his surroundings. Nothing appeared out of the ordinary, but he was still worried. So many of these infidels looked so much alike.

"And the prince?" Masoud asked. "He is well?"

"As well as anyone who embraces apostasy can be. He fills the hours with his vile proclivities—alcohol, gambling, women. And even now, with the sun high, he still sleeps. Yesterday his decadent indulgences caused me to miss prayers."

Mahfuj began to feel his rage building again. His brother's reactions seemed all too indifferent. He merely drank some more of the hot, dark liquid.

"Did you not hear me?" Mahfuj asked through clenched teeth.

"It is the will of God," Masoud said. "But, please, drink. Have you forgotten your manners just as the prince has forgotten his?"

"Do not compare me to him, even in jest."

Masoud lowered his head in apology.

"We should not stay here too long," Mahfuj said. "Tell me, is everything in place as it should be?"

"Yes, and no." Masoud's expression turned serious. "The Russian had to kill two American agents the night before last. They discovered us meeting."

Mahfuj felt a tightening in his gut. "What? How has this affected the plan?"

Instead of answering immediately, Masoud took another drink and then swiveled his head in a relaxed manner, surveying the room once more.

"It is under control," he said. "But the resulting surveillance has made it problematic for me to meet with him. I have been unable to provide him with the rest of the funds he needs to procure the equipment tomorrow night."

"Does Father know of this?"

"He does," Masoud said. "But, my brother, all is well. We have figured out an alternative plan. Remember, ultimately, this must look as if it can be traced back to Autry."

Mahfuj considered that. He knew the plan involved centering the blame on the eccentric rancher to forestall any subsequent American intervention once the military coup had begun. That part was essential. At this point there was no way the army of his people, divided by the monarchy for decades with their recriminations, could stand against the military of the Americans. Not yet, anyway. But while he understood his father's complex machinations, Mahfuj also knew that the simplest of plans was often the best.

His training had taught him that the intricate series of complexities offered a host of variables where something could go wrong. It was not like building a timepiece. He had tried to tell his father that, but to no avail. The Desert Falcon, the watchmaker, thrived on the intricacies of the parts all working in unison. It was how he viewed life itself. And now Mahfuj and his brothers were essential parts of that timepiece. So every night Mahfuj prayed that he would be proven wrong, that his father's plan would succeed. That his country would be able to throw off the yoke of oppression. Now the specter once again loomed that his prayers would go unanswered.

"What is this alternative plan? Does it have a good chance of success?"

Masoud placed his palm on Mahfuj's bandaged hand. "It has been arranged. The Russian has made a plan to attain the money by other means."

"Other means? What other means?"

Masoud touched Mahfuj's hand again. "You need not concern yourself."

Mahfuj felt the anger rising within him, but he knew he had to keep it under control. He had discussed every eventuality with his father before leaving, and surely his father, the Desert Falcon, had done the same with Masoud.

"All right," Mahfuj said. "And what of the puppets?"

"Two students, recruited by the Russian. He should have them in custody soon."

This part of the plan bothered Mahfuj, as well. "They are Muslims?"

Masoud nodded. "Shi'ites."

This made their use and sacrifice more acceptable. "As long as they are not Sunnis."

Masoud reached over and removed the plastic lid from his brother's cup. "Now, drink, my brother. Drink to our success, and the success of our father. A new country, a new world is about to be opened to us."

Slowly, Mahfuj gripped the paper cup with his left hand. He could feel the still-present heat radiating through the paper. The temperature of the artificially cooled air made his body feel strange, out of sorts. Perhaps a hot drink would restore his equilibrium. Bringing the cup to his lips he took a quick gulp. The hot liquid seared his tongue and tasted almost too sweet, but suddenly it felt deliciously warm on the journey down his throat. He paused, and then took another sip.

Masoud's smiling face loomed before him like an expectant child. "See? I told you it would be good, didn't I?"

Mahfuj smiled, too, and rewarded his younger brother with a quick nod.

Perhaps this was a sign, a good sign, that even in this decadent, hostile, foreign land something pleasant could come from something so unexpected and signaled the rewards that waited for both of them.

CHAPTER EIGHT

Desert Warfare Training Center

Bolan and Grimaldi hung back and let the rest of the attendees funnel out the doors as they headed across the parking lot toward their vehicles. The afternoon session had consisted of classroom instruction on tactics and a few practical rehearsals in the main building. It was an expansive brick structure with a lot of classrooms and a full-sized gym. The prince and his entourage had arrived late in the afternoon and sat near the back for only part of the sessions. When the training programs had started, the prince and his retinue abruptly left. Bolan had managed only a quick hello to Draper during one of the breaks, saying he would call him later.

Draper had nodded.

As they stepped out into the late-afternoon heat, Grimaldi emitted a heavy sigh.

"Well, that's eight hours of my life I'll never get back," he said. "Not to mention my audition for the *Nutcracker* suite." His face contorted into an exaggerated wince.

"We can stop by a sporting goods shop and buy you a cup," Bolan said as they approached their Escalade. He clicked the remote to unlock the doors.

"Yeah, that's probably a good idea," Grimaldi replied. "Especially if we have to participate in those urban assault practicals tomorrow. You think His Royal Highness will show?"

"Who knows?" Bolan said as he opened the rear passenger door and removed two bottles of a popular sports drink, handing one to Grimaldi.

His partner grinned. "Hey, where'd these come from?"

"I stashed them under the seat this morning. Figured it would be our reward after a hard day's training."

Grimaldi twisted the cap and took a long drink. "Some reward. This stuff tastes like a glass of water from the Dead Sea." He drank some more. "But I appreciate that you're always prepared for everything."

Bolan started the Escalade and set the air-conditioning on high.

Grimaldi drained the rest of the liquid in the bottle and leaned back in the seat. "Well, what do you say we grab a shower and then go get a couple of steaks at the Peppermill? I'm starving."

Bolan shifted into gear and took out his cell phone. "Let me check in with Hal first."

A rather pained expression stretched over Grimaldi's face as he shook the empty plastic bottle. "Man, you don't know the meaning of the word quit do you?"

"Not in my vocabulary." Bolan pressed the button and waited for Brognola to answer. When he did, Bolan put the phone on speaker.

"How's the class going?" Brognola's gruff voice asked. "Learning anything new?"

"Only that I should have brought my cup supporter," Grimaldi said.

"Huh?"

"Remember the ball-buster that I mentioned earlier? Jack had an unfortunate slip on the obstacle course this morning," Bolan said.

Brognola's deep laugh resonated. "I'll FedEx a cup."

"You find out anything about our buddy, George, or his militia pals?" Bolan asked.

"As a matter of fact, yeah."

Bolan heard the shuffling of papers and more clicks on the keyboard. Then the big Fed said, "Okay, first things first. The People's New Minutemen Militia is a fairly new organization. It sprang to life about six months ago, coincidentally right about the time that our buddy Rand Autry lost his appeal in that court case with the BLM over paying those back taxes."

"Go figure, huh?" Grimaldi said.

"And that's not all," Brognola continued. "They have a website, your typical militia stuff about freedom, the right to bear arms, protect the citizenry, etcetera, but the interesting thing is their IP address traces back directly to Autry's place, Camp Freedom. It's almost like it was created there on the ranch."

"Is there anything suspicious in their file?" Bolan asked.

"No," Brognola said. "Not much at all, other than posting their manifesto and the standard propaganda stuff on their website. They don't ask for any donations or recruitment or anything of the sort."

"So, they're more like Autry's private security force," Bolan said. His cell phone chimed with an incoming call. He ignored it, knowing it would go to voice mail.

"Exactly," Brognola agreed. "And while we're on

the subject of Autry, like I told you before, his finances are kind of suspect. He's got a net worth of about ten million in assets, and owes about twice that much to his creditors and in legal bills, not to mention his back taxes."

"You don't mess with the IRS," Grimaldi said.

"Glad to hear you're back to being as ballsy as ever, Jack," Brognola said. He cleared his throat. "But getting back to Autry, it's amazing that he's still solvent. My guess is he's doing some under-the-table stuff somewhere. This recent anti-everything campaign may be just a smoke screen."

"Any more info on that arms deal?"

"Only that the Russian *mafiya* is involved," Brognola said. "Aaron's intercepted a few emails that mention that some special cargo's coming in through Mexico."

"Special?" Bolan asked. "Any inkling as to what that means?"

"I don't know. They're playing this one close to their vest, but we'll keep digging."

"And what about George Duncan?"

"Yeah," Brognola said. "We traced him through his emails to the New Minutemen website. He's twenty-four, served a tour in Afghanistan but was separated from the military on a general discharge. Works for a PMO called McGreggor, Inc., which is the same company that bought out Colonel Coltrain for his desert warfare training school. They've been in business about eleven months. It's a seventeen-person operation. The CEO is a guy named Frank Andrews. He's the only guy named Frank that I've found so far, by the way. The Secret Service ran background checks on all of McGreggor's employees prior to approving the prince's enrollment in the class. Nobody had any criminal history."

"Seventeen members," Bolan said. "I wonder how many of them are in Autry's militia. Anything on this Andrews guy?"

"Nothing on the radar."

"Does he have a military record?"

"Nothing in the system," Brognola said.

"Keep digging. He's had some training. They've got a pretty impressive setup out here," Bolan told him. "They must have somebody with deep pockets bankrolling them. Could it be Autry?"

"Not that we can find," Brognola said. "We'll keep digging on that, too."

"Sounds good. In the meantime, email any satellite surveillance photos of Autry's place. It sounds like some more extensive recon might be in order."

Grimaldi groaned. "What about Peppermill? Our steak dinners?"

Bolan ignored him and clicked off with Brognola. He then checked his cell for the missed call and voice mail message. It was brief and to the point.

"Agent Cooper, this is Special Agent Gila Dylan. Please, give me a call as soon as you get this." She rattled off a cell number.

Bolan dialed it.

"I'm glad you called," she said. "I just wanted to tell you we located those two BLM rangers. I'm afraid they've been murdered."

"What's your location?" Bolan asked, covering the speaker with his palm as he glanced at Grimaldi. "Looks like that steak dinner is going to have to wait."

Camp Freedom

FEDOR ANDROKOVICH STOOD OFF to the side in the brightly lit barn and watched as they taped the stencils over the side panels and made sure they were properly aligned. The air was heavily laden with the paint fumes, and both the painters wore masks. The Russian reflected that if he spent much more time inside this enclosed space, he would probably get a bad headache. But the two painters kept moving with an animated efficiency.

Strogoff had done well recruiting these two men to perform this task, and he wouldn't even have to kill them afterward. Once they realized their inadvertent complicity in the attack, they would no doubt come forward and provide yet another of the links connecting the Autry family to the incident and his other illegal dealings. They were too stupid not to comply. Androkovich had to admit that in spite of their obvious lack of intelligence, they were adept at painting the vehicle. It was a time-consuming process. Each section had to dry before the next overlay could be painted, hence the rows of high-wattage lamps that sped the process as it baked the fresh paint.

Tedious, yes, he thought, but perception was reality, and this one had to look perfect.

He glanced at his watch. It was almost time for supper. Keep the men fed, and then pull them out once darkness fell so they could again resume their training for hitting the armored car. This next phase had to go down like clockwork. It would be a good dry run, plus, it would be lucrative. This subterfuge had not been part of the original plan, but when Masoud had called him and expressed his concern over the ongoing "government surveillance" and his reticence to meet with the next portion of the funding, Androkovich had suggested this new adjustment. It would enhance their plan. It would look as if the Autrys, desperate for money to purchase the Semtex, orchestrated the armored car hit to obtain the funds. The robbery would eventually be traced back to them, even though the Arabs would be putting up the actual money. In the end, it would mean more money for him.

He heard voices outside and slipped out the door and into the late-evening sun. He saw Ibrahim Shabahb talking to Shane Autry. Androkovich felt a flash of anger. He had told that fat Arab to stay out of sight, and now here he was having a conversation with the boss's son. The Russian slipped out the door and closed it behind him.

"Pancho," Shane Autry was saying, "you got to be the laziest Mexican I ever seen."

"Trouble, boss?" Fedor asked, stepping forward.

Shane Autry whirled, a look of surprise on his face. "Huh? Oh, hi. I've been looking for you, but old Pancho here said you weren't around. Shoulda known he was full of shit."

Androkovich grinned. "What's up?"

Shane ambled forward. "I wanted to ask you, what the hell happened between you and Eileen? She liked to tore me a new one about them devices she seen you putting up on that back end. Those the motion detectors you told me to tell her about?"

Androkovich nodded. He had to proceed carefully here, but he also figured that Shane was so stupid he wouldn't even know a Claymore mine if he was sitting on one. "Yeah. With all the snooping around going on, I figured we needed a little bit more of an edge."

"Motion detectors, huh?" Shane grinned. "You mean those kind they use along the border?"

"Right. And some other stuff, too."

Shane shrugged. "Hell, sounds like a good idea to me. After all, we don't want anybody sneaking up on us at the wrong time, do we?" He grinned and winked.

Autry pointed to the building Androkovich had just exited. "Hey, what's going on in that barn there? I thought I saw some lights on in there before."

The Russian considered the best way to deal with this idiot. The time wasn't yet right to dispose of him.

"My men are doing a little vehicle maintenance is all," he said. "It's taking them longer than they thought."

"Vehicle maintenance?" Shane scrunched up his forehead. "On which one?"

"The Jeep. It needed a brake job."

Shane reached into his pocket, removed a circular can of chewing tobacco and stuck one of the white pads inside his mouth. It caused his lower lip to bulge outward grotesquely. "I thought I saw you driving it yesterday."

"That's when we noticed it," Androkovich said. "I wanted to make sure it was fixed before tomorrow night."

Shane spit and cracked a smile. The tobacco had discolored his teeth. "Yeah, we have a shipment coming in, don't we? Lots of snooping rangers around, too."

"Don't worry, we'll check out the area before they come in." He turned to Shabahb. "Were you looking for me, too?"

The Arab smiled. "*Sí. Es* supper time, *no*?"

Shane grinned. "He's not one to miss a meal, is he? Hey, Pancho, how you say fatso in Mexican?"

Shahabh's brow creased. Androkovich knew the Arab's knowledge of Spanish was limited to a few words, and even those sounded artificial.

"It's *gordo*. That's how they say it, right, Pancho?"

Shabahb smiled and nodded. "*Si.*"

Shane spit in the dirt near the Arab's feet. "It's still fatso in English, *gordo*."

After sharing what he obviously felt was a commiserating laugh with Androkovich, Shane said he might as well eat, too, and turned and ambled off. The Russian watched him go and then turned to Shahabh.

The Iraqi smiled nervously.

Androkovich grabbed the man's upper arm and squeezed, causing him to grimace.

"Didn't I tell you to stay out of sight?"

The Arab nodded, gritting his teeth from the pressure.

"The last thing I need," Androkovich said, exerting a bit more force to his grip, "is for someone, especially one of the Autrys, to figure out you're no more Mexican than I am." He gave the Iraqi's arm one more final squeeze, and then shoved him away. "Now get the hell out of here."

"But, my food…"

"I'll have someone bring you something. Now go back in your hole."

As the Iraqi scurried off, Androkovich took out his cell phone and dialed. Strogoff answered immediately.

"Is George with you?" the Russian asked.

"Affirmative."

"Come in the back way in and don't go by the main

house." Androkovich turned and watched Shane's progress. "Park the Jeep in the barn with the van."

"Roger that."

The Russian ended the call and slipped the phone back into his pocket. The Autrys were no more than a minor distraction, something that could be dealt with easily. The old man was a senile fool, his son a greedy idiot. The daughter was the only one with any intelligence, but her naiveté was her undoing. She wouldn't allow herself to believe that her family was involved in something illegal. It was all a balancing act, but right now the Russian was more anxious to talk with George Duncan about those two men he'd seen the day before. There was something about them that disturbed him, set off a warning bell. He had no doubt they could be dealt with, though. After all, a good commander had to be prepared for every eventuality.

BOLAN SAW THE three police cars ahead on the highway. To the right a cluster of more official-looking vehicles were pulled off the road on the sandy shoulder. Twin ribbons of yellow crime scene tape, affixed to periodic metal poles, fluttered in the desert wind, forming a makeshift path that led to a group of people. They appeared to be preoccupied with a small, squared-off area perhaps a hundred feet from the highway.

He pulled to a stop as a uniformed officer walked up to the driver's door of the Escalade, holding his hand out and motioning them to drive onward.

"Keep it moving," he said.

Bolan held up his DOJ identification and said, "We're looking for Special Agent Dylan."

The officer did a quick scan of the ID and pointed to

the cluster of other vehicles. "You can park over there. Stay inside the tape as you go up to the scene." He paused and gave the Escalade an appraising look. "Nice ride."

"We always go first-class," Grimaldi said. "Works wonders with the chicks."

The officer grinned, and Bolan parked behind a familiar-looking dark sedan that he assumed was Agent Dylan's. They got out and walked to the designated parking area.

"Think they'll be able to get any tire tracks or footprints?" Grimaldi asked.

Bolan surveyed the scene, and then looked down at the path. The indented footprints in the sand were already filling in from the noticeable breeze. "Doubtful, but it depends on how long they've been out here. Probably be a better chance for fingerprints if they've recovered the vehicle."

As they neared the end of the path, Bolan saw a group of crime techs working the scene with systematic precision. One female CSI snapped photos with an impressive-looking camera, as a man pointed to different places. A third individual with a camcorder was taping both of them. Two other men, both wearing blue shirts with FBI stenciled on the back in large, yellow letters, snapped photographs, as well. A group of perhaps five more individuals, four men and one woman, stood off to the side conversing in hushed tones. Bolan recognized the big, barrel-chested sheriff, Dundee, he'd seen at the Autry standoff. The woman was Agent Dylan, and from her expression, she did not look happy.

"I agree that the timing of this whole thing stinks,"

DESERT FALCONS   115

Dundee was saying. "But until we can find a definite connection, we've got nothing to go on. No PC."

"Don't talk to me about probable cause," Dylan interrupted. "I'm well aware of the deficiencies. At the very least, I do expect some interagency cooperation."

The big sheriff towered over her. He straightened and pushed back his hat. "Seems to me that I've been giving you that in droves."

"Then tell me you'll cover the Autry ranch with round-the-clock surveillance until we get enough for a warrant."

Dundee seemed about to say something else, then looked over at Bolan and Grimaldi. "Well, as if we didn't have enough separate agencies crowding into this crime scene," he said, "the Justice Department has arrived. How did you guys get wind of this?"

Bolan said nothing.

"I called them," Dylan said. "I was under the impression that we're all on the same side here."

Dundee's face darkened. "Well, maybe they can help you with that round-the-clock surveillance then. My department's a bit understaffed right now." He turned away, shouting directions to the crime scene techs.

"Hey," Grimaldi said, leaning closer to Bolan. "She kind of reminds me of me."

"Looks like she has the same propensity for ticking off the local constabulary."

"Yeah," Grimaldi said. "And she's almost as good at it as I am."

Dylan smiled as she walked over.

"Thanks for coming," she said.

"We aim to please," Grimaldi said. He pointed toward two piles of sand next to two distinct, corpse-sized holes in the desert floor. "Those the rangers?"

"We believe so," she said. "We're waiting on positive ID now."

"You find their vehicle?"

She nodded, pointing north. "It's about a quarter mile in that direction, in an arroyo. Another team's processing it now."

"How you find them?" Grimaldi asked.

"We had some drones flying over the area using some special, infrared scanning devices. They show any recent disruptions in the earth's surface."

"Ah," Grimaldi said. "That explains why you didn't need my pilot expertise."

"Any preliminary ideas about cause of death?" Bolan asked.

She glanced over her shoulder. "Pending the autopsies, it appears both of them were shot to death."

"The sheriff's department handling that part?" Bolan asked.

Dylan bit her lip as she nodded. "Technically, it's their jurisdiction, so they're taking the lead, but the Bureau's involved, too. We've got our people here as well, assisting with the processing."

"How's that going?" Bolan asked.

She shook her head. "It looks as though they've been out here for at least twenty-four hours, probably more. The winds are very strong out here, and any tire tracks or footprints have been pretty much obliterated." She kicked the sand angrily. "Dammit, I know that Autry's bunch is involved in this. I just can't find anything to connect him."

"Let the techs do their job," Bolan said. "Autry's

obviously planning something big or he wouldn't have risked killing two park rangers."

"He stashed the bodies pretty far from Camp Freedom, didn't he?" Grimaldi said. "Any chance you might be able to get any satellite photos from the past few nights?"

"I hadn't thought about that," Dylan said. "I've never worked that angle before."

"Well," Grimaldi said, grinning broadly, "let me look into that for you. I'll see what I can find out."

Bolan felt the chances of that were dubious at best, but he let it go. He knew Grimaldi wouldn't be at his best unless he was trying to impress a pretty girl. Plus, he had an angle he wanted to pursue, too.

"Why don't we check back with you later regarding this?" he said. "If we do happen to find out anything, we'll give you a call."

"Thanks." Dylan smiled wearily. "You two look like you've just come from a war."

"Aw, shucks, ma'am," Grimaldi said, giving his words his best Western drawl, "we been in so many different wars, we lost count."

"Which is another way of saying we have to get going," Bolan said, tapping Grimaldi on the shoulder as he turned and started back down the path. "Like I said, we'll be in touch."

He suddenly felt the urge to take a closer look at Camp Freedom after dark.

Riyadh, Saudi Arabia

MUSTAPHA RAHMAN AWOKE, as was his custom, about thirty minutes before dawn. The king's Rolex sat on the small tray next to his bed along with the false watch, the one that contained the poison pills the Russian had given him. He checked the hands of the Rolex and verified the time with his bedside clock. Four-twenty-seven. The king's watch was now keeping perfect time. The old monarch had inquired as to how much longer Mustapha was going to take to finish the repair, saying that he was considering giving it to the prince upon his graduation from the military training school in the United States.

"You have not forgotten we are traveling there soon," the king had said. "Have you?"

"No, my king," Mustapha had replied.

"And the watch will be ready?"

"It shall, my king," he'd said. "Soon."

And soon it will be, he thought.

He checked for any messages on his smartphone. There were two, one from each of his sons.

All is well, said the first one. It was from Masoud. Met with Mahfuj. He is well.

He read the one from Mahfuj.

The watch was adjusted by Masoud, it read. Still keeping good time.

This one troubled him slightly. An adjustment? What exactly did that mean?

He estimated that it was now only 7:30 p.m. of the previous day in the desert city of decadence in the United States. Which son should he try to call? And did he dare? If the Americans were listening in, with their ubiquitous security devices, everything could unravel. Mustapha debated the quandary for only a few seconds more, then punched in the number for Mahfuj on the satellite phone.

A good commander does not hesitate, he thought.

And intelligence is the key. Plus, they'd discussed the particular code words to use to cover every situation.

It was several rings before his son answered.

"Greetings, Father."

"And to you," Mustapha said. "You are well, my son?"

"I am. And you?"

"I was worried about the watch. Is it still keeping good time?"

"I had to reset it," Mahfuj said. "But it seems to be working well now."

"And your brother?"

"He, too, is well. We met this morning after prayers."

Everything seemed to be going according to the plan, Mustapha thought. Perhaps his alarm was unwarranted. "It is almost time for prayers here."

"Then pray for us both, Father," Mahfuj said. "Pray to God to give us strength and we will be united soon."

Mustapha said he would and ended the call, feeling somewhat relieved, yet still harboring a niggling of doubt and concern. Mahfuj had hinted that some slight adjustments were made, but that the plan, designated as the watch, was still on track. Surely, if anything significant had happened, he would have expressed it. Mustapha knew his first son could be something of an alarmist at times. He was the strongest, but also the most inflexible. That was why Mustapha had chosen Masoud to go to the United States to lay the groundwork there. He was young, but with an uncanny ability to adapt to virtually anything. He could fit into the decadent, Western society like a chameleon and not be noticed.

A glance out of his apartment window told Mustapha that dawn was only moments away.

It was time to pray.

Everything would be fine, he told himself as he performed the ritual washing then knelt on his prayer rug and placed his hands in the proper positions. His plan would succeed on all fronts. This he knew as certainly as he knew the sun would rise over Mecca. It was the beginning of a new day in Arabia, and he was one step closer to his ultimate goal.

It was indeed the dawning of a new age.

CHAPTER NINE

Unincorporated Clark County, Nevada

"Any idea how long this'll take?" Grimaldi asked as he drove along the highway toward the back entrance to Camp Freedom. "I'm bushed already, and we got that damn class again tomorrow."

"It'll take as long as it takes," Bolan said.

"All the way, sir," Grimaldi said with a grin as he mimicked the traditional airborne ranger refrain.

Bolan told Grimaldi to slow down to about five miles per hour about a hundred yards from the rear gate area of Camp Freedom. The Executioner waited for the big SUV to de-accelerate a bit more, and then opened the door and slid out, holding his satchel. He hit the ground running and then veered off into the soft earth of the road shoulder. The tall, cyclone fence separating the easement from the ranch property was about twenty-five feet away, and had three strands of barbed wire strung along the upper section, which didn't make it look very inviting. Leaving the bag, Bolan flattened out and did a low-crawl to the edge of the fence. Each post had been mounted with a concrete base, which meant the structural integrity of the fence was secure. He probed the ground underneath the bottom wire shards of the section closest to him. A substantial layer of gravel had been sprinkled there.

The sign of a man who likes to maintain his privacy, Bolan thought. Going under would require an entrenching tool, which he hadn't brought along. But he did have bolt cutters.

Taking a quick survey of the area with his night-vision goggles, Bolan was satisfied that no roving patrols or infrared cameras were in the immediate area. He did a quick trek back to the satchel and retrieved the cutters and his radio. Since there were no repeater towers in the area, the range of the radios was fairly limited, but he knew Grimaldi would be staying fairly close.

"Jack, you read me?" Bolan said into the mike.

"Lima Charlie," Grimaldi answered.

"I'm going through at the drop-off point."

"Roger that."

Bolan clipped the radio to his belt and inserted an ear mike. Once in place, it served as both a receiver and microphone. He then began clipping the wires of the fence. It took him less than a minute before he had a section large enough. He replaced the cutters in the bag and left it on the ground next to the cut section. After pulling the ruptured fence back only far enough to allow him to slide through the opening, he set it back in place and marked it with a spray of paint that would be invisible to anyone not wearing night-vision goggles. He did a quick equipment check. He had his weapon, NVGs, radio, and two stun grenades he'd stuck in his pocket as an afterthought.

It's dubious I'll need them, he thought, but, as they said, it was better to be prepared.

The soldier set off at a quick trot toward the asphalt road that led to the lighted buildings of the ranch.

Welcome to Camp Freedom.

Bolan kept on a course that was parallel with the road, but far enough away that he felt he would be hard to spot. He heard the high whine of an automobile engine and hit the dirt, flattening out and scanning the area through his goggles.

A topless Jeep was barreling along the road with three men in it. The vehicle was towing a trailer. They appeared to be intent on getting to some destination and made a right turn that took them off the paved road. Bolan increased the telescopic vision on the goggles but saw little. The Jeep was proceeding south, in the opposite direction from him, and whatever was in the trailer was covered with a tarp.

A roving patrol?

No way to tell, but he had been able to ascertain that the man in the passenger seat of the vehicle was holding a rifle of some sort.

It was another indication that Rand Autry put a high premium on maintaining his privacy.

After checking the rest of the area, Bolan got to his feet again and resumed his trot. When he was within approximately one hundred yards of the outermost group of buildings, he heard voices and stopped to use the goggles again.

A group of seven men stood close to one of the prefab barn-like buildings. An empty semitrailer truck had been parked nearby, and a white van was also parked there. Numerous sets of floodlights lit up the area, and several wooden sawhorses formed a rectangle section about twenty by ten feet. Two men holding rifles stood in front. Two more, also armed, were on the right side, and another pair was in back, although they were staggered about fifteen feet apart. This last group had their rifles slung. The seventh man was separated from the group and was yelling directions, like a coach making a football team rehearse a play. Two men ran to the back of the trailer and swung open the doors, then lowered a ramp of some sort—the type for loading livestock. The white van drove up the ramp and into the empty trailer. The men lifted the ramp upward, closed the doors, and ran to the front of the trailer.

"Timing is everything, people," the leader shouted. "Let's do it again, faster this time."

The men opened the rear doors of the trailer and the white van backed down the ramp.

Bolan flattened again and used the telescopic feature to get a better look at the players. They all wore their black baseball caps, so it was difficult to see their faces clearly. The group leader looked familiar: the guy with the red hair who appeared to be Andrew's second in command. Bolan thought he detected a trace of a Southern accent in the guy's voice as he continued to bark out orders, making them repeat the drill over again.

The van circled back to its original position by the sawhorses. Two men ran to an assigned position, off to the side. The rest were in the back. The leader said, "Go!" Two men ran forward, one kneeling and holding something on his shoulder, his partner running to the left side of the sawhorses.

The three men by the van ran forward, two curling to the left side of the sawhorses. One man remained totally in back, at the starting point.

The leader yelled more instructions. "Sixty-five seconds! Move it!"

More scrambling. The man at the rear ran up, made a quick slapping motion, then darted to the side. Each man froze for about ten seconds, then would run forward again, joined now by the two men from the side. They went inside the rectangle, formed a straight line, and began making motions as if they were in a bucket brigade. Bolan saw they were passing sandbags, one after the other, into the van.

"Three minutes, forty-five seconds," the leader yelled. "Speed it up."

He directed the two standing by the front of the sawhorses to take up what appeared to be cover positions, as if they aimed their rifles into the darkness. The three at the rear filed out at a quick, double-time pace. They ran about ten feet to the last man. The two in the front cover spots also got up and ran to the back.

All but two of them piled into the white van. The last two pulled open the trailer doors and lowered the ramp again. The van's tires spun on the loose soil as it bounced up the ramp and disappeared into the trailer. The two outside men raised the ramp, closed the doors behind it, and clamped the locking mechanism down. They ran around to the cab portion of the semi.

"That's way the hell too long, ladies," the leader shouted in his Southern twang. "We gotta get the time down. Do it again."

The group groaned and protested a bit as they loaded the sandbags back inside the sawhorse perimeter and then reset themselves in their original positions.

"This time we do it with our masks on," the leader yelled.

More groans of protest.

"Shut the hell up," the leader said. "I don't wanna hear it. Masks." He began tossing them each some kind of face masks. Bolan couldn't tell exactly what they were, but as they began to take off their baseball caps he recognized one blond-haired individual.

George Duncan.

Looks like Jack won't be the only one who's a little tired during the classes tomorrow, Bolan thought.

THEY HAD JUST pulled up, and Fedor Androkovich was listening, more than watching, for the small plane's approach. The pilot had made the trip so many times that it should be second nature to him. Fedor heard the distant whine of the twin prop engines, as he jumped out of the passenger seat, slung his rifle, and began undoing the bungee cords that held the tarp over the generator.

"Damn, Frank," Shane Autry said. "Sounds like they're coming in early."

"No sweat, sir," the Russian said, including the honorific to butter him up. Autry was wearing his usual cowboy attire, with a long-barreled .357 Colt Python strapped to his leg in an ornate leather holster. The man fashioned himself a mythic cowboy, one from the old movie era. He bragged about being named after one of them. Perhaps that was why he'd chosen an old-fashioned wheel gun over a more modern, semi-auto, despite Autry's ignorant claim that he liked revolvers because they "don't jam."

Any gun could jam if it was not kept clean, Androkovich thought, but had offered no argument to Autry's admonition. Rather, the Russian had used the man's venality to manipulate him, like a marionette. Soon it would be time to cut the puppet's strings, but not quite yet.

Androkovich flipped the generator switch to the On position and turned the key. His fingers nimbly explored the belt, making sure it was properly wound, and then pressed the rubber nipple to prime the starter. Gripping the handle, he pulled back on the belt, and the generator roared to life. As the motor went through a few cycling belches, he plugged the heavy-duty extension cord into the generator socket and then jumped down from the trailer. He held the cord in his left hand as he ran to the metal post that rose about two feet from the ground and connected the extension cord to the socket that extended from the post. Then he flipped the toggle switch on the post and watched as the oval lights on either side of the landing strip came to life.

"I could say you were cutting it kind of close," Autry said, peeling a patch of chewing tobacco out of his round can. He slipped the tobacco into his mouth and rolled it between his lower lip and gum line. "But I won't."

That's right, the Russian thought. Don't.

He looked forward to the time when he didn't need the Autrys anymore and could finally give this hamboned idiot his just deserts. But for the moment, Androkovich knew it was imperative to keep playing the faithful employee.

They stood side by side and watched the small, twin-engine aircraft approaching out of the dark velvet sky toward the strip, its engines cycling down as the plane slowed in descent. The plane's nose elevated slightly as the larger, strutted wheels hit the runway with the skidding sound of rubber on crushed gravel.

Autry sent a looping stream of spit on to the ground in front of them. "Damn, he sure can fly that thing, can't he?"

"He sure can." The Russian slipped the M-4 off his shoulder and adjusted the strap so it hung in front of his chest for easy access.

"Expecting trouble?" Autry asked.

"Just getting ready for it."

Autry grinned.

Androkovich motioned to Simmons, the guy who'd been driving the Jeep.

"Cut the lights."

Simmons, who was already at the post, nodded, and the landing strip went dark again. The plane coasted toward them and came to a stop. They waited until both propellers had ceased rotating before they moved closer. The side door opened, and three large men got out. They all wore dark clothing and had holstered sidearms.

"*Buenas noches, mi amigo*," the first one said, holding out his hand.

Androkovich deliberately held back as Autry moved forward and shook the Mexican's hand.

"*Buenos* whatever to you, too," Autry said, his right hand returning to rest on the butt of the Python. "How much goodies you bring me this trip?"

"Three hundred kilos of our finest Acapulco gold, my friend." The Mexican smiled. "And a bit less of *zee coco.*"

"All right, have your boys load it into the trailer. I'll have my man give him a hand." Autry motioned for Simmons to assist.

The Mexican barked some instructions in Spanish, and the two men began opening the cargo bay door.

"And," the Mexican said, "you have something for me?"

Autry nodded and pointed to the Jeep. "Gimme my briefcase, Frank."

Androkovich stepped over to the Jeep, keeping the Mexican in his peripheral vision. Although they'd been dealing with this cartel for months, he never was one to lower his guard. He grabbed the briefcase from the rear floor compartment and brought it to Autry.

He took it and handed it to the Mexican, pausing to spit some more tobacco juice off to the side. If the Mexican took it as a sign of disrespect, he didn't show it. He simply accepted the briefcase, opened it, perused the contents, and then snapped it closed again.

"Ain't you gonna count it?" Autry asked.

"For what reason?" The Mexican smiled again. "That is not how my employer does business."

Autry spit once more, trying to look tough and not really succeeding. "Like I said, it's all there, minus my percentage for transportation fees."

"*Claro*," the Mexican said. "But of course."

Androkovich knew this meant that if the money was short, some cartel goons would come calling for the rest of it. Besides, once the marijuana was loaded on to one of the company trucks and transported to its ultimate destination in Denver, the second payment, the one to Autry, would be made. There was more than enough money to be made by all, and everyone knew it. Being greedy would only cause undesired consequences. At this point that was something neither Autry nor the cartel could afford. So the need for a low-key operation kept everybody honest. He also knew that Shane Autry had been keeping a portion of the cocaine for himself.

He'd developed a nasty little habit, which would ultimately be his undoing. At least, that's how the authorities would be made to see it. This, too, figured well in the overall plan.

"One of these days I'm gonna have to thank the great state of Colorado for making this whole pot thing so nice and easy for us," Autry said with a laugh.

The Mexican laughed, too.

With everyone having such a good time, the Russian was almost tempted to tell them that this unfortunately would be their last transaction together. When the plane came next time, there would be no one here to turn on the lights.

His radio crackled. "Boss, we've got possible trouble."

Androkovich walked a few steps away and keyed his mike.

"What kind of trouble?"

"Sensor alarm went off in quadrant five. Could be a jackrabbit or something."

"Assume it's not. Check it out and get back to me."

"YOU GET A FIX on that plane?" Bolan whispered as he keyed his mike.

"Yeah," Grimaldi's voice said in Bolan's earpiece. "It landed somewhere on the south end of the ranch. They must have a strip or something."

Bolan considered that. An obscure landing strip and small planes in the dead of night indicated something wasn't quite aboveboard at Camp Freedom. Plus, Brognola had said that Autry was financially strapped. Desperate times often called for desperate measures. Could Autry's recent dispute with the BLM be due to some illicit shipments of something flying up here from south of the border?

This whole mission was starting to seem like an exercise in futility. If Autry was blowing smoke with his anti-Muslim threats to cover his own shenanigans, that meant the prince wasn't really in that much danger at all. Those two BLM rangers might have stumbled across some illegal activity. Maybe the rest of this one would routinely wind down, and he could turn the investigation over to the Feds and locals. Let them sort it out.

He took one more quick survey through his night-vision goggles. The seven-man drill was still taking place. Another guy, wearing some kind of plastic mask, walked out of the barn, removed the mask and lit up a cigarette. This guy was dressed in baggy overalls and didn't look like a soldier or militiaman. Suddenly Bolan heard a new buzzing sound. He swept his night-vision goggles, still in binocular mode, over the area beyond him. Three all-terrain vehicles, the kind with oversized tires, were speeding toward his location.

Had he tripped some sort of alarm?

He took a quick survey of the area and caught a metal rod with a sensor device attached to it. A motion detector, most likely, the same kind the Border Patrol used, and he'd totally missed the thing. It was odd that Autry would have that kind of sophisticated equipment.

He slipped the night-vision goggles over his head and began to get to his feet. As he was pushing up, his fingers brushed something that had an eerie, familiar feel to it. He glanced down.

A rectangular plastic box about the size of a thin, decorative brick with two wires running from it was mounted upright against a small hill of dirt. The face-plate told the story: Front Toward Enemy.

A Claymore mine.

Score another one for Autry and his sense of privacy. Those no-trespassing signs meant business, but this type of armament was certainly in the realm of overkill. Bolan reached down and pulled the scissor-like legs of the Claymore out of the ground, gently twisting it so it faced away from him and back toward the ranch. He pressed the legs back into the soil.

Where there was one Claymore mine, there were usually more, and with those ATVs bearing down on him, the soldier knew he didn't have time to look. He keyed his mike as he began running toward the hole in the fence.

"Jack, I got burned," he said. "Get ready for a pickup."

"Roger that."

He had perhaps a quarter mile to cover, which he could do quickly, but not as fast as an ATV. He needed some sort of diversion. As he ran, he reached inside his pants pocket and pulled out one of the two flash-bang grenades he'd brought. It was nonfragmentation but would provide enough flash and bang to do the job. The fingers of his left hand sought the circular, wire ring as he gripped the grenade with his right.

No time to straighten out the flanges of the pin, he thought. He'd have to do this John Wayne style.

As soon as he'd threaded his left index finger through the circular part of the pin, he pulled hard. The thin metal bit into his flesh, then gave way as the flanges straightened when they slid through the hole. The grenade would be live as soon as he released the spoon.

Three-second fuse, he thought as he ran.

Bolan twisted as he cocked his arm back, looking like a quarterback going for a long Hail Mary pass.

More like an outfielder trying to send one home, he thought as he did a bouncing three steps in reverse and threw the grenade for all he was worth.

One second.

Two seconds.

Three…

The grenade exploded.

"WHAT THE—" AUTRY SAID, glancing back toward the ranch.

Androkovich looked in that direction, too. It had sounded too loud for a rifle shot. An explosion? One of the Claymores? And was it related to that sensor going off in quadrant five?

He brought up his radio. "Give me a sitrep."

The reply was nervous and garbled. "Intruders! At least one. They've got grenades."

Grenades? The Russian keyed his mike again. "How many and where exactly?" He had to sort out the details to figure this out, which was virtually impossible to do at a distance.

"*Qué pasa*?" the Mexican asked, taking out his big Colt Government Model and snapping down the safety. "What is happening? *Policía*? You set me up!" He turned and shouted to his two henchmen, who immediately stopped unloading the plane, and pushed Simmons back.

"Hey," Autry said, his jaw jutted. "Keep unloading that stuff, you stinking Mex."

The Mexican swore in Spanish and spit at Autry

who then snatched the big Python from its holster and pointed it straight at the other man. Androkovich turned in time to see the Mexican bringing up his .45. From the look in the man's eyes, he wasn't playing around.

Shit, he thought. This was spinning out of control. The last thing he needed was a gunfight, but at this point there was no way to avoid it. He couldn't afford to lose Autry just yet. Androkovich swiveled the barrel of the M-4 toward the Mexican and fired off a short burst. The big man curled forward on to the ground. The two other Mexicans by the fuselage were pointing their guns, as well. The Russian did a quick sidestep, bumping hard into Autry and knocking him down, as the M-4 lit up in his hands at the same time. The two Mexicans by the plane twisted and fell.

The Russian's hearing was temporarily affected by the auditory shock. He moved forward and checked each Mexican, making sure all were dead. After kicking away their weapons, just to make sure, he turned back to Autry who had gotten to his feet, his face looking pale and white in the moonlight.

Simmons ran up and pointed to Androkovich's radio. His lips were moving, but no sound was audible.

"I can't hear you," the Russian said, his own voice still distant and indistinct.

Simmons mouth moved again, and he pointed to the radio. Androkovich held it to his ear. The ringing was still too loud for him to decipher anything. He turned to Simmons who had taken his small notebook and pen from his pocket and was scribbling furiously. He finished writing and held the tablet toward the Russian. It was hard to read, but he made it out:

He says he's gonna detonate the Claymore.

Goddammit, Androkovich thought, just when he thought things couldn't get any worse. He held the radio to his mouth and yelled, "Negative. Do not detonate the Claymore. Do you copy?"

Even though he couldn't hear his own words, Simmons' sudden cringe told the Russian that he'd been too late.

BOLAN HEARD AND then felt the concussive wave of the Claymore exploding behind him. Since none of the 700 steel balls had torn into his back, he assumed it had been the mine he'd turned around.

Front Toward Enemy.

Prophetic words, he thought.

Since his adversaries apparently had no compunction about turning him into hamburger, he slipped his Beretta 93-R out of his tactical holster as he ran. He flipped the selector switch to 3-round burst mode, aimed the weapon under his left armpit and fired off two 3-round bursts, hoping to give himself some cover fire. The escape port in the fence was about a hundred yards away now, but the buzzing sound of the ATVs was getting closer. A few rounds whizzed by him, kicking up dirt to his left. He fired off two more bursts.

Fifty yards to go.

The whining buzz of the ATV's engine was extremely close. Bolan took a quick peek over his shoulder and saw one of them bearing down on him, perhaps twenty feet away. Another one trailed it by about forty feet. There was no sign of the third one. Had the reversed Claymore gotten him?

More rounds drilled into the earth near his feet.

Bolan pivoted to his right as he sensed the ATV almost on top of him. At the same time he lashed out with his right hand, which held the Beretta. The weapon collided with the ATV rider's face, knocking the man off the vehicle. The riderless vehicle's momentum kept it going for several more feet before it came to a stop. Bolan ran to it, swung his leg over the center, holstered his Beretta and pushed the accelerator with his thumb. The ATV zoomed toward the fence. He zigzagged a bit, trying to make himself a harder target. The fence still loomed a long fifty yards away. More rounds zipped by. Bolan didn't dare take his hands off the handlebars, the way the front tire was bouncing off the uneven earth. The only saving grace was it made it problematic for his pursuers to acquire a decent sight picture.

Suddenly, Bolan saw headlights barreling down the highway.

Grimaldi in the Escalade.

The big, black SUV veered off the road and on to the shoulder.

"Is that you in the lead?" Grimaldi's voice asked in Bolan's ear mike.

"Roger that," Bolan said.

"Figured as much," Grimaldi replied.

The front of the Escalade smashed into the fence with a resounding crunch. Several sections of chain-link shook and separated from the perpendicular fence posts. The driver's window of the Escalade lowered and the barrel of an M-16, with an M-203 grenade launcher attached, extended through the opening. Bolan heard the popping sound of the M-203 and thought he saw the zooming trace of the projectile shooting by. Seconds later the roar of the explosion sounded behind him.

That one was no stun grenade, he thought. Leave

it to Grimaldi to know how to make an intimidating statement.

He slowed the ATV as he rolled over the broken fence and turned in by the right side of the Escalade. Bolan let the ATV coast to a stop as he jumped off and ran to the SUV. As he was getting in he heard the popping report again. Grimaldi had punctuated the incident with another grenade.

"Ready to boogie?" the Stony Man pilot asked.

Bolan nodded. "Anytime."

Grimaldi pumped the M-203 once again and sent another round flying into Camp Freedom.

"That is," Bolan said, "if you're done having fun."

Grimaldi grinned, twisted the wheel and accelerated back toward the solid surface of the highway.

CHAPTER TEN

Desert Warfare Training Center

"We'll have to see about getting a new vehicle after the class tonight," Bolan said as he drove the Escalade into the parking lot.

He pulled up in front of the circular concrete base of a light pole. He figured it would hide the front-end damage a bit, in case anybody was looking. Grimaldi's earlier plunge through the cyclone fence had broken out the left headlight and caused a rippling wave of dents and scratches over the sloping hood, grille and front fender.

"As well as another couple cups of coffee," Grimaldi said. He groaned and took another drink from the large foam cup, and then blew out a slow breath. "It's going to be a long day, and I'm really dragging."

"Your buddy, George, will be just as beat as we are," Bolan said, shifting into Park.

"Hell, on my worst day I could still knock the stuffing out of that two-faced little creep. I wonder if he was one of the ones that got hit by that Claymore?" Grimaldi drank some more coffee. "Or maybe by my little presents?"

Bolan shook his head. "From what I saw he was with a group down by the buildings. They looked to be practicing some kind of attack drill."

"Attack drill?" Grimaldi shook his head. "I wonder what that one's all about."

"Me, too," Bolan said. "I left a message for Agent Dylan to call us. Perhaps it's something she can use."

Grimaldi grinned. "I'm all for that. She's a real babe." He yawned and drank some more coffee. "I wonder if His Royal Highness is going to honor us with his presence today?"

"I guess we'll find out shortly," Bolan said, shutting off the engine. "But my money is that he will." He pointed to a black sedan parked by the main building that housed the offices, classrooms and gymnasium. "If I had to guess, I'd say that Draper and his crew are here early to check things out, which seems to indicate that he'll be here."

Grimaldi squinted at the vehicle and then took another drink of coffee. "Ah, well, all I got to say is, it's a good thing that this town never shuts down. You can always get a good cup of java someplace. I'll bet those poor guys are just as worn out as we are, staying up all night watching their charge." Grimaldi drained his cup and reached over to the tray for his second cup of coffee. "You sure you don't want this one?"

Bolan shook his head.

They got out of the Escalade and walked toward the building. Draper and another agent came out, heading toward the black sedan.

"Hey," Grimaldi called. "How's your royal babysitting job going?"

Draper's head swiveled. When he saw who it was, he smiled.

"You two guys look like you had a long night," Draper said. "Partying on the Strip."

"I wish," Grimaldi said.

"Doing the ground work for the prince's attendance today?" Bolan asked.

Draper told the agent with him to go call in, then he turned back to Bolan and Grimaldi. "Just the usual routine safety checks. The prince should be on his way shortly. We'll be monitoring the training today and tomorrow."

"Too bad you missed yesterday," Grimaldi said. "That obstacle course was something else."

Draper grinned. "Yeah, I heard it was a real ball-buster."

Grimaldi's eyes narrowed, and he cocked his head to the side. "How'd you know about that?"

"We have our ways." Draper's face took on a serious expression. "By the way, I called that number you gave me, and they verified your story."

Bolan nodded. "We'd have been disappointed if you didn't."

"Okay." Draper compressed his lips. "Just to bring you up to speed, then, we've been guarding the prince 24/7. All he's done so far is party-hardy. He had us inform the instructors yesterday that the long journey and time change were adversely affecting him. However, today he is scheduled to attend some of the classes."

"That's real ambitious of him," Grimaldi said. "The guy's a real ball of fire, isn't he?"

Draper's mouth stretched into a grin. "That's one way of putting it."

"I assume you ran background checks on all the instructors at this school," Bolan said.

Draper nodded. "Yeah. Why?"

"We were checking out the Autry place the day before yesterday. He had a face-off with the local and federal authorities."

"I heard our side blinked," Draper said.

"Autry's got a small group of armed men acting as security for his ranch," Bolan stated. "They're calling themselves the People's New Minutemen Militia."

Draper nodded again. "We already ran a check on them. From all appearances, they're just a small fringe group. They don't seem to be an overt threat. Pretty mild, in fact. Just a bunch of guys posting parts of the Constitution on some website, who like to dress in camouflaged outfits and play army once in a while. Autry's hired them as security for his place, which is not against the law as long as they stay on private property and don't have illegal weapons."

"Like fully automatic rifles and Claymore mines?" Grimaldi asked. He drank some more coffee.

Draper's brow furrowed. "Claymores?"

"At least one of these guys works here," Bolan said, redirecting the conversation. "His name is George Duncan."

Draper's eyebrows rose. "Now, that, I didn't know." He took out a pen and notebook. "I'll run a check on him."

"We already did. Nothing comes back, other than he was bounced from the army, after a tour in Afghanistan, on a general. It may be just a coincidence, but I thought we should let you know."

"I appreciate that. It's something we should've caught, but like I said, the militia members aren't listed by name on that website." He paused and looked at Bolan. "How'd you guys come up with that info?"

"We recognized him yesterday," Grimaldi said,

breaking into the conversation. He winked and held up his coffeecup in a mock toast. "Always glad to help out a brother agent."

"According to the course program, we're working on urban assault tactics today," Bolan said. "What precautions have you got in place?"

"We got here about two hours ago and checked out each of the buildings for any type of booby traps," Draper said. "We also did another check of the weapons you're going to use. They're all fitted with Simunitions barrels." He turned and pointed to the array of mock buildings about fifty yards away. "Additionally, I've got two snipers in fixed positions there and there, and a roving patrol on the perimeter."

"Sounds like you've got things pretty well covered," Bolan said.

"We've also got an undercover, four-man PMO contract team enrolled in the course, as well," Draper said. "They're not officially part of the Service, but they've worked with the G before in Iraq and Afghanistan, so they're used to this rigorous kind of stuff."

Grimaldi almost choked on his coffee. "Those four smart-asses are yours?"

Draper smirked. "How do you think I knew about your little mishap on the obstacle course?"

"So the prince is definitely coming today?" Bolan asked.

Draper held his left wrist to his mouth and spoke into it. "What's our status?" He listened, then said, "Roger that."

He turned to address Bolan. "His Royal Highness has just awakened to face the day. His entourage was up early, and is now milling about. We expect Royal Dissidence to be on his way within an hour or two."

"I'm glad he's not letting the possibility of learning something interfere with his beauty sleep," Grimaldi said. "Why is he even enrolled in the damn thing?"

"He's being groomed for a top spot in the Saudi military one day," Draper explained. "In fact, his grandfather, the king, is coming to D.C. in honor of the prince completing this class. There's going to be a ceremony in the Rose Garden."

"Sounds like a good photo-op," Grimaldi said.

Several more cars had been pulling up, and the rest of the class was beginning to filter toward the main classroom building, including the four-man PMO team. The short guy nodded and grinned at Grimaldi as he passed.

"Hey, you bring your cup today?" the team leader asked.

Grimaldi held his coffeecup up in another mock salute and grinned. "See you on field, short-stuff." As the four guys moved past him, Grimaldi drained the remainder of his coffee and crushed the now-empty cup.

Draper touched his earpiece and listened, then murmured an acknowledgment into his wrist mike before looking back at Bolan. "The prince is getting ready. One of his entourage is out getting some medical supplies and said he should be set to go in an hour."

Bolan nodded and tapped Grimaldi on the shoulder. "Looks like it's time."

The Grand Marquis Hotel and Casino

MAHFUJ WAITED BY the fountain once again. As he watched the water pouring over the large statues, he thought of the wretched excesses of the prince, and how much he'd come to despise the man. Not only had he spent another night in wasteful dissipation, drinking alcohol and consorting with jezebels, he had missed all of his prayers. Mahfuj had stood by, dutifully watching as the prince danced and jerked his way around the casino and then moved the party up to his room, inviting a bevy of the Western whores to accompany him. When he could stand the sight no longer, Mahfuj had begged to take his leave, citing the pain of his hand injury and his need to rest. The prince had been more than accommodating, holding his hand above Mahfuj's embarrassed head while proclaiming, "This is the hero who saved my life. He is an example of a true *Bedouin* warrior."

At least the *Bedouin* warrior part had been true, Mahfuj thought. He flexed his still-bandaged right hand as he waited for the signal from the cell phone in his left. Finally, it came.

Mahfuj looked at the text.

Do you desire coffee, my brother?

Masoud's humor irritated Mahfuj. Why did he feel the need to make jokes when the jihad was underway? Perhaps he had spent too much time in this sea of infidels. He did a quick glance around to make sure none of the Secret Service agents had followed him and then, assured that they had not, turned and walked inside the huge entrance of the casino. The instant clacking and ringing of the infernal gambling machines greeted him.

Finally, after what seemed like an eternity of walking but what was in reality only a few minutes, Mahfuj managed to make his way to the small coffee shop. He saw his brother sitting at the same table as on the previous day, the same boyish smile on his face.

"Good morning, my brother," Masoud said, holding his hand toward the chair on the other side of the small table. "Sit and refresh yourself." He pointed to a white paper cup with a plastic lid on top. He held an identical one in his left hand. A wisp of steamy vapor rose from the small perforation in the lid.

"*As-salamu alaykum*," Mahfuj said in his normal voice. "*Hah-lik keef*?"

Masoud winced and gave his head a quick shake. Mahfuj sat but did not touch his cup.

"Be careful not to draw too much attention to yourself," Masoud whispered. "It is not wise to speak Arabic here."

Their eyes met, Masoud's sparking and full of light. Mahfuj purposely kept his expression dour. "Sometimes I worry about you, my brother."

Masoud emitted a slight laugh. "Worry not. All is well."

Mahfuj still felt his core muscles tighten. "What of the developments you mentioned yesterday?"

Masoud brought the white cup to his lips, purposely making him wait. This angered Mahfuj. He felt the rage burning up his neck, and he wanted to grab hold of his younger brother and slap the playfulness out of him like he would with a recalcitrant child. Instead, he reached forward and pinched a piece of skin on his brother's wrist. Mahfuj's powerful fingers pressed together, the fold of skin trapped between them.

Masoud jerked in a grimace. "What are you doing?"

"Getting your undivided attention," Mahfuj said, his words coming between clenched teeth. He held the pinch a moment longer, then released it and kept his voice in a low whisper. "I know that father would be concerned at any modifications to his plan. What is happening now?"

"Nothing," Masoud said, rubbing the underside of his wrist. "I told you, it is merely a small wrinkle in the rate of delivery."

"Small wrinkles may develop into large creases."

Masoud continued to massage the inner aspect of his wrist, the space between his dark eyebrows still knitted into a frown. Mahfuj grew impatient and reached across the table, but Masoud quickly leaned back and withdrew his hands.

"Don't touch me like that again," he said. "I am not a child."

"Then stop acting like one," Mahfuj replied. "What is going on?"

The sly smile appeared on Masoud's face once more, and he reached for the cup but stopped short of touching it. He leaned forward, placing both elbows on the table.

"The Russian says that it is still too dangerous for us to meet at the moment," he said sotto voce. "The Americans tried to gain a closer look inside the compound last night. There was a brief skirmish."

"Skirmish? Have the Americans discovered us?"

"They have not. This only means that the ranch is currently under a strict surveillance."

"Surveillance? But is he not taking the two Shi'ite puppets there for safekeeping?"

"He assures me that this will not be a problem." Masoud smiled. "We merely have to be more careful about when and where we will meet. That is all."

"The Russian has enough money to complete the necessary transactions?" Mahfuj asked.

Masoud nodded.

"The money must not be traced back to us," Mahfuj said.

"Trust me, it will not. He is making it appear that it was obtained elsewhere."

"Where?

Masoud shook his head. "A robbery. It will eventually be traced back to the infidels." He leaned forward and whispered, "Do not worry. Have I not spent the past year over here working with the Russian to ensure all the pieces would be moved into the proper spaces? Everything is cool."

But Mahfuj was worried. His younger brother was even starting to sound like the infidels, adopting their decadent expressions.

"Do not speak in the manner of the infidels," he said in Arabic.

Masoud brought a finger to his lips. "And you," he said in English, "would once again do well to remember we are in their country."

"The Russian, will he be able to obtain all of the necessary materials? Are we certain he is trustworthy?"

"I am. Do not worry, my brother. All is well."

Mahfuj could still feel the tightness in his neck and gut. "I don't like the idea of placing so much trust in this Russian. Remember our uncles died in the jihad with the *mujahideens*."

Masoud smiled. "And now, their sons and nephews, the new *mujahedeens,* fight the Americans. *Inshallah*, my brother."

Mahfuj blew out a slow breath and looked at his

watch. "I must go. The prince is getting ready to attend that class this morning. I am supposed to be getting new bandages for my hand."

"And how is your injury?"

Mahfuj shook his head. "It is nothing, and nearly healed. I use it only as a pretext to meet with you."

Masoud smiled once more, with that same impish, childhood grin that Mahfuj remembered from their childhood. "Then, go, my brother. May God watch over you and grant you strength."

Mahfuj got to his feet and nodded. The next time they met, it would be the penultimate phase of the plan. He took a deep breath and recited a silent prayer. When they met again, the four desert falcons would be on the cusp of triumph, and it would be a new day for his country. A new day for Arabia.

Desert Warfare Training Center

ANDROKOVICH MOTIONED FOR George Duncan to join him in the shaded area on the side of the building. He looked at Duncan's face, which had a big scrape down the right side. The young idiot had been so fatigued he'd fallen during the training session the previous night.

Perhaps I'm pushing him a bit too far, the Russian thought. I do need him, and the rest of them, as well, to be combat ready for the next part of the mission. The little skirmish had put three of his men in the hospital. Luckily, he was able to cover it with a half-assed explanation of an accidental explosion while trying to remove some tree stumps. All of them were now in intensive care and not talking. They didn't know enough about the big picture to do any lasting harm anyway.

Once the plan was complete, and the authorities tracked them down in the hospital, the Russian knew he'd be long gone. And the headlines about another marathon bombing would be keeping the authorities busy. And Mustapha would be settling in as the first president of Saudi Arabia. He would probably be the last one, too, since the Russian doubted that Mustapha planned to give up the power once he had it.

It should make for an interesting new world, Androkovich thought. If it all comes together like the Arab planned.

"Did you check their vehicle?"

Duncan nodded. "Dents and scratches all over the hood and front fenders. Broken headlight, too. They're the ones."

This only confirmed what the Russian already knew. Now he had to assess the information. "Let me see their apps again."

Duncan handed him printouts of the two applications. Both men were purportedly from the Justice Department. That, in itself, didn't seem too logical. Why would the Feds send employees to a class run by a private military organization? Of course, with the Saudi prince taking part, it was a bit more understandable. Were they extra security? But there was more to this than just sending a couple low-level government jokers to help guard some royal Arab. Plus, they'd already jumped through all the hoops set up by the Secret Service regarding the prince's security.

But all that aside, why would these two guys break into Camp Freedom in the middle of the night? And where did they get all that firepower?

The first grenade had only been a flash-bang. A diversionary tactic, probably. But the ones fired by the guy who smashed down the damn fence had been the real deal. Forty millimeters, delivered by an M-203, no doubt. Sophisticated equipment… Way too sophisticated and way too much firepower for a couple of Feds on a standard bodyguarding detail. And their MO—breaking and entering—certainly wasn't standard government law enforcement procedure, either. That was why Androkovich hadn't been overly upset once he'd seen the damage and reasoned it all out the previous night. The two Feds, Cooper and the other guy, had committed numerous felonies breaking through the fence and entering Autry's property, not to mention their little interlude with the security patrol on their graceless exit. They'd never be able to get a warrant based on illegal actions like that.

Hell, if I had the time, cover and inclination, the Russian thought, I'd probably have Eileen file a lawsuit.

But that wasn't in the cards, either. Besides, explaining how one of the new "motion detectors" had exploded might reopen their previous little dispute.

Having to shoot those damn cartel goons was another unexpected wrinkle. Once their errand boy didn't return with the plane and their profits from their stores up in Colorado, they'd send someone to check on things. But acting as if it was business as usual would give him the few days he needed to pull off the Arab's scheme and then take off. He'd assured Shane Autry that the matter was a mistake that could be blamed on the American DEA, or somebody. He told Autry to hold off sending the drugs up to Denver in the cattle truck, just like always, and he'd square things south of the border.

Androkovich smiled at the thought. He'd square things, all right. It would make the Autry's ultimate fate all the more obvious to those putting the pieces back together. And by the time the cartel's bloodhounds traced their missing plane and personnel to the Autry place, Androkovich would be long gone.

Perhaps he'd settle in Spain once he got the final payment from the Arabs. He had a thing for dark-eyed, pretty maidens who spoke Spanish. Central America was too volatile, except for perhaps Costa Rica. But that was too close to the U.S. Still, it did offer a convenient place to disappear. One thing was certain: this was an endgame for him.

Duncan's voice shook him from his reverie. "So, they got urban assault today. You want me to arrange some kind of a training accident for those two assholes?"

"That's the last thing I want." Androkovich wasn't even upset by Duncan's idiotic suggestion. "Haven't you ever heard the expression, keep your friends close and your enemies closer?"

Duncan looked perplexed. "But what if they saw us practicing the drill last night?"

"Don't worry about it, George." The Russian raised his hand and patted the other man's shoulder with as much ersatz affection as he could muster. "You just go and get ready. It's almost time for us to shove off."

"We still good to go?"

Androkovich nodded, gave him another reassuring pat and gently pushed him toward the Hummer.

Duncan moved toward the big SUV but paused. "Like I said, I'm pretty sure they saw us."

As the Russian waved him away with casual assurance he considered Duncan's last words, and then thought, I hope they did see you, moron. In fact, I'm counting on it. He took out his cell phone to call Strogoff.

BOLAN NOTICED THE prince's somewhat low-key entrance into the back of the dimly lit auditorium where the two lecturers were going over urban assault techniques on a podium as large, colorful images from an overhead projector danced against the huge screen behind them.

First Draper and two of his men entered the room, followed by the prince and his six bodyguards. They'd discarded their traditional *thobes* and *ghutras* for standard, desert camouflage BDUs, with the prince's outfit being obviously tailored. The rest of them looked to be wearing off-the-rack uniforms. The seven men took seats in the back row, with Draper and three others standing in the rear.

Grimaldi shifted a bit in his slumber, and as his head lolled back he began snoring. Bolan elbowed him, and Grimaldi shifted again, his head flopping forward. The snoring stopped, for the moment.

Bolan had no problem letting his partner grab a combat nap. The classroom instruction, while well produced and sound in its tactical approach, was nothing that both Bolan and Grimaldi hadn't lived through on countless occasions. While paying scant attention, the soldier used the time to better advantage, sizing up the other members in the class and assessing the effects of his little side trip of the previous night. Duncan, and whomever else had been at the practice drill, would no doubt notice the front-end damage to the Escalade, if they hadn't done so already.

If Rand Autry wanted to push the issue, he could certainly call the local authorities and make a report. But Bolan had a hunch that was the last thing they wanted to do. In fact, he was beginning to see Autry's bellicose rants as more of a facade. That twin-engine plane had landed on an airstrip in the middle of the night on the back end of Autry's ranch, and one of the men in the Jeep going to meet it had appeared to be Autry's son, Shane. It wasn't the way business was usually done.

The Autrys were hiding something. Some drug business, most likely. That could explain why they were so against the BLM nosing around. It could explain the murder of those two park rangers, too. What if they'd stumbled on to some clandestine meeting and seen something they weren't supposed to see? And what about the rumblings of an impending arms deal? Autry's well-armed militia boys obviously had a plethora of military-grade equipment. He made a mental note to check those satellite photos of Camp Freedom that Brognola had emailed.

Grimaldi shifted his head again and suddenly woke up.

"What did I miss?" he whispered to Bolan.

"Nothing you don't already know."

"That's good news."

The lights in the auditorium suddenly came on, and the two men on the podium addressed the audience.

"That concludes the lecture part of our presentation," one said. "You will proceed to building A for equipment. We'll also be serving lunch. Those of you who are armed will be required to store your weapons in the lockboxes in the gymnasium. No real weapons are allowed to be brought into the training area."

"Better safe than sorry," Grimaldi said in a hushed voice.

Bolan nodded. It was a sensible move, stressing safety and making Draper's job of guarding the prince a little easier.

"After lunch," the instructor continued, "you will all proceed to Ambush City for the practical application of the aforementioned techniques. I want to warn you, each team will be in competition with the others during this exercise, and only one will emerge victorious." The instructor paused and smiled. "May the best team win."

Grimaldi grunted. "Well, that's us."

"Don't be so sure," Bolan said. "Look behind you."

Grimaldi glanced over his shoulder and grinned. "Well, well, well. Looks like we're going to get a little royal jelly on our biscuits, after all."

ANDROKOVICH WATCHED THE rear section of Autry's big truck-and-trailer parked on the side of the freeway one hundred yards ahead of him. He was in the freshly painted ambulance bearing the blue-and-white logo of the First Responder Ambulance Service. He had to admit, the jokers that he'd hired to do the paint work had done an admirable job. It looked like the real deal. He'd left the white canopy shell that fit over the top of the ambulance back at the barn. It was filled with a mixture of shaped fiberglass, wood putty, nail, and lined with Semtex. Once it went off, it would send shrapnel flying in every direction to inflict massive casualties, just like the Saudis wanted. It was an incident that would shock the American government, especially when it became evident that Saudi nationals were involved. But it wouldn't be prudent to affix it before the actual operation. Too much could go wrong, although Androkovich felt he had planned for every eventuality, even looking the part this day. He'd slipped into a tan, nondescript uniform shirt and white baseball cap that could easily pass for a paramedic's uniform. He also had an orange-and-yellow vest on the seat beside him in case he had to direct traffic.

Scrolling his cell phone, he found Strogoff's number and pressed the button.

"How's it going?"

"They're leaving the Mandalay Bay now," Strogoff said. "Where are you?"

"Waiting on the freeway," Androkovich said. "Just south of the entrance ramp. We'll fall in behind you. Text me when they're getting on."

"Roger that."

He terminated the call and dialed Duncan in the big semi to brief him. As soon as he terminated that call, his cell phone went off with the chime of an incoming text. Glancing at it, he saw it was from Strogoff.

They're getting on now.

Androkovich pressed the button on his wristwatch to reset it to the timer mode.

Everything was on track.

CHAPTER ELEVEN

Desert Warfare Training Center

Neither Bolan nor Grimaldi had seen any trace of George Duncan at the facility. After being fitted with the standard safety gear for the urban assault training, protective helmets, throat guards, vests and groin protectors, the group took a quick lunch break in which the catered sandwiches and drinks were brought in. The food was very bland, and Bolan noticed that the prince and his entourage had specially prepared meals that were separate from the rest of the food.

Draper and his men took turns on watch, eating quickly in separate shifts. Bolan was impressed with them and felt His Royal Highness was in little danger while under their watchful eye. He let his thoughts drift to the goings-on at the Autry ranch and made a mental note to contact Special Agent Dylan about an ongoing surveillance.

"What're you mulling over?" Grimaldi asked, handing Bolan one of the two cups of coffee in his hands.

Bolan shook his head, and the Stony Man pilot shrugged. "More for me, then, and, man, do I need it."

He drank from the cup in his right hand, and then took a sip from the one in his left.

"Just make sure it doesn't come back to haunt you

while we're doing our urban assault drills," Bolan said. "You did say you wanted to teach a few people some lessons, right?"

Grimaldi's mouth twisted into a frown as he nodded, then walked over to the large plastic garbage can and unceremoniously dumped both cups into the circular hole.

"You're right," he said. "Never go into a hot zone with a full bladder, if you can help it."

The training resumed in a section of four, flat-roofed, brick buildings along a paved section of asphalt that was approximately half a block long. The structures varied between one and three stories and were devoid of windows, although each had a "breakable" front door that could be reset after a forced entry. The interiors of the buildings had numerous hiding places and afforded both cover points and killing zones. The whole place was nicknamed "Ambush Lane."

The group of attendees had dwindled to twenty-seven, the desert heat getting to many of them. They assembled in the makeshift street, holding their cumbersome helmets under their arms, as two of the course instructors addressed everyone in loud, commanding voices.

"For this phase of the training," the instructor said, "you will all be given 9 mm Glock 19 pistols. Make no mistake, these weapons are real." The instructor paused as the second man held up a blue-colored gun.

"However," this second instructor said, "they have all been equipped with a special barrel that will not fire a live round. Instead, they're designed to fire a Simunitions round. These rounds—" he paused again and held up a fully loaded magazine filled with plastic bullets in his other hand "—are made of plastic and contain a nontoxic, colored substance that will identify a hit on an opponent."

His partner picked up a ballistic shield, and the armed instructor aimed the Glock at it and fired. The gun emitted a subdued cracking sound that was similar to, but not as loud as, a real gunshot. A pink flower blossomed on the middle of the shield.

"These Sim rounds can cause injury," the instructor said, "if they hit someone in a vulnerable spot, like the eyes, throat and groin. This is why all participants must wear the protective apparatus at all times."

"If you get hit in a nonprotected area," the second instructor said, "it'll hurt like hell."

Both of them grinned.

"Each team will be sent into Building Alpha," the first instructor said. "It contains paper targets of both enemy combatants and hostages. The goal is to effect a breach of the front entrance, and then proceed through the building eliminating the hostile targets. Each operation will be scored and timed, and the team with the longest time, the lowest score, will be eliminated. This procedure will be repeated in Buildings Bravo and Charlie, at which point, the two remaining teams will compete for the best time in the final assault on Building Delta. Building Delta will contain live role players who will be armed with Sim guns and will shoot you."

"Are there any questions?" the second instructor asked.

When no one raised his hand, the two instructors began dividing the group into four, five-man teams. Bolan and Grimaldi were placed on separate teams, with Bolan being placed with the undercover PMO agents. The short guy grinned and winked at Grimaldi, who stood there fuming. The prince stated that he would be "commanding and observing" from an appropriate point initially, along with the member of his entourage with an injured hand.

Bolan figured this was a break for Draper and went along with his new teammates. The short guy, Grimaldi's nemesis, shifted his helmet and offered his hand to Bolan.

"I'm John St. Alban," he said. "SAC Draper said you and your partner were from DOJ."

"Right," Bolan said, shaking St. Alban's hand. "Matt Cooper."

"Glad to meet you, Coop." He smiled as he lifted his helmet and began to slip it over his head. "Looks like your partner's a little bit miffed at getting stuck with the B Team, but to tell the truth, we were hoping we'd get you."

Bolan said nothing. While this game mattered little to him, he looked at every opportunity to test himself as good training. And being split up from Grimaldi had a slight advantage, as well. It would afford the soldier a chance to size up and assess the skill levels of the other participants. And Bolan had no doubt that Grimaldi, despite his protestations to the contrary, would do the same. Bolan was also curious to see how the Arab contingent would fare. From the looks of things thus far, the group did not seem to be very serious or professional, but a group was often defined by its leader. From what he'd heard from Draper, the prince was more interested in partying than learning any new tactics.

Bolan glanced over at His Royal Highness and happened to lock eyes with the bodyguard with the injured hand. The man gave off an aura of competency and authority.

It was too bad he was injured.

I'd like to see the guy's moves, Bolan thought. But maybe I will down the road.

MAHFUJ WATCHED AS the others donned their helmets and protective adornments. Part of him wished he was there with the rest of the team, but he knew it was better if he stayed off to the side at this point. Besides, it would give him an opportunity to observe the others and assess their abilities. He was particularly interested in the two big Americans whom he'd noticed watching them in the auditorium. Had he seen those two before? He thought so, but where?

He searched his memory. The possibilities were few since the time they had landed in this forsaken place. Then it came to him. It had been at the airport shortly after the plane had landed. Those two had been there with the contingent of Secret Service agents. Mahfuj assumed they, too, were U.S. governmental agents, but there was something about them, especially the dark-haired, larger man, that made Mahfuj feel somehow unsettled.

He shook off his concerns and set upon watching this little game unfold before them.

The prince slapped him on the arm and leaned close, a smile stretched across his face.

"It will be a pleasure to watch our brothers best these Americans at their own game," the prince said.

Mahfuj nodded, stiffening slightly at the permeating odor of alcohol emanating from the breath and skin of the sweating prince. The man disgusted him to no end, and Mahfuj wished he could end this tedious charade today, with one swipe of his knife. He fingered the smooth handle with wistful regret. In true Arab tradition, he knew that one did not draw one's weapon unless it was going to draw blood, and now, he reminded himself, was not the time.

No, he thought. Not quite yet.

THE FIRST BUILDING on Ambush Lane was about what Bolan expected. He let St. Alban lead the group, since they were used to him being in charge, and Bolan was playing the role of an add-on. They were obviously used to working together as a team. Bolan volunteered to do the initial breach on the first entry, which placed him first by the door, and then last into the room. The others all had obviously rehearsed their positions countless times before, and the Executioner figured this would be the best place for him to fit in. It would also mean that he would enter the structure and assume the position of rear guard. St. Alban, who was team leader, would enter right behind the point man, followed by the left and right flanking team members.

Their team was first, so that meant they had to set the time to beat for the rest of them. The others would also have the benefit of watching and learning from any mistakes or unanticipated problems. They squatted in a circle in front of the buildings at the designated starting point, guzzling bottled water as they conferred.

"Okay," St. Alban said, pointing to a diagram he'd drawn of the target building. "Once Coop here makes the breach, we'll enter by the numbers. Point man goes straight ahead, I cover the stairway, right and left flankers clear the first floor, rear guard assumes cover position, and Coop and I go up the stairs and clear the second floor. Any questions?"

Everyone shook their heads. The plan seemed solid to Bolan. It was basically standard tactical entry procedure. He locked back the slide of the Glock 19 and rechecked the specially designed barrel, which was just like the regular barrel except the chamber was much smaller. After inserting the magazine, he pulled back on the slide, chambering the artificial round. The others were doing the same. After donning their helmets, they were given a final safety inspection by the course monitors and told to line up. Bolan holstered his weapon, picked up the battering ram and took his place at the front of the line.

The front entrance was approximately thirty feet away. The solid-looking metal door had a breakaway panel by the jamb, which was designed to give way if hit by a solid blow. Bolan regretted that they hadn't had time to rehearse the approach as a team. His mind drifted back to the practiced rehearsals he'd witnessed the previous night, and he wondered what it was they'd been preparing for.

"Remember," the instructor yelled, "this is a timed event." He held up the stopwatch in his left hand. "There will be both hostile and nonhostile targets. You will be penalized for shooting a nonhostile target or for any friendly fire incidents. So choose your shots wisely, and be aware of all of your surroundings at all times."

Bolan was sweating inside the helmet and heavy vest cover. It also made it difficult to breathe. He purposely took a couple deep breaths to build up the oxygen level in his blood.

The instructor dropped his arm, signaling the race had begun.

Bolan sprinted toward the door, holding the heavy metal ram. He slowed with his final three steps, positioning himself squarely in front of the door and bringing the ram up and back, then swinging it forward. The solid, round end struck the door right below the breakaway plate, which gave way just as it was designed to do, and the door swung inward. He stepped back, twisted slightly to drop the ram behind him and drew his Glock as the others rushed past him. He went in last at the ready position and began scanning the room.

St. Alban's group was already spreading out in front of him. Dual targets, lifelike paintings of two men holding pistols, appeared in the hallway. St. Alban and his men fired several quick rounds, taking out the targets.

Since the instructors had made a point of referring to the place as Ambush Lane, Bolan anticipated that there would be a few tricks set up. Across the room a target popped up from behind a sofa. Bolan put two rounds through the target, neutralizing it.

One ambush down, he thought.

The sounds of more gunshots echoed in the other rooms. Bolan finished clearing his section and then concentrated on covering the stairway until St. Alban and his men had secured the first floor.

"All clear, first floor," St. Alban yelled as he motioned for Bolan to join him at the stairway. It was eleven steps upward, Bolan surmised, and he moved to a key cover position against the wall. If there was going to be another ambush, this would be the place.

St. Alban seemed to sense that, as well. He began moving up the stairway, his weapon at the ready, hugging the inside railing so as to give Bolan as clear a field of fire as he could.

Seconds later a target popped out from above. This one was a man holding a woman in front of him, his left arm encircling her waist. His right hand held a gun.

St. Alban hesitated for a split second, but Bolan had anticipated something of the sort and acquired an immediate sight picture on the bad guy's head. He squeezed off a round, and a neat hole appeared between the male target's eyes. St. Alban took the rest of the steps quickly and assumed a cover position as Bolan rushed up the stairs. Three rooms were spread out on the second floor. The temptation would be to try to beat the clock by separating and doing the rooms individually. St. Alban rushed into the first one on his left. Instead of moving to the second one, Bolan stepped inside the first room and assumed a cover position at the door. He heard the sound of a shot and knew that St. Alban had to have dispatched another hostile.

Seconds later St. Alban gave Bolan's shoulder a tap and said, "Clear."

They moved to the next room. Bolan went in first, clearing the room with a sweeping motion. A target popped out of a closet, and he moved his Glock to center mass but did not fire. The target was a woman holding a baby. Another target slid into view: a small boy, about ten.

After checking the remaining sections of the room, Bolan moved beside St. Alban and tapped his shoulder. "Clear."

One more room.

They probably saved the best for last, Bolan thought.

Obviously, St. Alban had similar thoughts as he moved into the room quickly. Bolan took up a cover position and suddenly a target dropped from the ceiling.

A man holding a shotgun.

Bolan reacted instantly, shooting a hole in the target's lifelike face.

Behind him, he heard St. Alban's gun go off several times.

Another target dropped from the ceiling. Bolan put two rounds in this one, as well.

St. Alban was beside him again, slapping his shoulder.

"Clear," he said.

Bolan sensed from St. Alban's voice that the man was starting to relax, but the Executioner saw one more point, a closet about three feet away, that they needed to check. He motioned to it, assumed a stance on the other side of the door, and placed his hand on the knob. St. Alban assumed a ready position in front of the door, but Bolan pushed him a bit more to the side. St. Alban nodded and adjusted his stance. Bolan's hand gripped the knob, and he twisted and pulled.

As the door opened the closet appeared empty. After a four-second delay another hostile target, a man with a submachine gun, dropped down from above. St. Alban's Glock came up, but Bolan's had already fired, leaving a hole in the target's throat. St. Alban put another one in for good measure. They did a final sweep as they moved back downstairs and out the front door.

The instructor clicked the stopwatch and nodded.

"Not bad," he said. "Three minutes, fourteen seconds. Looks like that's the time to beat."

I-15 South, Las Vegas

THE HOURS OF following the armored car had paid off.
Their pickup route never varied. Androkovich trailed
them again in the ambulance as they got on I-15 South
after hitting the last casino on the strip, the Mandalay
Bay. They would now head to the final two, the Silverton and the M casinos, which were farther out of the
metropolitan cluster.

He kept several car lengths behind them, although
he doubted the driver would have much concern over
a trailing ambulance. It was a noticeable vehicle, but
hardly one that seemed threatening. Still, it was better
not to take a chance, and he used his radio to tell Strogoff, who was driving the white van, to take over the
closer shadowing.

"Roger that," Strogoff said as they passed each other
by the large snake decoration on the side wall adjacent
to the freeway.

Androkovich dropped back and watched them take
the exit to head to the Silverton Casino. He kept going.
He'd station himself on the parkway down by the M,
their final stop. The area, called Southern Highland,
was perfect for the hit. The area was upscale, but the
neighborhoods were separated from the roads by high
walls and security gates. And many of the sections in
between were vacant, sandy fields waiting to be sold
and transformed into more luxury homes. The ambush
point was ideal: sparse traffic, no proliferation of buildings, no pedestrians.

Strogoff advised him that they were en route now,
ETA seven minutes. Androkovich put the ambulance
in Park and checked with the men in the semi. They

were in the position ready to pull out when the armored car arrived. He waited about five hundred feet west of the intersection. This was the hardest part for him. The waiting.

He wondered if the two men in the armored car had ever been cognizant of this most vulnerable point of their route. The Russian doubted it. They were two uniformed middle-aged security guards, both flabby and out of shape, one even carrying an old revolver in a worn holster. Hardly a challenge for a well-trained team. And they had practiced the take-down drill over and over.

It should go down like clockwork, he thought.

He surveyed the setup one more time. The semi was in position, ready to pull across the road on his signal, and Strogoff and the men were also ready and in position. He saw the armored car in the turn lane with its signal on. They had only to wait about thirty seconds more for the heavy-duty vehicle to pull off of Las Vegas Boulevard and on to St. Rose Parkway to proceed to their final stop before the bank depository. Thirty seconds, but it seemed like an eternity.

Like all men of action, he wanted to be at the forefront, instead of watching at a distance, but as a good leader, he knew he had to stay above the fray in this one.

Androkovich had pulled the ambulance off the road on St. Rose Parkway and donned his orange safety vest. With the baseball cap, vest and nondescript jeans, he looked like any other roadside construction worker. He grabbed the Road Clsoed sign from the rear of the ambulance and jogged to the intersection, arriving just as the armored car, followed by the white van, made the turn. He set the sign in the middle of the road. Traffic was relatively sparse this time of day anyway.

The armored car turned on to the deserted stretch of St. Rose Parkway before they'd make the turn on to Volunteer Boulevard to drive around to their pickup point at the back of the casino. Only an empty field on one side and a long, high privacy wall on the other.

Seventy yards ahead on Volunteer Boulevard, the semi rattled forward, its big diesel engine emitting a thunderous, percussive sound, followed by the squeal of air brakes. It blocked the two eastbound lanes with ease, and then stopped. The armored car turned on to the street, then slowed down, coasting to a stop perhaps fifty feet from the intersection.

Androkovich ran back to the ambulance and pulled up to the intersection, next to the Road Closed sign. His fingers gripped the toggle switch, ready to activate the overhead red-and-blue lights on top of the vehicle. It would be an attention-getter and would prevent people from driving down the street.

Americans would disregard a road construction sign or drive around a police car in a heartbeat, he thought, but everyone respected an ambulance.

The armored car was stopped in the road, with nowhere to go. The trailer truck blocked both lanes, and the white van pulled up in the middle of the street behind it. Androkovich watched the area about forty yards ahead as his squad disembarked from the van and semi and descended on the stopped armored car wearing their colorful, full-faced, Mexican wrestling masks. The two men in front, one holding the PTRD antitank rifle. He raised the antiquated weapon, aimed and fired. The massive 14.5 mm round would no doubt leave a gaping hole in the vehicle's rounded front end.

The armored car was still vibrating from the force of the round as the Russian saw the rounds from an SKS perforate the windshield, no doubt taking out the driver. A trail of dark smoke slithered upward from the front of the armored car. Two more of his men were behind the fortified vehicle, and one ran up and placed the triangular, explosive sleeve against the rear door. He stepped back and away. They looked like devils in their red, white and black masks.

Seven seconds later the muffled roar from that explosion rippled across the empty field. The rear door of the armored car flipped open. Two of his men placed the barrels of their rifles in the space between the broken metal door and the frame.

Androkovich glanced at the intersection. A smattering of cars was approaching, but they were all stopping. He flipped the toggle switch activating the emergency equipment lights on top of the ambulance and pulled on to the street, effectively blocking the lanes that led to the carnage. A dark plume of smoke billowed upward. Several cars slowed, but none stopped or turned on to the street.

The burp of automatic gunfire sounded.

He glanced back at the scene. The second guard had tried to resist and had been taken out.

He looked at the timer: Three minutes, forty-five seconds.

Androkovich cut the lights on the ambulance and watched as Strogoff pulled his nondescript, windowless white van up next to the truck, the rear doors swinging open. Four of them worked in unison transferring the sacks of money from the damaged armored car to the white van. The big semi's engine emitted a strained roar as it rolled forward and turned to pull forward, ready to exit the area. It jerked to a stop, and even though he couldn't see them, Androkovich knew his two men were now opening the rear trailer doors and lowering the ramp, ready for the white van's ascent into the back. It was all going like clockwork, just as they'd planned.

Then he heard something else: sirens.

He turned and saw two marked police cars speeding toward the scene.

How the hell had they gotten there so fast? It wasn't in their original plan.

He couldn't tell if they were highway patrol units or municipal police. He tapped his horn twice—the signal for approaching police, and then shifted into Reverse and pulled off to the side.

The two squad cars roared around the corner, their tires squealing as they shot past him, twisted and stopped. Both officers jumped out, one holding a shotgun, the other a handgun, and took cover behind the hoods of their vehicles.

Not bad, tactically speaking, Androkovich thought. The engine blocks would afford them a modicum of ballistic cover.

He pulled the ambulance forward, angling it so that he had a clear view of the two officers as he lowered the window on the passenger-side door.

They were perhaps twenty yards away. One of them, the one holding the shotgun, turned and gestured frantically for Androkovich to leave. The man was talking into his radio.

The Russian brought up his P-223 pistol and shot that man first.

He'd loaded it with the special, old, Soviet-style steel projectile rounds that he knew would penetrate their vests. He watched the first cop jerk backward from the impact.

He fired again, this time drilling the round into the officer's forehead, and acquired a sight picture on the second cop. This one was crouching, having fired his handgun a few times, still using his squad car for cover.

Androkovich shot the man in the head and watched him slump forward.

He felt a tinge of regret having to shoot two such brave, dedicated civil servants, but only a tinge. They were professionals, just as he was, and therefore knew the risks.

Glancing toward the disabled armored car, he saw that this unexpected little foray had cost them precious seconds in the money transfer. He checked the opposite direction and saw more cars on Las Vegas Boulevard, clustering at the intersection.

The other days they'd followed the armored car the traffic hadn't been this heavy.

No matter, he thought, as he watched Strogoff slam the doors and flash him the ready signal. He jumped into the van as it took off for the rear of the trailer and the loading point. In the distance the Russian could hear more sirens. But those approaching units would have no reason to stop an ambulance or a semi-tractor/trailer getting on the freeway. They'd be too busy looking for a bunch of armed suspects in a white van. He flipped off his own red lights and drove around the carnage toward the entrance to the freeway.

Not bad for an afternoon's work, he thought, as he wondered how much the take would be.

He glanced at his watch again and pressed a button that would freeze the time.

Seven minutes and fifty-three seconds… Not a bad time, all things considered.

Desert Warfare Training Center

THE ARAB TEAM performed better than Bolan thought they would. Despite their lack of attendance, they had a respectable time and were in second place after the initial round. Grimaldi's team was disqualified after the first round due to all of the nonhostile targets being shot. When that was announced, Grimaldi grinned and patted himself on the chest with a subdued gesture obviously aimed at Bolan. Draper and three of his men stood in the background.

After moving through Beta and Charlie Buildings, only Bolan's group and the Arabian team remained. The instructors gathered everyone outside the last building. At five stories, it was the largest of the four. On the right side, a hollow plastic tube extended downward from the roof into a dumpster garbage bin with a large, digital clock affixed on the top edge.

"This is the final part of this training phase," the instructor said. "It is a timed exercise. Five floors up. Your goal is to move up to the roof area as quickly and as safely as possible, locate this basketball—" he paused and held up a red, white and blue ball "—and drop it into the chute." He pointed to the plastic tube. "Once the basketball strikes the bottom of the bin, your time will be recorded on the digital clock. Whichever team has the fastest time, and the lowest number of casualties, wins. Be advised, there will be a minimum of four adversaries inside the structure. These four are live, armed participants and may be anywhere inside. They are to be treated as enemy combatants and dealt with accordingly. You will be able to carry ballistic shields, if you so desire. Are there any questions?"

Bolan looked at the other members of his team. St. Alban had done a credible job leading the group thus far, so Bolan saw no reason not to let him do so in this final exercise. The PMO team looked a bit worn, and tired men made mistakes. St. Alban echoed his concern.

"Look," he said, "I know you're all beat, but we've got to suck it up this one last time." He motioned for them to get into a huddle and added sotto voce, "We're not going to let a bunch of Arabs beat us, are we?"

"I will wager ten thousand U.S. dollars that my Saudi team will beat yours," a voice said.

Everyone glanced over to see the prince strutting toward the group, his face a picture of amusement. The wiry guy with the bandaged hand walked a few steps behind him, his dark eyes continually searching and probing the other groups.

That guy took his bodyguard duties seriously, Bolan thought. He looked totally focused on his surroundings. Bolan saw that Draper and his contingent were being equally observant.

"Well, do I have any takers?" the prince continued in a loud voice. "Or are you Americans all bluster and no substance, as I have heard?"

When no one spoke, the prince's head lolled back in laughter. "Oh, perhaps I need to lower my wager?"

"Perhaps you ought to try stepping up to the line yourself," Grimaldi yelled.

"A true leader chooses his battles and knows how to direct his men," the prince said. "A concept that would be wasted on a commoner, such as you."

Grimaldi drew his head back and pretended to sneeze, instead emitting the word, "Bullshit!"

Bolan shot him a hard glance, and Grimaldi lowered his eyes.

The prince glared at him but said nothing.

"Your Highness," one of the instructors said. "Since you're our honored guest, we'll give you the choice of deciding if you want your team going first or second."

The prince stared at the instructor and then to his men, looking as if he were reviewing a cluster of camels before a race. He shrugged and sighed. "It does not matter. My men will best your Americans regardless." A crafty smile crept over his bearded face. "But are we not in Las Vegas, your gambling capital? Why not throw a coin in the air?"

The instructors exchanged glances, and one of them reached into his pants pocket, removing a quarter. He looked at St. Alban and said, "You want to call it?"

"Sure," St. Alban said. "Heads."

The instructor flipped the quarter in the air and watched it rotate end over end until it reached its apex and then dropped. It bounced twice on the hard asphalt surface and lay on its side. He bent over and looked down. "Heads it is."

St. Alban grinned and said, "We'll go second."

It made sense to choose that option, Bolan thought. The first team would be at a slight disadvantage not having an established time to beat, and the amount of gunfire emanating from the building would be a good tip-off to how many, and where, the assailants would be.

Bolan saw the guy with the bandaged hand whispering something into the prince's ear. His Royal Highness stepped forward, clapping his hands and saying, "Wait, I have changed my mind. I wish to invoke my right to choose after all."

St. Alban's head shot up, but he said nothing.

"We shall let you Americans go first," the prince said. "That way my men will know what they need to do so as not to embarrass you too badly." The prince lifted an eyebrow and locked eyes with Bolan.

"Looks like the fix is in," St. Alban said in a low voice.

"This stinks," one of the team members added.

"Let's not lose sight of our primary mission here," Bolan said. "As far as this little charade goes, it's like all training exercises. We're only in competition with ourselves."

"Cooper's right," St. Alban said. He extended his hand into the center of the huddle. "Come on, let's do this."

Each man placed a gloved hand on top of St. Alban's, forming a spoke. The team straightened and moved to the starting point.

Camp Freedom

ANDROKOVICH WAS GOING over the details in his mind as he and Strogoff closed the big door to the south barn that now housed the semi-tractor and trailer. He wanted to be present when they counted the money, but he also wanted to make sure he had crossed all his *t*'s and dotted all his *i*'s. A debrief of his men was also in order. They still had a few more tasks to perform before he was through with them. The arrival of the two police officers had been somewhat unexpected, but he had factored in a police response in one of his many contingency planning sessions. And he'd dealt with it effectively. It would no doubt raise the heat level a bit. A bunch of dead cops and armored car guards would do that. At least none of his men had been shot or wounded. Once the inevitable police assault on Camp Freedom began, many of them would no doubt bite the dust, as they used to say in the old western movies, but he would be long gone by then.

He smiled at the thought.

Rich, footloose, and fancy-free, somewhere. Lately, he'd been thinking that Brazil might be a better choice than Spain or Costa Rica. The women there would be just as dark and lovely.

Suddenly he heard a feminine voice call his name. Not his real name, but that of "Frank Andrews." He turned and saw Eileen Autry walking toward them with a determined gait.

Strogoff looked at him. "Looks like trouble."

"Nothing I can't handle."

"What do you want me to do?" Strogoff asked.

"Go around the long way, so she doesn't see you go into the barn. Then watch the men as they count the money."

"Want me to have them take the van out of the trailer first?"

Androkovich thought about that. "No. Leave it in."

It would be better to tie the Autrys to the armored car robbery that way.

His partner walked away, pausing to tip his hat to Eileen Autry as he passed her. She didn't acknowledge him at all.

Androkovich smiled. "Ms. Autry. Where's your horse?"

"Never mind that," she said, "what exactly went on last night? I heard some explosions."

The Russian reviewed his possibilities. This bitch was turning out to be the unforeseen wrinkle in every plan.

"Sorry you were disturbed," he said. "It was…inadvertent."

"Inadvertent?" Her mouth puckered into that haughty, familiar-looking pout. "What exactly was going on?"

He stood there in silence for a good fifteen seconds. She was a rather handsome woman, and he wondered if he'd get the chance to taste her sweetness before this was over. Her breasts strained against the fabric of her blouse, her legs looked long and shapely inside the snug jeans.

"Did you hear me?" she said, the color reddening her cheekbones. "I asked you a question."

"We had some intruders sneak on to the property," he said. "We repelled them. I didn't want to upset you."

"What?" The color darkened in her cheeks. "Who were they?"

He shrugged. "I'm not sure."

"Did you report this to the sheriff?"

He shook his head. "We felt it best not to."

The space between her eyebrows furrowed. "You aren't making sense. What is going on around here?"

"Perhaps you should talk to your brother. He can explain it better than I can."

"My brother?" Her tone was more subdued now.

"What's Shane got to—or should I say, what have you gotten him mixed up in?"

Androkovich let his eyes roam over her body, imagining her under him and naked, a look of terror in those blue eyes. "As I said, you need to talk with your brother."

Her nostrils flared. "You can bet that I will. And he better have some good answers, too."

She turned and strode back toward the main house. He watched her go, admiring the tightness of her buttocks in its blue denim prison.

Soon, he thought. Soon.

CHAPTER TWELVE

Desert Warfare Training Center

The interior first floor of Delta Building was devoid of furniture or any other obstacles, which made clearing the expansive room a fairly easy task. At Bolan's suggestion, St. Alban split the team in two, with him taking three men up the farthest stairwell, and letting Bolan lead one man up the closest one. They used the same, standard stairwell and room clearing techniques they'd used in the other buildings. This time the pace was a bit slower due to the weight of the shields. They encountered live adversaries on the second, third and fourth floors. Both stairwells ended on the fifth floor, and the two teams met in the middle. One last double staircase led to the roof. It had two alternating sets of stairs, with a platform in the middle.

"This is it," St. Alban said. "Think there's somebody up there waiting for us?"

"Most likely," Bolan said. He took the shield from his point man, who was obviously depleted from the long trek upward. "Time for me to do some of the heavy lifting."

St. Alban grinned and did the same. The others formed a line behind the two leaders as they moved up the stairs.

"Make sure you keep a rear guard," Bolan said. "I've got a hunch there might be more surprises in store."

St. Alban nodded and told one of his men to assume that position.

As they got halfway up to the middle platform, the door below them burst open. Two adversaries ran in firing wildly. The rear guard was ready and took out both of them with a series of shots. Just as this was occurring, the door to the roof opened, and a hand dropped a flash-bang on to the floor.

"Grenade," Bolan yelled, and managed to kick it on to the lower set of stairs. In the three seconds that it took for the grenade to explode, he ran up to the door and thrust it open, holding the shield in front of him and his pistol at the edge. He knew the only way to get out of an ambush was to fight your way out. This sudden move apparently startled their adversary on the roof, and Bolan shot the man twice, the second round hitting him in the clear visor part of his helmet. St. Alban was beside him now, and they took time to clear the roof as the rest of their team burst through the door. After clearing the area and posting one man at the door monitoring for anyone trying to flank them, Bolan pointed to the red, white and blue basketball. St. Alban grabbed it, ran to the tube and dropped it down. He slipped off his helmet and wiped the sweat from his forehead.

"The prince's team will have the advantage of knowing what's coming," he said. "Especially that damn flash-bang. Good move kicking it out of the way."

Bolan took off his helmet, too. The air, as hot and dry as it was, felt good against his skin.

"Sometimes you get lucky," he said. "Now let's get some of that water."

Their time was fourteen minutes and fifty-two seconds.

Bolan and his team moved to the row of ice coolers filled with water bottles and sports energy drinks. Grimaldi came ambling over and grabbed one. Bolan introduced him to the members of the undercover Secret Service team, and they shook hands all around.

"St. Alban, eh?" Grimaldi said, tipping his bottle toward the other man. "Usually I'm suspicious of anybody with a saint-something in their name, but in your case I'll make an exception. I was watching your moves. You did all right."

"Thanks mainly to your partner, here," St. Alban said, giving Bolan's shoulder a light tap. "Let's see how our Saudi competitors are doing."

They walked back to the front of Delta Building and watched as the numbers on the LCD screen of the digital clock continued to ascend. It was at seven minutes and counting before they heard the sounds of any rounds being fired.

"From the sound of it, they're either moving kind of slow or they're not encountering the same kind of resistance you guys did," Grimaldi said.

After a few minutes more gunshots sounded. The clock was at fourteen twenty-eight.

Bolan watched St. Alban and the rest of the team. Their eyes were glued on the advancing numbers. The Executioner knew this type of competition had a way of bringing out an atavistic sense of competition in men. While he viewed it simply as a game, his competitive juices had been slightly aroused. He wanted to win and found himself slightly amused at the thought.

Fourteen thirty-five…thirty-six…

"I haven't heard a flash-bang yet," one of St. Alban's group said.

Fourteen forty-five...forty-six...forty-seven...

The sound of two more gunshots filtered down from above, along with voices shouting in Arabic. After a seemingly long twenty seconds, the plastic tube vibrated, and the basketball plunked down into the bin.

The numbers on the digital clock were frozen: *15:08.*

The members of St. Alban's team emitted a cheer.

"All right," Grimaldi yelled, as he turned toward the prince and his bodyguard with the bandaged hand and gave them a raspberry.

The prince's dark eyes narrowed, and the fury was obvious in his face.

"Easy, Jack," Bolan said in a low voice. "Remember why we're here."

"This was a sham," the prince said. "It was rigged to let the Americans win. I should have known it would not be a fair contest."

Grimaldi snorted. "Just be glad nobody took you up on your little bet."

A dark scowl twisted over the prince's face. "You are right. It was a rather small wager, at that. Next time I'll make it two times your yearly salary, for sport."

The Stony Man pilot started to say something more, but caught himself.

The Saudi team began filtering out of the front entrance. One ran to check the clock and said something in Arabic. They looked disappointed.

The two instructors were leaning over conversing in hushed whispers. One of them straightened and spoke in a loud voice.

"After evaluation of the scores and techniques, the

competition between the two teams has officially been declared a draw," he said.

The group of Arabs stopped as a huge smile spread across the prince's face. He said something in Arabic, and they were suddenly all grinning.

"Hey, pal, wait a minute," Grimaldi said. "These guys had a better time." He pointed to Bolan and St. Alban.

"It isn't always about having the best time," the instructor said. "The interior judges can assess penalty points if they see any tactical irregularities."

"Tactical what?" Grimaldi said. "That's total crap."

The instructor flushed and repeated his statement.

Grimaldi was about to continue his discourse when Bolan placed a hand on his shoulder.

"Jack," he said, lowering his voice to show he meant business. "Drop it. It's not important."

Grimaldi turned, his mouth twisting into a frown, and nodded, adding, "Sorry."

St. Alban nodded. "We appreciate it, bro, but the big guy's right. It's all about politics."

The instructor announced that all equipment and Simunition weapons had to be returned to the gymnasium. "Those of you who stored weapons in the gun lockers may also retrieve them."

Everyone began filtering toward that large, flat-roofed building. Special Agent Draper caught up to them and offered his condolences. "For what it's worth, we all know you guys got robbed."

Bolan allowed himself a slight smile. "Let's save our sentiments for something important."

About midway to the gun lockers Bolan's cell phone

vibrated. He removed it from his pocket and saw that it was from Agent Dylan.

"Sorry it's taken me so long to return your call," she said. "I got your message, but we've had a rather busy day."

"Likewise," Bolan said. "We've had a long day ourselves. We're finishing up our Desert Warfare class."

"I figured that's where you'd be," she said. "Actually, I'm in that area. Mind if I stop by and meet you there? I need to talk to you about something."

"Not at all," Bolan said. He gave her directions and terminated the call.

A row of mats had been set up inside the gymnasium. A series of plastic buckets with rolls of paper towels and sanitary wipes had been positioned about every four feet. The instructors asked that those who participated in the final exercise remove and clean their helmets and protectors before retrieving their weapons. Bolan picked up one of the wipes and began using it on his helmet. St. Alban and his team began to do the same. The Arabs merely set theirs down and made no effort to clean them.

"Those lazy jerks," Grimaldi said.

"Saudi men feel that certain types of manual labor are beneath them," Bolan stated. "That's why they've imported so many foreign workers into the kingdom."

"Hey, it's beneath me, too, then," Grimaldi said. He kept walking, saying that he hadn't worn one during the exercise anyway. He grabbed the basketball and dribbled a few feet away to the end of the gym and began taking shots at a hoop. The ball banged against the backboard and bounced wildly, careening out of control, its trajectory sending it straight toward the prince, who had been standing off to the side. Only the quick reflexes of the bodyguard with the bandaged hand kept the ball from striking the prince. He managed to tip it away at the last second.

Grimaldi jogged toward it. He started to say, "I'm sorr—" when the prince moved forward with a cat-like grace and grabbed the bouncing ball.

"Is this yours?" he asked in a mocking tone as he brought the ball back to his chest, holding it with both hands, and then thrust it forward, throwing it directly into Grimaldi's face. He brought his hands up at the last second, but the ball still bounced off his forehead.

The pilot looked more surprised than stunned, but seconds after he recovered he jumped toward the prince, only to be caught by the bodyguard and pushed back.

Bolan dropped his helmet and rushed over, grabbing Grimaldi and holding him back.

"That was a cheap shot, pal," Grimaldi said.

The prince blew out a derisive breath. "You should be glad that ball did not strike me."

Grimaldi held up his fist. "Care to give me a second chance?"

"I would not sully my hands with you," the prince said. "But perhaps you would care to affirm your truculence against Abdullah." He gestured toward the largest of the bodyguards. The big Arab stepped forward, removing his shirt to display huge, sinewy arms and shoulders.

"Sure," Grimaldi said. "Bring him on."

"Okay, guys," Special Agent Draper chimed in. "This has gone far enough."

"I agree," Bolan said, pulling his friend back.

"Let me go. I can take him."

"He's a little bit out of your weight class," Bolan said.

"Ah, the bigger they are, the harder they fall."

"I knew it," the prince said, his mouth twisting into a sneer. "You are cowards. Both of you."

Grimaldi tried to leap forward again, and as Bolan moved against him, trying to grab his partner's flailing arms, Abdullah shoved both of them, staggering the Executioner and knocking Grimaldi to the floor. In a reflexive action, Bolan shoved the big Arab back.

"Ah," the prince said, "you have at last mustered enough courage for a physical confrontation after all." He snapped his fingers and nodded. "Are you not a true man? Do you wish to engage further?"

"No, thanks," Bolan said.

"That is too bad," the prince replied. "Because we do." He said something in Arabic that Bolan recognized as a command to attack.

Abdullah smiled and balled up his fists as he assumed a fighter's stance and then lumbered forward.

"Oh," the prince said, his grin outlined by his dark beard, "did I forget to tell you that he is renowned in my country's National Guard for his boxing and fighting prowess? I fear for your health, American."

Bolan raised his arms but held his palms facing outward. "Look, we're not looking for trouble. Let's act like gentlemen here."

"That's right, Your Highness," Draper said. "We need to let cooler heads prevail."

The prince made a kissing sound with his mouth—the standard Arab pejorative expression for "No."

"Abdullah," he said. "I command you to beat this infidel like the dog he is. Show no mercy."

"Saying that was a big mistake," Grimaldi said, cocking a thumb at Bolan. "You see, he likes dogs."

As the big Arab advanced, Bolan closed his fists and backed in a semicircle to his right. Abdullah's stance was orthodox, and Bolan figured to move away from the Arab's power hand. As they continued to circle, Bolan noticed something else: his opponent was big, but slow-moving. Tossing out a quick, darting jab, Bolan's fist smacked the other man's cheek. Enraged, Abdullah stepped forward and swung a looping right hook. Bolan stepped inside the arc of the punch and delivered a quick left, right one-two to the big Arab's midsection, then danced away.

Abdullah grunted and leaped forward, this time swinging a looping left that Bolan easily avoided. The Executioner pivoted and drove a short right cross to the Arab's side.

Another grunt from the big man. He surged forward again, but once more Bolan anticipated the move and slipped the overhand right. Pivoting again, the Executioner smashed a left hook into Abdullah's side. The blow made a thudding sound as it collided, and Abdullah took two more steps and sank to one knee, gasping for breath. His dark eyes glared up at Bolan.

The Executioner drew his right fist back, but he didn't throw the punch. Instead he stepped back and away as he watched the big Arab holding his right side as his ragged breathing continued. The shot to the liver had taken the man's legs.

"This is over," Bolan said. He waited a moment more, then stepped forward and offered an open hand to Abdullah.

The big Arab snorted and shook his head, remaining on one knee.

"You're damned right it is," Draper said. "Prince Amir, on behalf of the U.S. government, I apologize."

"Apologize?" Grimaldi repeated. "They started it. Where was your concern when I got hit in the face?"

"Back off," Draper said.

Grimaldi smirked. "You Secret Service guys are really something."

Draper's face reddened. "What was that remark?"

"Want me to repeat it into your earpiece?"

"Jack," Bolan said, "let's go get some air." He began heading for the doors.

"You know, I would've gone with a one-two punch in the jaw," Grimaldi said, falling into step beside him. "How'd you know those body shots would stop a big lug like that?"

"They usually do," Bolan said. "Remember what Joe Frazier used to say, kill the body and the head will die."

"Besides, there's less chance of hurting your hands, right? You know, I should go back and talk to His Royal Highness about what we call a good, old *American* liver shot."

"I think you've said more than enough already."

"Yeah, I know," Grimaldi said. "Sometimes I don't know when to keep my big mouth shut."

"I think this is another one of those times."

"Huh?"

"To keep your mouth shut," Bolan said.

MAHFUJ WATCHED THE two Americans go through the doors leaving the gymnasium. The bigger one was obviously the leader. He had performed well with the substitute team without even knowing their capabilities, and his leadership qualities had shown through. This was obviously a very capable and dangerous man. His persistent presence at the same places as the prince made the hairs on the back of Mahfuj's neck stand up.

Obviously, the man was an American government agent, but he did not appear to be affiliated with the Secret Service guards. He and his partner were a separate entity, probably assigned to watch over everyone. But why, then, would he allow his associate to behave in such a manner? Perhaps that was merely a facade.

"We shall leave this place at once," the prince shouted.

He turned toward Agent Draper. "Go fetch my limo."

Mahfuj could see that the Secret Service agent flushed at the tone of the command. He spoke into his wrist microphone. After a few seconds he extended his palm toward the door and said, "It's on the way, Your Highness."

Abdullah was still on one knee, holding his side. The prince was a fool, causing this humiliation for no reason other than his own petulance. If he truly knew anything about leading men, he would have avoided pushing Abdullah into a fight he was not certain to win. Not only were they on the enemy's home ground, but the big American was obviously a seasoned warrior. He had defeated the redoubtable Abdullah with only a minimum of effort. Their experiences with him in the field exercise should have told the prince that much. For the rest, he could have looked into the man's eyes, as Mahfuj had. He saw no fear, only the serenity and confidence of a man who has fought many battles.

Yes, he thought. This American was a formidable

adversary. Obviously, the U.S. had sent their best man to monitor the situation, even if they had sent a hothead to accompany him. Yet even that man, despite his temper, did not look like one who could be easily outfought or outwitted. They were both formidable foes.

Mahfuj filed that information away in a special place in his brain as the others helped Abdullah get to his feet.

"You have disgraced us," the prince said. "If we were on Saudi soil, I would have you given one-hundred lashes for making such a fool of yourself."

Abdullah muttered a polite apology as he took a few tentative steps toward the doors.

"You will not ride with the rest of us," the prince said. "Ride back with the Americans. Nor shall you stay on my floor at the hotel."

Mahfuj purposely trailed behind them, placing his palm on Abdullah's shoulder as the big man walked. Ridicule and scorn often opened the door to opportunity. Perhaps it would not be too difficult to recruit Abdullah to his side.

"It is not important, my brother," Mahfuj whispered. "We shall win next time."

Abdullah gave a fractional nod and kept up his slow pace.

And it is also a good reminder for me, Mahfuj thought. If and when the time comes that I must face those two Americans, I shall give them no chance, and show them no mercy.

BOLAN SAW THE black Ford sedan heading toward them as they stood in the hot, desert air under the overhang of the gymnasium. He figured it was Agent Dylan and her partner.

"Hey, I'll bet that's her," Grimaldi said.

The sedan pulled to a stop, and Dylan got out of the front passenger door and extended her hand. She was wearing business attire today, a white blouse and navy skirt. Bolan assumed her jacket was in the car. A delicate gold necklace, with a Star of David medallion, gleamed in the sunlight.

"I hope I'm not disturbing you gentlemen," she said.

"Not at all," Grimaldi said, grabbing her hand and shaking it heartily. "We're always available to help a fellow government agent."

Just as he said that, a long, black limousine, a dark brown Hummer and two other black Ford sedans pulled up in front of the building. Several men, some clad in black tactical outfits, others in suits and ties, got out of the vehicle. One of the men opened the right side door of the limo. As if on cue, Draper pushed through the exit doors, followed by the prince and his entourage. Draper's face was flushed, and he shot a dirty look at Grimaldi and Bolan. The prince glanced at them, as well. His eyes swept over each of them, lingering for a time on Dylan. He turned and said something in Arabic, and the other Saudis stared at her, too. Laughing, the prince ducked into the capacious rear section of the limo, followed by the bodyguard with the bandaged hand and three others. They laughed, as well.

After seeing them all safely into the limo, Draper got in the Hummer and slammed the door.

Bolan saw that Dylan's face was red.

"You all right?" he asked.

Her mouth puckered. "His Royal Highness wasn't aware that I speak fluent Arabic."

Bolan cocked his head. He spoke a little Arabic also

and hoped she hadn't heard the derogatory term the prince had used when he'd looked at her.

"What did he say?" Grimaldi asked.

She took a deep breath, looked at the ground and then lifted her head. "It's not worth translating. Suffice it to say, he noticed my necklace and doesn't like Jews very much."

Grimaldi snorted. "Yeah, well, he can go to hell as far as I'm concerned. He's what you'd call a *schmuck*."

Her eyebrows rose.

"Well, not you directly." Grimaldi smiled sheepishly. "I mean, that's Hebrew for a guy's who's a real… Well, you know what I mean, right?"

"Yeah," she said, suppressing a laugh. "I'm impressed. I didn't know you were bilingual."

"Actually," Grimaldi said, "I'm a lot more than that. I know how to ask an attractive woman out to dinner in eight different languages."

"And I'll bet you've been turned down in at least ten," she said, but her smile was still engaging.

Two other agents escorted the big Arab Bolan had knocked down to the Hummer. He, too, shot a look of utter contempt toward Bolan as he managed to get into the vehicle with some amount of difficulty. Whether it was due to the man's size or the soreness of his body, Bolan didn't want to speculate. He filed the big Arab's vulnerability away, just in case they met again.

"I wonder what's eating him?" Grimaldi asked.

"Which one?" Dylan asked. "The big guy or Agent Draper?"

Grimaldi laughed. "Draper's just a little sore because we made his easy babysitting job a little more challenging. The big Arab's PO'd because we had to knock him down a peg after he picked a fight with us."

Dylan arched an eyebrow. "Sounds like you two are taking this desert warfare class a little too seriously."

"What was it exactly you wanted to speak with us about?" Bolan asked.

"Sheriff Dundee called me a little while ago. It seems someone paid a nocturnal visit to Camp Freedom last night."

"What happened?" Bolan asked.

"That's a good question," she said. "It seems to depend on whom you ask. The complainant said two men in black, both heavily armed, entered their ranch, private property, by cutting a hole in the fence, and then set off several explosive devices before doing more damage to the fence as they drove off."

"Who's the complainant?"

"Eileen Autry."

"Did Dundee have any theories about it?" Bolan asked.

Dylan smiled. "He actually had the gall to ask me if the Bureau was involved." She laughed. "I told him that no respectable federal agent would act in such a reckless manner."

Bolan said nothing.

"Then to make it even more untoward," she said, "Ms. Autry called him back an hour or so later and told him to drop the whole thing. Strange, isn't it?"

"Very," Bolan said. "Obviously, the Autrys have something illegal going on. It's just a matter of finding enough manpower to stake the place out till they make a bad move."

"That's more or less what I told the sheriff," she said.

"You might want to tell him that a private plane landed on the far south end of the ranch last night," Bolan said. "They must have a private landing strip out there. That could explain why they've been at loggerheads with the BLM."

"Yeah," Grimaldi added. "They've got to be mixed up in drugs or smuggling illegals or both, which is why the daughter didn't want to pursue anything. Plus, I have it on good authority that they have some pretty heavy ordnance at Camp Freedom."

"Interesting," she said. "And you know this how?"

Grimaldi grinned. "An anonymous informant told me."

Dylan's smile faded completely. "Well, I hope this anonymous informant also told you how frustrating it is to try to build a solid case when there are a couple of—" she held up her fingers forming quotation marks "—vigilantes taking matters into their own hands and doing illegal acts."

Grimaldi's grin slowly faded, as well.

"Because," she continued, "any type of information gathered through these illegal actions, even solid evidence of wrongdoing, would be totally inadmissible in court." Her voice rose an octave as she spoke. "It would all be considered fruit of the poisonous tree. I'm sure you've heard of that, haven't you? You two are Department of Justice agents, aren't you?"

"Justice," Grimaldi said, "is our middle name."

Bolan sensed the frustrations of the case were getting to her. She looked almost ready to cry.

"Maybe we can give you something to work with," he said. "We've got some satellite photos of Camp Freedom from a few nights ago. The same time those BLM rangers disappeared. Want to take a look at them?"

Her eyes widened. "Where did you get those?"

"We got friends in high places," Grimaldi said. "And low ones, too."

Nice, France

MUSTAPHA SAT IN the shade of the lush, green garden of a private airport and smiled as he toyed with the watch and reflected on the irony of the situation. It was as if he had the ability to turn back time itself. They had left Riyadh at ten o'clock that morning, and it was barely 10:35 a.m. The king wanted to rest in Nice for a few hours as his plane was refueled and serviced, but Mustapha wasn't fooled. The old monarch had taken frequent trips to France. Mustapha suspected the king was being treated by a doctor here for some unknown affliction. Perhaps he was suffering from some fatal disease. That would indeed explain his push to get his favorite grandson, Amir, through that ridiculous desert warfare training in the U.S. As a true Bedouin warrior, he had no doubt forgotten more about the art of fighting in the desert than the wasteful prince was likely to learn in a hundred such classes. Still, Mustapha couldn't denigrate the fighting ability of the Americans. They had proven themselves redoubtable foes, so long as their political leaders were interested in the fray. As soon as their will was sapped, however, they were anxious to depart, not caring what destruction and instability they left in their wake. That was why he knew his plan would succeed. Once the news of the prince's involvement in the marathon bombing was discovered, it would eliminate any desire or will that the Americans might have to intervene in the coup in Arabia. It was foolproof.

As long as everything worked in unison, like the watch.

He fingered the king's Rolex again, marveling as the second hand glided in its continuous, circular rotation with elegant precision. All the small wheels and gears working together in unison. He placed it back into his pocket and took out the ersatz copy, the one he was supposedly working to repair. After glancing around the private villa, as if to appreciate the verdant richness, he saw that his nearest associates were ordering some refreshments from the attractive French waitress.

Even though her hair was uncovered, and her dress clung to her shapely body, she did not disturb him. In fact, it set him thinking about the reforms he would initiate once he was firmly in control as president. Building up the Arabian military was his first priority, as well as ending the indulgences of the royal family and its many scions. The loyalty of the *muftiate* would have to be ensured, but this would be accomplished once he was firmly in control. The clerics would fall into line behind him, just as they had done with the House of Saud.

He glanced around again, taking in the scenery as well as the locations of the others in his party. He was on his own on this part of the journey, a solitary desert falcon seeking to meet with the three others: Mahfuj, Mamum and Masoud. Mamum, the trustworthy, who was still in Riyadh, with Hafeez, Samad and Matayyib; Masoud, the lucky, who had been in the land of the infidels, in the belly of the beast, learning the ways of the Westerners so that one day their throats could be cut; and Mahfuj, the protector...the strongest.

Mustapha wondered how his first son was faring with the plan. He should be with the Russians securing the sacrificial goats. He longed to call his son, ask for a progress report, but the time was not right. The king's bodyguards were too ubiquitous here. It wouldn't do for them to see him texting or calling someone, especially his sons, who were in the United States. No, he had to wait. He would have to just believe that everything was moving according to the proper timetable. And, surely, Mahfuj would have notified him if something had gone awry. But there was so much to worry about, so much that could go wrong, so many interdependencies.

The complexities of the operation concerned him once again. The plan, albeit brilliant, was so complicated, so convoluted…like the workings of the watch. His strong, nimble fingers twisted the rear plate of the ersatz Rolex, and he looked at the small white pills stored inside. Soon it would be time to use them on the king. But that wouldn't be until they had reached the United States. Until then, he knew he had to be content that he was, in some small, artificial way, turning back time.

The Lucky Seven Motel,
On the Outskirts of Las Vegas

ANDROKOVICH WATCHED THROUGH his binoculars as Ibrahim Shabahb ushered the two Saudi students into the motel room. He'd told the Iraqi to dress all in black, to fit the part of an urban terrorist mastermind. Shabahb had responded by complaining that the only clothes he had that fit were the worn jeans and cowboy shirt that he'd been wearing for the past week. The Russian allowed him to keep on his pants, but gave him a black BDU shirt to put on. It fit too snugly over the man's fat belly and couldn't be buttoned.

"Who will believe a terrorist with a gut like that?" Androkovich said, giving the man's abdomen a smack. They had made a quick stop at the first store they passed and purchased a 3XL black T-shirt.

"Now I feel ready," the Iraqi said with a simper. He made his fingers into gun shapes and pretended he was shooting a machine gun. "How do I look?"

"Get all your clowning out of the way now," the Russian said. "I want these two pigeons to think you're the real deal. You're sure they won't detect something from your accent?"

The Arab looked wounded. "I was an expert translator for the Americans when they took over. I know how to sound like a Yemeni." Shabahb grinned. "Do not worry. All will be well, as long as we can stop at the liquor store on the way back. I'm all out of beer in my room."

"We can do that. Would you like me to find seventy-two virgins for you as well, so you can start your time in paradise a little early?"

"Where are you going to find any virgins around here?" Shabahb laughed. "Besides, they're no fun. You have to teach them all the tricks."

The Russian didn't like having to depend on this fool, but at this phase it was crucial. He had to make sure those two Muslim students were tucked away in the motel for the night, certain they'd stay put until tomorrow. He thought about just taking them hostage and storing them at the rented house on Billman Street, where he had the ambulance stashed. But that would entail expending more manpower for guards, and he was running a bit short with those injured in the break-in the previous night. He blew out a slow breath and went over the options.

The two Shi'ite students were from the Eastern Province of Saudi Arabia and had been recruited through the jihadist website. They were fired up and ready to go. Shabahb had assured him of that. Plus, although they'd been studying in the U.S. for the past year, they were now in a strange place, on a religious jihad, waiting for instructions, and, most importantly, without a car. The Russian had stocked the room with plenty of food and water. They'd keep until the next day. He was certain of it.

He felt the vibration of his cell phone and looked at the screen. The name surprised him: the Autry ranch.

He pressed the button to answer it. Eileen Autry's voice came through.

"Andrews, where are you? I've been looking all over for you."

"Ms. Autry, I'm not at the ranch right now," he said. "What can I do for you?"

"You can get back here immediately. We need to talk. And why are so many of the buildings locked up? We don't even have the keys."

Androkovich thought for a moment. He needed to avoid any more problems with her. She was starting to become a bit more than a nuisance.

"I'm sorry," he said. "I thought I gave duplicate keys to Shane. I'll double-check that ASAP."

"ASAP." Her tone was full of contempt. "And what have you gotten Shane mixed up in?"

"Did you speak to him about that?"

"I did," she said. "And he told me some cockama-
mie story about motion detectors. But I know when
my brother is nervous, and I know when he's lying.
I want some answers. Fast. Or I'm firing all of you
and calling the sheriff to have you removed from our
property."

That was the last thing he needed at the moment. He
saw movement at the door of the motel room. Shabahb
paused, said something to the two students and closed
the door. The Iraqi began waddling toward the car. The
Russian knew he had to end this current Autry problem
sooner rather than later.

"Look, Ms. Autry," he said in a calm voice. "I'm
sorry for any misunderstanding between you and Shane.
Why don't I call you when I get back? I'm on the way
now. I should be there in about twenty minutes. We can
talk." He hated kissing this bitch's ass, but he had no
choice at the moment. Besides, Shabahb was almost at
the car and would no doubt open his big mouth as soon
as he plopped his ass down.

Androkovich flipped the locks to keep him temporarily outside.

Finally, Eileen Autry's voice came back on the
phone. "All right, Mr. Andrews. I'll wait for you to arrive. But I'm warning you, you'd better have some good
answers." She rattled off her cell phone number. "Call
me as soon as you get here."

She hung up before he could say anything else.

Shabahb tried the door and his hand slipped off. His
face twisted into a pitiful-looking frown—an over-
wrought clown about to cry for his audience.

The Russian put his phone away slowly, and then
pressed the button to unlock the doors. It was all about

constant reminders of who was in control…something he had to keep in mind when next dealing with that woman.

AFTER REVIEWING THE satellite photos of the Autry ranch, Bolan was certain of two things: there was indeed a relatively new airstrip on the south end of the property, and the two BLM Park Rangers who'd been murdered had made some sort of traffic stop on the highway that intersected with the back road into the place. The images of the vehicles, four of them, were too minute to make any positive identifications.

"These photos are great," Dylan said, leaning over the table where Bolan had spread out the eight-by-tens. "How on earth did you get them?"

"Like I told you," Grimaldi said, handing her a freshly brewed cup of coffee. "We got friends in high places."

She accepted the coffee with a smile and took a sip before turning back to the photo array. "If only they were bigger. Do you have a magnifying glass?"

Bolan shook his head. "If you have a laptop, I can put the files on that, and you might be able to enlarge them that way. I don't know how much detail that will afford."

Dylan sipped her coffee again. "It's worth a shot." She turned to her partner, who was already on the way to their car.

Bolan had taken the precaution of downloading the files Hal Brognola had sent him to a flash drive. Even though he knew Aaron Kurtzman had all sorts of safeguards preventing anyone from tracing electronic transmissions back to Stony Man Farm, Bolan felt that it was always best to rely on proper security measures on all levels.

Dylan's cell phone rang, and she set her coffee down and went to her purse on the sofa.

As Dylan conversed on her phone, Bolan immediately picked up that something had upset her. He watched and waited. The space between her eyebrows creased as she kept nodding and replying in monosyllables. After about a minute she said, "Yes, sir, I understand. We'll get right over there."

She hung up and turned to Bolan.

"Looks like our computer review of your photos will have to wait," she said. "There's been a new development."

Bolan raised an eyebrow.

"Earlier today an armored truck was robbed," she said. "Two of the guards and two police officers were killed."

"Damn," Grimaldi said. "Where'd this go down?"

"A few miles south of the main Strip, out by the M Casino," Dylan replied. She bit her bottom lip and put the cell phone back into her purse. "That was my supervisor. He wants us to put everything else on hold and respond to offer assistance in the investigation."

"We'll come, too," Bolan said, holding up the flash drive. "Why don't you ride with me? You can review the files on the way."

Dylan nodded, her expression somewhat distracted. "I hate cases where police officers have been killed. It's so tragic."

"Me, too," Grimaldi said. "And we've worked a lot of them. I could tell you quite a bit."

"You can do that later." Bolan tossed him a fresh,

black BDU shirt. "You ride with Agent Dylan's partner, in case we get separated."

Grimaldi frowned as he slipped on the shirt.

Bolan chose to follow Dylan's partner, so she could review the files as they proceeded to the scene. After several attempts at enlarging the photos, she sighed in frustration.

"It's no use," she said. "I can't get enough pixel resolution on this laptop. I wonder if the photos could be enhanced."

"I'll see what I can do," Bolan said. As he approached the exit for St. Rose Parkway, he saw the red oscillating police lights in the impending darkness. They exited the freeway and drove toward the silhouette of the casino and hotel, standing like a thin, lighted wedge over the sea of red and blue lights. Numerous uniformed police officers motioned the passing traffic to continue south on Las Vegas Boulevard. Even at this hour it had created a "gaper's block." Several more squad cars, their lights rotating, were parked in the street amid fluttering ribbons of yellow crime scene tape.

Beyond the squad cars Bolan could see more tape and two vacant, bullet-ridden marked squad cars sitting diagonally, open driver's doors facing them, in the middle of the street. Obviously, they'd been positioned as cover by the responding officers. Perhaps forty feet beyond them another vehicle, the armored car, or what was left of it, still sat in the middle lane of the road. The rear door had a huge piece missing. All of the tires were flattened, and the front end of the armored truck rested on the asphalt in a thick pool of oil. Huge floodlights illuminated a section in the encroaching darkness almost as brightly as if it were day. Dylan's partner flashed his credentials and was waved through by one of the traffic cops. Bolan pulled up and showed his as well, saying, "We're with them."

The officer shone his flashlight on the ID and then motioned for the Executioner to drive into the protected zone, adding, "You can park over there."

After stopping in an abandoned field next to a host of other marked and unmarked police vehicles, Bolan and Dylan got out and walked toward the scene. They were joined by Grimaldi and Dylan's partner, Agent Banks. As they approached, Bolan immediately picked out the hulking, barrel-chested figure of Sheriff Wayne Dundee standing off to the side of one of the two shot-up squad cars. A group of processing crime scene techs swarmed over the area with organized precision, the intermittent flashes of their cameras now winking in the darkness. Dundee was in full uniform, minus his hat. The big man's expression was grim as he extended his hand toward Bolan and Dylan.

No one dispensed any superfluous amenities. Dundee got right down to business.

"I'm mad as hell. I just came from the hospital and trying to console those two officers' families." His mouth settled into a tight line. "There's nothing I hate worse."

Bolan gave him a commiserating nod. "We've been there ourselves, Sheriff. My condolences on the loss of your men."

Dundee took a deep breath and pushed out his lower lip. "I tried to comfort the families of the two security guards, too." He shook his massive head slowly. "What the hell can you say? I ended up tripping over my words."

"I'm sure they appreciated it," Bolan said. "They might not have said so, but they did."

Dundee nodded, closing his eyes for a few moments.

"The Bureau is here to offer you every assistance," Dylan said. "What can you tell us about the incident?"

Dundee sighed again and opened his eyes. Bolan saw a slight glistening there, but Dundee shook off any emotion as he pointed to the battered shell of the armored car.

"As near as we can piece it together," he said, "it was a well-planned, well-executed operation. The armored car had just finished its regular pickups from four casinos. We're still trying to get a handle on how much was taken. They exited the freeway at St. Rose Parkway here, off of LV Boulevard, then turned on to Volunteer. A semi rig pulled across the road, blocking it. That's when all hell broke loose. At least seven assailants, all wearing those full-faced, Mexican-style wrestling masks, hit the truck from all sides. They must have taken out the engine with some kind of powerful gun. Left a baseball-sized hole in the grille, went right through the radiator, and pierced the engine block like a hot knife stabbing into an English muffin."

He paused and motioned for them to follow him around to the front of the armored car. They managed to skirt the inky tendrils of the oil slick. The hole in the front end was indeed impressive. It had to be at least four to five inches in circumference. The bulging hood had been sprung by the pressure of the powerful round. Bolan took one look at the ruined engine and had one thought: antitank weapon.

"Your techs find any shell casings for this one?" he asked.

Dundee nodded. "They found a whole bunch. Mostly 7.62 mm. SKS or AK-47 rifles most likely." He pointed to a small yellow tag on the street about thirty yards away. "The one that did this damage is over there. You should see the size of it."

"Fourteen point five millimeter?" Bolan asked.

Dundee raised an eyebrow. "Yeah. How you guess that?"

"I'd say the weapon used was a PTRS-41," Bolan said. "Russian made. It's designed as an antitank weapon. That's some pretty heavy ordnance floating around."

Dundee nodded. "Cop killer bullets, too." His expression hardened. "My two officers were shot with a 9 mm, rounds that went right through their vests. Not that those damn rifle rounds wouldn't have, but, hell, the vests should've afforded them more protection against a handgun."

"More than likely it was old Soviet ammunition," Bolan said. "The projectiles were steel-core."

Dundee nodded, his lower lip jutting. "I'm gonna get these damn bastards if it's the last thing I do."

"As I said," Dylan told him, "the Bureau is offering whatever assistance you might need."

Dundee nodded. "Duly noted and appreciated. I've got a team of detectives working on it, tracking down leads, but unfortunately, they seem few and far between. These assholes seem to have vanished into thin air. We've got an appeal for anybody who witnessed anything going out on the news tonight. I hate to act like we're desperate, but like I said…" His voice trailed off.

"Any cameras in the area?" Bolan asked.

"None." Dundee pointed toward the two squad cars.

"We got a little bit from their in-car cameras, but because of the straight-ahead viewfinder and the angle they parked at, there's not a lot to see. Come on, one of my techs has it downloaded."

They walked over to an open van filled with electrical equipment. Inside two men sat with laptops, talking and pointing. They looked up when Dundee approached.

"Len," he said, "you got the video loaded from the squad cars ready?"

The tech nodded, clicked a few buttons on his keyboard and shifted the laptop around for them to see.

"Here's the first one," the tech said. He pressed a button and the color image filled the screen. It showed the view through the squad car's front windshield as it darted through traffic.

"The camera's automatically activated when the emergency lights come on," the tech said. "This is the view as the first squad got the radio call of a robbery in progress and responded. I have audio, too, if you want."

Bolan nodded.

The sounds of the dispatcher updating the officers of multiple offenders, shots fired, accompanied the videos of the squad car driving around other cars, most of which were stopped or in the process of pulling over to the right.

The officer's voice could be heard on the audio advising that he'd arrived on scene.

The camera's viewfinder showed the squad car making a wide circle to the right. As it straightened, an orange diamond-shaped sign was quickly visible, followed by a flash of blue and white—a vehicle of some kind was captured momentarily.

"Stop it there," Bolan said. "Replay that part again. Can you make it slower?"

The tech played with the mouse. He reran the section again in slow motion.

Bolan studied the screen. "Was that a road construction sign?"

Dundee nodded. "It must've been part of the setup. No construction was in the area this morning."

Bolan watched the slow-motion replay again. "That looks like an ambulance of some kind. The camera caught the front end just short of the insignias on the side. The crew might have seen something."

"We figured the same thing," Dundee said. "But no luck so far tracking them down."

Bolan nodded. He motioned for the tech to continue the playback.

When the video resumed, Bolan saw the armored car was disabled, with a trail of dark smoke emanating from the front end. The rear door was damaged and hanging open. Several men in full-faced masks labored in metronomic fashion, removing bags of money from the open rear door of the armored car. The long, blue trailer of a semi-rig was stretched across the street in front of the armored car. A windowless, white van was pulled up next to the rear section of the armored car.

A jolting motion was discernible, most likely as the officer exited the vehicle, and then his voice could be heard on the audio once more: *"Multiple offenders wearing masks,"* the officer's recorded voice said. *"Armed with assault weapons. AK-47s or SKSs."*

His voice ended abruptly, drowned out by the sound of automatic gunfire. The camera's viewfinders suddenly showed a series of round holes, surrounded by a web of cracks in the windshield. More booming retorts could be heard.

"At this point we estimate that the two officers who reached the scene were attacked from behind," Dundee said. "Shot in the back."

After several more seconds, the gunfire stopped, but the camera stayed focused through the splintered glass. The movement of men could be partially discerned, continuing for several more seconds. Something blue moved on the other side of the ruined windshield, then something white, as well. The view settled into a steady image of the fractionated view through the broken glass of the motionless armored car.

The tech pressed a button and froze the screen. "Want to see the one from the other squad? It's pretty much the same as this one."

"Let's see it," Bolan said, although something had already clicked in his memory. He'd seen the entire operation being rehearsed the night before at Camp Freedom.

The second video yielded little more than the first one. Bolan had the tech play them both again, freezing the images at certain points. When they'd watched both numerous times, he turned to Dundee.

"I need to talk to you about this one, Sheriff," Bolan said.

Dundee's eyes narrowed. "I'm all ears."

Dylan looked surprised, as well.

After hearing Bolan's account of his unauthorized trip into the Autry compound, the relentless drill tactics the militia members were undergoing, the van being driven up into the back of the trailer, the minefield and the ensuing firefight, Dundee seemed both impressed and irritated.

"Claymores?" Dundee said, looking incredulous. "Are you sure?"

"Positive," Grimaldi stated.

"Dammit," he said through clenched teeth. "You hand me a sledgehammer that'll knock down a wall and then tell me you stole it and I can't use it."

"You've got the 'who,'" Bolan said. "All you have to do is figure out the 'why,' and you'll be able to start breaking that wall down."

"Yeah," Grimaldi added. "Just use extreme caution. Like my partner said, they've got some heavy ordnance out there, and from the looks of it, they used some here, too."

"You know," Dundee said, "I had a call from Eileen Autry complaining about someone breaking into their place. Then she called back a couple hours later leaving me a message that the whole thing, her complaint, had been a mistake."

"A mistake for them, maybe," Grimaldi said.

Dundee wasn't amused. He looked directly at Grimaldi and asked, "Who are you two, really? I've been around long enough to know that the Department of Justice doesn't operate this way."

"Look, Sheriff," Bolan said. "The Autrys are into this up to their necks. They're obviously planning something big. This robbery and the murders are only part of it. Give us twenty-four hours to run this to ground. In the meantime, if I may, I'd suggest that you set up a round-the-clock surveillance of Camp Freedom, and tag the truck or van if they're seen leaving the property."

"And I'll see about getting you some assistance from the Bureau," Dylan said. "I'm certain that they were tied into the murders of those two BLM Rangers, as well."

Dundee stared at Bolan for several moments, then nodded and took out his cell phone. Dylan did the same. As the two of them were punching in numbers, Grimaldi tapped Bolan on the shoulder and motioned for him to step to the side.

"And just how in the hell are we going to bust this thing wide open, all nice and legal enough to suit them, in twenty-four hours?" he asked in a hushed voice.

"We'll just keep beating the bushes," Bolan said. "Something's bound to jump out."

CHAPTER THIRTEEN

The Grand Marquis Hotel and Casino

Mahfuj took what he knew would be his final look at the massive, obscene fountain in front of the hotel. Despite finding its audacity disgusting, he had, in a strange way, grown to look forward to visiting it each day. Certainly, it represented the decadence against which they struggled, but it also was a precursor to seeing his brother.

This morning's meeting with Masoud was the preamble to the final phase of their father's plan. Waiting for it all to unfold in sequence had been a trying, difficult task. Mahfuj reflected on the beginning, at the nightclub in Bahrain, grabbing the barrel of the rifle, feeling the hot metal searing his flesh… His hand was all but totally healed now, no longer requiring the bandage he still wore, which gave him the pretext each morning for going out of the hotel to meet Masoud. And he had a lot to tell his brother this time. They had a powerful new ally to their cause. The first convert of their cause.

He knew that he had Abdullah with him when the big man joined him for dawn prayers. The soft knock on his hotel room door, shortly before dawn, had come as only a mild surprise. Mahfuj had opened it and saw Abdullah standing there holding his prayer rug and asking to pray with him. Mahfuj had agreed and silently gave thanks for sending such a redoubtable ally to the jihad. Mahfuj had always liked the big man, and dreaded the thought of killing him when the time came. Now, perhaps, he could allow Abdullah to live, just as the prophet had spared those who converted.

They prayed side by side, and afterward Abdullah confided his ongoing embarrassment at the beating he had sustained at the hands of the American, of the shame he felt being derided by the prince for losing. Mahfuj brushed away his words. He told him that they were both part of a larger plan that was destined for greatness.

"What plan?" the big man asked.

Mahfuj wanted to tell him, to take him fully into his confidence, but he did not know if he should risk it. Instead, he reached over and held Abdullah's hand.

"You must trust me, my brother," Mahfuj said. "Believe in my word as you might believe those of a prophet. And there will come a time, soon, when I shall reveal all to you and ask that you accompany me. Will you do that?"

Abdullah's face set itself in a grim-looking expression. Mahfuj felt he suspected something, but he didn't know what exactly. His massive head nodded, and he bowed, looking at the floor. "Of all of us, Mahfuj, you have the most powerful will, the strongest faith. How I envy that strength. Would, that I could be like you."

Mahfuj placed a hand on Abdullah's shoulder. It felt like a pile of rocks. It most certainly was a sign that at this eleventh hour, on the eve of this final part of the plan, that a formidable *mujahadeen* would come forward pledging allegiance and loyalty without even knowing the particulars.

His cell phone vibrated.

Do you desire coffee, my brother?

Even the insouciance of Masoud's impish behavior could not upset Mahfuj this day. Victory was almost within their grasp. He could feel it. Turning, he strode to the coffee shop with a proud defiance in his gait. Although he walked in the land of the infidel, he walked as a lion.

His brother sat at the same small table with two paper cups and a plastic bag in front of him. His dark eyes were gleaming with a look of anticipation.

"*As-salamu alaykum*," Mahfuj said, not caring who heard the Arabic. He was a lion now, and let the infidels fear the roar of the beast. He sat down and smiled.

Masoud's mouth drew into a thin line. He leaned across the table and said in a hushed voice, "Do you not remember my admonishment to you from yesterday? About speaking only in English?"

Mahfuj laughed. The plan was in its final phase, and he felt vindicated by supreme rectitude, at having recruited Abdullah to their side. He decided to push it. "*Loa-sah-mahht*," he said. "I am sorry."

The combination of the two languages made Masoud's body jerk. He winced, as if he'd been slapped.

Mahfuj smiled broadly, but said nothing else. His brother did have a point. Overconfidence had been the undoing of many a warrior. "And you are totally correct, my brother," he said in English, withdrawing an envelope from his pocket and shoving it across the table.

"This is a detailed diagram and log of our location and procedure for dropping off the prince after the class each day." His nostrils flared with a defiant superiority. "It should be the same for this evening, as well. Do not forget to be there."

"We will not."

"And you have something for me?" Mahfuj asked.

This made Masoud smirk as he pushed a colorful plastic bag and a cup of coffee across the table. "Perhaps these will help you prepare for your final day of desert warfare class? I take it the prince has done well?"

Mahfuj emitted a snort of derision. The bag was exceptionally heavy. He opened the top of the bag and saw some sort of garment, a T-shirt, emblazoned with a bird. Mahfuj looked closer. It was a falcon. A desert falcon. A smile stretched over his lips. He reached inside the bag and felt the hard, angular surface of the pistol, and two other long objects affixed to it. One of them was round, the other more angular.

"It is a 9 mm Beretta," Masoud whispered. "With two fully loaded magazines and a sound suppressor. I have also included a knife with a spring-loaded, retractable blade."

Mahfuj nodded and closed the bag.

Masoud drank from his cup and glanced around. The shop had a line on the other side, but no one was in the immediate vicinity. "There is a laser sight on the pistol, as well. You will not be able to use the sights of the weapon with the suppressor attached. Do you wish me to show you—"

"Show *me*?" Mahfuj felt like slapping him. "I know how to use it. How dare you question my knowledge, my ability?"

Masoud smiled. "I would never do that. I was playing a game, returning the teasing of your bilingual greeting. It was my turn." He started to get up. "You'd better not be late on your last day."

Mahfuj reached out and grabbed his arm. "Everything else is set? For tonight?"

"Everything is ready," Masoud replied, the impish smile still on his lips. "Text me tonight when you have finished your…assignment."

Mahfuj nodded. The upcoming events of the day and the night flashed through his mind. In a few more hours they would either be waiting to execute the final, crushing blow, or they would be dead. Either *mujahadeens* or *fedayeens*, triumphant warriors or those martyred in battle. They were close to the end of the game, and he couldn't help himself as he whispered, *"Inshallah."*

Desert Warfare Training Center

"MAN, IT'S WONDERFUL what a good night's sleep will do for a person's disposition," Grimaldi said, yawning before he took a gulp of coffee from his paper cup.

Bolan nodded as he pressed the button to contact Brognola. As usual, he answered before the second ring in his customary gruff tone.

"About damn time you called in. Everything going okay?"

"It could be better," Bolan said, putting the phone on speaker. "We lost four more of the good guys yesterday in an armored car robbery. I'm convinced our buddies at Camp Freedom were behind it, but we're lacking solid proof."

"Solid legal proof," Grimaldi chimed in. "Which

we've assured the local and federal authorizes that we'd provide in twenty-four hours, of which we have about twelve or thirteen left."

"Sounds like a tall order," Brognola said. "Anything I can do to help?"

"Plenty," Bolan said. "First, were you able to make any high-resolution enlargements of those satellite feeds you sent us?"

"Aaron's been working on that, and more," Brognola replied. "We're not exactly sitting on our hands back here, you know."

"That's good to know," Grimaldi said. "I feel better already."

Brognola snorted.

"Anything more on that pending arms deal?" Bolan queried.

"Yeah. Our sources are saying it's set for tonight. We're working through channels to trace the transaction via a drone."

"Got an idea on the location?" Bolan asked.

"Not a good fix yet. Aaron's been reviewing satellite feeds from the past month trying to figure out where the last one went down." Brognola sighed. "There's so damn much smuggling traffic going north through the border that it's like looking for the proverbial needle in a haystack."

"Tell Aaron to concentrate on small planes coming up from Mexico," Bolan suggested. "Autry's got a private airstrip on the south end of his property. A plane landed there the night before last."

"Will do," Brognola said. "Anything else?"

Bolan thought for a moment. "Check into Autry's finances again. There might be something there. In the meantime, we've got to get to our final day of class."

Grimaldi emitted an exaggerated moan.

Brognola laughed. "Yeah, I owe you guys for putting you through that one, all right. But how's our Royal Highness doing? You keeping him safe and sound?"

"Between us and the Secret Service," Grimaldi said, "he's just fine."

"Make sure he stays that way," Brognola said. "The President's very concerned, and the Saudi king is due to land in D.C. tonight. All this other stuff, Autry, the arms smuggling, the robberies…if it doesn't directly tie into the prince's safety, let the locals handle it, okay?"

Bolan felt in his gut that it all did tie in somehow. He just wasn't sure how.

Camp Freedom

ANDROKOVICH STOOD IN the shadows of the barn and scanned the highway with his binoculars. The white car sat on the shoulder approximately one-hundred yards from the rear gate.

"There's another one by the front entrance, too," Strogoff said. "The sentries say they've been there all night."

Police, no doubt, Androkovich thought, and tried to factor this new development into the overall plan. He'd actually anticipated something of the sort after he'd killed the two police officers. They always overreacted when a couple of their own went down. Had it just been the two armored car security guards, the response wouldn't have been this extensive with the surveillance. But the fact that they were just watching meant something, too. They were suspicious, but had no evidence to make a move. Not yet, anyway. He remembered the two Americans and how they'd broken into the compound with impunity. They would pursue any means, apparently, and he had to figure that they were in collusion with the police. He thought of what else he had to do.

"Is the rest of the Semtex still on schedule?" he asked.

"As far as I know," Strogoff said. "They sent a text that they'll be landing at 0300."

"Tell them to move it back an hour or so. And have the men load the shell into the four-wheel-drive pickup."

His partner's eyes narrowed. "You're removing it now?"

"Yes. There's enough Semtex already packed in it to make a big enough bang for their buck." Strogoff nodded.

"We have to leave enough Semtex for the authorities to find here after the bombing. The trail must lead back here."

Once the authorities hit this place, Androkovich thought, they'll have the direct link between the bomb and the Autry militia, just as Masoud wants. Nothing will tie the operation to the Saudis. It will look like Autry engineered the whole thing, kidnapping and them assassinating the prince and the other two Arabs as a smoke screen. It should create enough confusion that any hint of a Saudi conspiracy would be delayed until after the military coup had succeeded. Mustapha will be in charge, as the new president, and the U.S. will still be wringing its hands with apologies over the kidnapping and murder of a member of the royal family on American soil, in conjunction with an act of domestic terrorism.

"Go get Ibrahim," he said. "We'll grab those two Arabs at the motel now. It's time they got their first taste of what awaits them."

"In paradise?" Strogoff asked with a wry grin.

"And tell Duncan we'll need him to drive the white Jeep out the south gate and draw the surveillance car away. We'll use the black Wrangler to go through the back pasture, the disputed territories, as the old fool calls them."

Before Strogoff could reply, another voice, female, cut in. "Is that how you refer to my father? The old fool? And did my brother give you permission to use his Jeep?"

Androkovich turned and saw Eileen Autry standing a few yards away. That she had sneaked up on them so effectively made him realize all the new pressure was having its effect on him. He should have been more aware of his surroundings, and of what he said.

Prying ears, he thought. But perhaps it was as good a time as any to deal with this particular problem. He stepped toward her, smiling as benignly as he could.

"Eileen," he said, reaching into his pocket. "I didn't hear you come up."

"Don't call me by my first name," she said. Her tone was vituperative.

Androkovich felt his fingers close around the elliptically shaped plastic handle. He withdrew the stun gun from his pocket, flipped off the safety and extended it toward her.

Autry started to scream, but it was stifled in her throat as the twin prongs caught her in the abdomen and upper left thigh. She stiffened and did a little pirouette to the ground.

"Take her inside."

Strogoff moved over, picked up the woman's still-rigid form and dragged her backward, careful to keep his hands from between the two prongs.

Androkovich kept the trigger depressed, giving her an extra jolt, after the initial, five-second ride, until they were inside the barn. As she came out of it she started to scream, and he gave her another jolt.

Her voice was reduced to a quavering moan.

"Gag her and tie her up."

Strogoff nodded and walked to the corner where a coil of rope hung on a post. "Should we kill her now?"

Fedor considered that option but decided against it. When it was time, all the Autrys would die together. It had to look like a murder-suicide, with Shane shooting his father and sister and then turning the gun on himself. Having one die too early would be a red flag to the coroner's office and throw off the timetable.

He looked down at her as his partner pulled her hair back and worked his cloth handkerchief between her clenched teeth. Androkovich knelt on her outstretched legs and held her arms to her sides. Her eyes flashed, and she managed to say, "You bastard."

He smiled, remembering the line from one of the old American movies, *The Professionals*, that his Russian instructors at the American training facility had made him watch over and over again during his youth.

"Yes, ma'am," he said, mimicking old-time tough-guy actor Lee Marvin. "An unfortunate circumstance of birth. But you…" He realized the line didn't totally fit, so he changed it slightly. "You, ma'am, are what they call a self-made bitch."

Strogoff was almost done completing the knotting of the handkerchief. Androkovich released her left arm and punched her hard in the stomach and then in the temple. The woman's body went limp as she sank into unconsciousness.

Desert Warfare Training Center

IT HAD TURNED into a relatively easy final day: more classroom instruction, with evaluation of the tactics used during the preceding day's raids, all of which had been recorded, and the final shooting competition following lunch. There were a variety of trophies, and Bolan caught Grimaldi eying the one for first place. It was about two feet high, with a figure standing in a Camp Perry style pose on the top, flanked by gold-colored wings.

Special Agent Draper came over and stood by Bolan and Grimaldi. "Hey, I wanted to tell you guys I was sorry about yesterday," he said. "No hard feelings?" He held out his hand to Bolan.

"Hard feelings about what?" The Executioner shook Draper's hand.

"About the little donnybrook. I know you guys didn't start it." He extended his palm to Grimaldi.

"Yeah," the Stony Man pilot said, shaking the agent's hand, "but my partner here sure finished it, didn't he?"

Draper grinned and leaned forward. "All I can say is tomorrow morning we put him on his private jet for D.C., and he's somebody else's problem."

"How'd the prince do last night?" Bolan asked.

Draper blew out a sharp breath and shook his head. "About the same as he's done every other night. Broads and booze till about two a.m. He keeps two or three of his bodyguards in the suite with him, along with one of our guys. We got to handle it in shifts, the guy's so obnoxious." He grinned. "I actually feel kind of sorry for the bodyguards. He treats them like shit. They just sit there in the other room while he entertains the ladies in his main suite."

"Sort of like being the piano player in the whorehouse, eh?" Grimaldi said.

Draper grinned again. "I guess that's one way of putting it. He was late getting up this morning. We practically had to ask Metro PD to escort, with lights and sirens, to get here on time. So many of the damn streets were blocked off."

"They're setting up barricades for the Las Vegas Marathon," Bolan said.

"Yeah, we were thinking of entering it," Grimaldi said, "but it doesn't look like we'll have time."

"I ran Boston again, this past year," Draper stated. "I was in it back in '13 when the terrorists hit it. I was about a quarter mile away from the finish line when the bombs went off." He shook his head. "I'll never forget that one."

"Few of us will," Bolan said.

As shooting competitions went, this one was pretty standard. Each round eliminated more shooters, based on standard bull's-eye scores. Bolan and Grimaldi advanced to the latter rounds without any problem, as did St. Alban's team and the Arab security squad. With each successive round, the targets were moved farther down the range while the time limit was decreased. Soon only three men remained: Bolan, Grimaldi and St. Alban.

The prince took this opportunity to frown and say something in Arabic to Abdullah, the big guy Bolan had taken out with the liver punch. The big Arab's face darkened as he stood stoically when the prince berated him. Bolan couldn't quite follow the rapid conversation, but knew enough Arabic to figure out the conversation was a dressing down of the big man and his teammates for not doing better.

Grimaldi walked over and smirked. "Looks like he's a real prince of a fella, doesn't it?"

Bolan said nothing, but he wondered how much loyalty Prince Amir had engendered among his bodyguards with his constant humiliations.

The three shooting finalists stepped up to the firing line. St. Alban went first, amassing a respectable score of 95. Grimaldi topped him with a score of 97, and Bolan fired last, scoring a perfect 100.

"This will be the last round," the firing range instructor said as the targets were moved to the thirty-yard line. "The two top shooters will fire in competition."

Grimaldi stepped up and waited for the clock to sound. Bolan watched the determined expression on his partner's face as he drew and fired his SIG Sauer. His score was again 97. He frowned in frustration as Bolan came up to the line.

"Show the rest of these ladies what you can do," he said.

Bolan nodded and signaled he was ready. The clock sounded, and the Executioner brought up his Beretta, putting nine rounds through the center of the bull's-eye. He paused for a split second and fired his last round.

The scorekeeper moved to the target, shook his head and pulled it from the framework. He trotted back to the line with the big paper in his hand.

"Looks like you would've had another perfect score," he said, "except your last round went way low." He pointed to the fourth ring. "Your score is a ninety-five."

"What?" Grimaldi said, his face an expression of disbelief, which soon transitioned to a broad grin. "You mean I won first place?"

Bolan extended his hand toward Grimaldi. "Congratulations, Jack. Nice shooting."

Grimaldi looked askance. "Come on. You let me win, didn't you?"

Bolan raised an eyebrow, smiled and said nothing.

St. Alban offered his congratulations, as well.

Draper came by with a big grin and slapped Grimaldi on the back as he was hoisting the trophy. One of the Arabs, the man who had sat out the training sessions with a bandaged hand, also stepped over, his face was a solemn mask.

Grimaldi froze.

"I wish to offer you my congratulations on your exhibition of your shooting prowess," the man said. He held up his bandaged right hand while extending his left. "Forgive me, but my injury prohibits me offering you the proper hand."

Grimaldi smiled and thanked him as they shook.

Bolan watched as the Arab then extended his left hand toward him. "And to you, sir, on your performance."

The man's grip was very powerful, and the palm of his hand felt like the edge of a brick. This was the first chance that Bolan had seen the man up close and assessed his build. He was wiry and formidable-looking. Not overly muscular, the way the big guy, Abdullah, was, but the Executioner got the immediate impression that this fellow had the look of someone who could handle himself. But then again, he wouldn't be a member of the prince's entourage of bodyguards if he couldn't. Bolan also noticed that as the man moved he nonchalantly kept pulling up his belt. He was wearing a fanny pack on his left side that his loose-fitting BDU was covering. Whatever was in it was bulky and heavy.

"We are leaving this place soon," the Arab said. "But perhaps we shall someday meet again. *Inshallah.*"

I wonder, the Executioner thought. Maybe we will sooner rather than later.

CHAPTER FOURTEEN

Ambulance Storage House, 4917 Billman Avenue,
Las Vegas

Androkovich shifted the black Jeep Wrangler into Park and took a long look around. The location was perfect: on the corner of a sparsely populated street inside the city limits and only a short drive to the finish line of the marathon. The nearest neighbor on this side of the street was an expansive, junk-filled yard away with a five-foot heavy metal fence around it, and the house immediately across the street was surrounded by a six-foot-tall privacy wall. The garage was more than spacious enough to house both the ambulance and the plastic canopy shell.

The final countdown had started. By this time the next day the deed would be done, and he would be on his way to his new life. Ibrahim Shabahb sat in the front passenger seat, munching on the hamburger and fries he had insisted on picking up as they headed to the Lucky Seven Motel to collect the two scapegoats. The Russian had humored him, not wanting to give any inkling that the Iraqi did not have much longer to indulge in his gluttonous ways.

Shabahb glanced at him, chewing and then speaking with a mouthful of food. "What is it, my friend? Is not everything proceeding on schedule?"

"Schedule?" one of the captive students said from the backseat. "What are you doing with us? Are you with the CIA?" His voice was muffled by the black, burlap sack that they'd tied over his head after they'd handcuffed them. The other was identically bound.

"Shut up," Strogoff said, smacking his open palm against the student's temple.

Androkovich grunted his approval and then said, "If you both wish to spare yourself a lot of pain, you will cease asking stupid questions and do as you're told. If you obey, and behave accordingly, we'll let you live. If not, you'll be killed immediately."

Shabahb turned and said something in Arabic, sending tiny speckles of food flying on to the seat.

Androkovich waited for Shabahb to finish, then asked, "What did you say to them?"

The fat Arab grinned. "I told them that we would not only kill them, but we would drop their bodies into a pile of pig shit." He laughed.

The Russian laughed, too, but only outwardly. The Iraqi disgusted him to no end, and he thought about how much pleasure he was going to get putting a bullet into the man's brain once his usefulness had ended.

"I have to go to the bathroom," the other student said.

"Should we move them inside now?" Strogoff asked, ignoring the young man. He sat between the handcuffed Arabs. They both struggled under the black burlap bags. He smacked his captives again and told them to be still.

Androkovich surveyed the deserted street. He shut off the engine and pulled the keys out of the ignition. "Let me go open the front doors first. We want this transfer to be smooth." He turned to the Iraqi. "Can you hold off on your eating long enough to keep watch?"

"Sure thing, boss," Shabahb said, licking his fingers.

Androkovich left the driver's door wide open to further obscure the view and strode quickly along the sidewalk to the recessed front doors. The jutting walls formed an alcove of sorts. If they exited this side of the vehicle, their walk to the front doors would be almost totally hidden. After unlocking the dead bolt and then the doorknob, he opened the doors. The Russian walked back to the edge of the recess of the house and did a quick glance up and down the street. Seeing no one, he looked to Shabahb, who gave him a thumbs-up. Androkovich quickly motioned for his partner to proceed. The rear door of the Jeep popped open, and Strogoff stepped out. He shoved the first Arab from the car toward the doors, and then pulled the second one out. Both of the young men were sweating copiously.

The Iraqi appeared at the edge of the door. "You want me to take them to the bathroom?"

Androkovich shook his head. "Just tie them up and leave them where we can watch them. In the room with no windows."

He glanced at his watch. So much to do, so little time.

Above the Atlantic Ocean

MUSTAPHA SAT BY the oval window, with the works for one of his spare watches spread out on a cloth on the pulled-down tray. He set his tweezers next to the numerous metallic instruments, which lay on the cloth, as well. He wondered if the other parts of his complex plan were working in complete synchronization: Mamum in

Arabia at the ready with the other army officers, Masoud and Mahfuj in the city of decadence in the American desert. It all rested on them now, especially Mahfuj. The king's plane was set to land at Dulles Airport near Washington, D.C., in about five hours, and it was already evening.

With things moving toward their inexorable conclusion, working on one of his watches was the only way he could relax. He looked out the window but saw only his own reflection set against the blackness. He knew that somewhere, on the other side of the world, the sky was blue and the clouds were forming castles in the sky. And somewhere as well, the desert falcons soared, preparing to swoop down on unsuspecting prey.

Hamid, the king's most trusted bodyguard, lumbered down the aisle and stopped in front of Mustapha's seat. His dark eyes and prominent nose and cheekbones gave his face a brutish cast. Mustapha knew the man's loyalty to the king surpassed his own will to live. The throats of those he considered threats to the royal family had been sliced open by the huge *jambiya* that hung sheathed on his waist. And he never drew it unless he intended to take a life.

"Is that the king's Rolex?" Hamid asked, his large fingers thrusting down at the scattered timepieces.

Mustapha looked up at him and smiled, thinking, once the time comes, I will have to kill him first. "It is not. I am still waiting to be certain I have repaired the king's timepiece in a proper fashion."

Hamid's nostrils flared. "The king is growing restless for its return. He wishes to give it to Prince Amir upon their reunion in the United States. It will be a gift to him for successfully completing the American military school."

"It shall be ready," Mustapha said, bobbing his head to fashion a slight bow, even though he was seated. "God willing."

Hamid stared down at Mustapha a few more seconds and then walked away.

Yes, my fearsome friend, Mustapha thought as he watched Hamid's broad shoulders and back. The king's watch will be ready. He took a moment to finger the two Rolexes in the pocket of his thobe, the watch that belonged to the king, and the identical one that contained the lethal tablets. God willing.

Desert Warfare Training Center

MAHFUJ COULD FEEL the sweat seeping through the fabric of his tailor-made desert camouflage BDU shirt. He glanced at his watch. It was 1540. They were scheduled to embark back to the hotel at 1600. That was where he had to make his move. His fingers went to the pocket of his pants, feeling for the cell phone. He longed to call his father, make sure that everything was still on track. Perhaps he should call Masoud.

No, that would be a mistake, he thought. If the prince, or even the Secret Service agents, saw him making a call, it might create suspicion.

He could hear the prince's accusatory tone: *To whom were you talking?*

That could be difficult to explain. No, he had to proceed with the presumption that everything was nearing completion.

"It is like all the parts of a watch, working together,"

his father had told him. "If one part fails, the entire mechanism stops."

He would not be that faulty mechanism.

As superficial as it was, the graduation ceremony was proceeding. The prince, in his supreme vanity, had elected to accept the certificate and award himself, even though he had not participated in any of the activities. He also decided to allow none of his Arab contingent to accompany him onto the stage.

His royal vanity would be his ultimate undoing, Mahfuj thought.

His eyes locked with Abdullah's. Mahfuj began walking off to the side and cocked his head for the big man to meet him. After they'd stepped away from the others, Mahfuj stopped, looked around, and then stared directly into Abdullah's eyes once again.

"My brother," he said, "our task is almost finished."

The big man sighed and nodded. His huge face acquired a sad cast. "The prince has told me that I am to be punished when we arrive back in Saudi. For disgracing our country."

"It is he who has disgraced us," Mahfuj said. He knew he was taking a risk, but if he had calculated correctly, Abdullah was a ripened plum, ready to be plucked. If not, it would spell death and disaster. He did not have enough rounds in the pistol that Masoud have given him to kill everyone now, and some of them, the Secret Service agents, were armed. He had to be sure, so he took another chance.

"Tell me, do you love our country?"

Abdullah's expression took on a baffled look. "Of course. Why do you ask?"

Mahfuj said nothing, still mentally calculating his next words.

"The way the prince behaves," he said. "The way he humiliated you in front of the infidels, the way he goaded you into situations that were stacked against you, just for his own amusement, to shore up his own inequities." Mahfuj watched the other man's face carefully. "And now he plans to reward your loyalty, your bravery with punishment and humiliation."

Abdullah's forehead furrowed. "Why do you speak like this?"

Mahfuj waited a few seconds before answering. "Because I believe in you, my brother. I believe you are a true Muslim, a true *Bedouin*, a true Arabian."

Abdullah looked even more befuddled, but Mahfuj felt that he had him.

"Soon I will come to you and ask for your help," Mahfuj said, placing his hand on the big man's solidly muscled shoulder. "I need to know that I can trust in you. Can I?"

"Of course. You are a hero."

Mahfuj smiled, shook his head slightly. "Soon, we will all be heroes."

"We will? How?"

"Are you with me, on your honor as an Arab and a Muslim?"

The big man's face hardened, and he nodded. "Tell me what I must do."

Mahfuj thought about his next words. Could he totally trust Abdullah? But what choice did he have? If he did not, he would have to kill him. An ally would be useful and assure the last phase of the plan would proceed with more ease.

Mahfuj placed his hand on Abdullah's shoulder again. "Listen now, my brother. I shall tell you of the pathway to a new Arabia."

THE GRADUATION CEREMONY was quick and to the point, with the two first-place teams being called on to the stage first to receive their plaques for the urban assault competition. Bolan told St. Alban, who had been team leader, to accept the plaque. He brought his guys up on the stage with him, but Bolan stayed on the sidelines with Grimaldi and watched. The Arab team was called up next, but the prince elected to go up on the stage alone to receive the plaque. His entourage stood at attention along the base of the platform.

Grimaldi leaned over to Bolan and whispered, "Man, he sure treats those guys like shit, doesn't he?"

Bolan said nothing, but he had been thinking the same thing. He also wondered about the type of loyalty that kind of treatment would imbue. Certainly, the Arab team had performed well and seemed competent, but he wondered how much of that would translate into loyalty to the prince, if push came to shove.

As they headed for the entrance, St. Alban ran up beside them.

"Hey, Cooper," St. Alban said. "Give me your address, and I'll have another one of these made and send it to you."

Bolan smiled and shook his head. "Not necessary."

"Come on, we couldn't have done it without you."

"You guys earned it," Bolan said. "It's yours." In reality, he had little use for such accolades.

"Well," St. Alban said, looking at the handsome plaque of polished wood and fancy script on an inlaid gold centerpiece, "thanks a lot." He reached into his pocket, pulled out a business card and handed it to Bolan. "Here's my card. It's got my email and cell phone on it. Maybe we can grab a beer sometime."

The two men shook hands.

Grimaldi held up his trophy and looked at it as St. Alban walked away. "I think I'll leave this one here, too."

"It's your call," Bolan said.

They pushed through the doors and into the pervasive heat of the early afternoon. Outside, the prince's limo was pulling up, flanked by the Secret Service vehicles. Draper's men, alert and vigilant, were positioned strategically as the prince was escorted to the lengthy vehicle, followed by four of the Arab bodyguards and one Secret Service agent. The prince paused on the edge of the sidewalk as the Arab with the bandaged hand opened the car door. Taking one more look around, his handsome face a picture of disgust, the prince slipped into the limo. The Arab with the bandaged hand got in next, followed by the rest. The last of the Arabs, big Abdullah, glared at them as he got into the rear of the limo.

Agent Draper walked over and extended his hand toward Bolan, who shook it, and then to Grimaldi.

"You two guys take care," Draper said. "I've got to run. It's time to escort His Majesty back to the hotel for the last night. We leave for D.C. in the morning."

"Good luck," Bolan said. "Stay safe."

Draper nodded and got into the front passenger side of a black Hummer. As soon as he'd slammed the door, the vehicle took off.

"You know," Grimaldi said, "he's a pretty good guy. I wonder if we'll run into him again?"

Bolan felt the vibration of his cell phone. He looked at the screen and saw the call was from Brognola.

"What's up?" he asked as he answered it.

"A new development with that arms deal," Brognola said. "We intercepted a message that said they're moving the shipment back until 0400."

"Okay," Bolan said. "You find out anything else?"

He heard Brognola's heavy sigh. "Yeah, they keep talking about bringing the special item. Got any idea what they got planned?"

Bolan thought about it. "Nothing concrete," he said, "but whatever it is, it can't be good."

CHAPTER FIFTEEN

I-15 North, Las Vegas

Mahfuj felt himself sweating despite the coolness of the interior of the limousine. He watched the scenery flashing by through the tinted windows: tall, gaudy buildings and billboards with displays of practically nude women. The entire culture of this place was built on decadence and obscenity, and worse than that, his royal charge reveled in it. Mahfuj would be glad to get away from this sordid place, back to his country…his new country, once the last parts of his father's master plan had been achieved.

At the instruction of the prince, the limousine driver raised the screen separating the two front seats from the passengers in the spacious rear compartment.

Mahfuj adjusted his view to be certain he could still discern the two silhouettes in the front seat through the opaqueness. He could.

The prince sat directly across from him, holding the awarded plaque that his men had worked so hard to win for him. His face was the picture of indifference. He tossed it on the seat beside him and turned to Mahfuj.

"Make certain you pack that in your luggage," he said. "My father will want to see it before I throw it in the trash."

Mahfuj picked it up, waiting a few seconds before answering. "Yes, Your Highness."

The plaque was similar to one of the solid blocks of wood he was accustomed to breaking in his Tae Kwon Do practices, except this one had many layers of a clear, hardening liquid to make it shine along with the fancy gold trim. He hefted it in his hand. It was heavy. It would do nicely.

The prince was babbling about his plans for the last night here as he took his cell phone out of his pocket and began scrolling through some of the numbers. He pressed a button and held the phone to his ear. Mahfuj halfway listened to the conversation, which was in English. The prince was saying something about making sure the girls were all blondes this time.

Mahfuj took out his cell phone and quickly located the text he'd earlier written to Masoud. He pressed the button to send it. Only a matter of minutes remained.

"What are you doing?" the prince asked in Arabic, holding his cell phone away from his mouth. "To whom did you send that message?"

Mahfuj bowed his head. "My brother is traveling through this area. It was my hope to see him before we leave."

The prince shook his head. "No, no, no. We will not have time. We will be leaving in the morning, and I have plans for tonight."

Mahfuj concealed his hatred for this apostate wastrel as he bowed his head in apology. "That is exactly what I told him, Your Highness."

The prince nodded and went back to his conversation concerning the women he was ordering.

The limousine slowed substantially, and Mahfuj

knew that they were now leaving the freeway. At a traffic signal they came to a complete stop. Mahfuj placed the plaque on his lap and slowly unzipped the fanny pack that held the pistol that Masoud had given him. He felt the hard steel of the barrel, and the long sound suppressor underneath the gun.

His cell phone vibrated inside his pocket. He knew he dared not look at it, but he was certain that it meant that Masoud had received his message and that he and the Russian were moving into position.

Would it be possible to attach the suppressor before they arrived at the hotel, or should he merely use the pistol without it?

There were two Secret Service agents in the limousine. One was in the front passenger seat next to the driver, and the other, in the back compartment with them.

He would have to kill the closer American, then the other members of the Saudi National Guard team. They were Arabs, just as he was, so he would make it quick. Their allegiance to the prince could not be questioned, although Mahfuj was certain he could have converted them to his side if he'd had the time, just as he had Abdullah. But that was the problem: time was something he did not have. The two Americans in the front seats would have to be killed next.

The limousine began moving. It would not be long until they were at the hotel.

Mahfuj continued with the task. He managed to align the barrel with the end of the suppressor and tried to turn it so as to catch the line of threads and screw it on to the barrel. The vehicle shifted, and it went around a turn. Mahfuj knew from past trips that they were only minutes from the hotel. The weapon was a Beretta, and the magazine held fifteen rounds. With one in the chamber, that gave him more than enough ammunition before he had to reload. The Secret Service agent in the front would no doubt draw his weapon if he heard the shots, but he wouldn't dare risk a shot through the screen due to the presence of the prince. The next rounds would have to kill him, and then the driver. The prince would not be a problem. The man was weak and undisciplined. He was also essentially a coward.

If the Secret Service agents from the first vehicle were not alerted by the sound of gunfire, they would follow the same, standard procedure they used every other day to whisk the prince out of the vehicle and across the rear entrance to the elevators. Once they were in the open forming a line to the door, Mahfuj could easily shoot the remaining ones, especially if Abdullah did his part with the knife.

Mahfuj tried to line up the threads once again. Fortunately, the barrel of the Beretta protruded slightly from the end of the framework of the pistol. It made the positioning a bit easier, but now he wished he had practiced the action without the benefit of setting the alignment with his eyes.

The limousine slowed and turned once again. Through the window, Mahfuj saw the approaching pillars of the underground entrance to the hotel. They would be there in about thirty seconds. His fingers were slippery with sweat. The noise of the weapon's report would most assuredly alert the entire contingent of Secret Service agents. It was imperative for him to complete this one, last preparation to ensure success.

He took a deep breath and slid the two metal pieces

together again, lining them up. Slowly, the wet fingers of his right hand twisted ever-so-slightly. The threads of the cylinder fell out of alignment again. He repositioned them once more.

The vehicle pulled into the driveway that went into the underground section. The interior of the vehicle darkened as they passed from the light.

He twisted the suppressor one more time and felt the threads catch. Quickening his movements, he completed the last turn and felt it lock into place.

"What are you doing with your hands?" the prince asked, his face twisting into a grin. "Thinking about the girls who are coming?" He laughed. "Don't worry, if you're good, I will save one of them for you." His head lolled back in mirthful laughter once again.

The limousine jerked to a complete stop.

The Secret Service agent next to him looked down at the plaque. Mahfuj brought the pistol upward and shot the man in the face. He reeled backward, grabbing his head as the hot shell casing ejected. Mahfuj turned the pistol toward his three Arab National Guard comrades.

Allah akhbar, he thought, as he shot each man in the forehead. More brass shell casings flew from the ejection port.

"What are you doing?" the prince shouted. His face had lost its mirth now.

"Sending you to hell," Mahfuj said as he slammed the edge of the plaque against the prince's right temple. His head jerked, and his eyes fluttered, showing only white. Mahfuj aimed the pistol at the two silhouettes visible through the opaqueness of the privacy screen, centering the red dot of the laser sight on the front seat passenger first.

He squeezed the trigger.

A small hole appeared in the screen and the silhouette slumped forward. Mahfuj swept the weapon to the left and shot the driver. That silhouette slumped down, as well.

The prince was unconscious. Mahfuj moved to the door of the limousine and opened it. Resting his arms on the roof of the vehicle to steady his aim, Mahfuj quickly shot the two Secret Service agents from the first vehicle, as well as the two who had been guarding the rear entrance of the hotel. As they twisted and fell, Mahfuj saw three civilians, two of them women in obscenely short dresses, exposing their breasts and legs. He shot the man in between them first, and then both of the harlots. On the other side of the yellow doors, behind the large window, Mahfuj saw people staring in shock and horror.

Observe the terror that is on your doorstep, he thought, as he sent two more rounds through the door window.

Abdullah was suddenly beside him, his huge hands and forearms splattered with blood. He was breathing hard.

"It is done," the big man said. "Which vehicle are we taking?"

"None of them," Mahfuj said as the sound of a racing engine echoed in the cavernous surroundings. A black Jeep was hurtling toward them at a high rate of speed. Abdullah started to turn, but Mahfuj grabbed his arm. "It is my brother, Masoud, and his confederates."

Abdullah's brow furrowed.

"Get the prince," Mahfuj said, wondering how Abdullah would react to the sight of his three dead countrymen.

It might be prudent to kill him now, Mahfuj thought as he held the weapon by his leg, ready to bring it up in a split-second. It would depend on the giant's reaction.

Abdullah emerged from the limousine carrying the prince by the collar and belt, as if he was hoisting a suitcase.

The side door of the Jeep slid open, and Mahfuj saw Masoud's impish grin.

"Greetings, brother," Masoud said. "Do you wish a ride?"

Mahfuj saw a Westerner with red hair in the driver's seat. Next to Masoud, in the back of the vehicle, another man squatted behind the rear seats, motioning to them.

Mahfuj assumed this was the Russian that Masoud had mentioned.

"Put him in here," the Russian said in English.

Abdullah hesitated. Mahfuj took this as a sign of loyalty, and he directed the big man to place the prince inside the vehicle. The Russian immediately pulled the prince's hands behind his back and secured them with a thin, nylon cord. Mahfuj and Abdullah got into the Jeep, and the vehicle roared off, moving away from the array of corpses and toward the exit.

The Russian was binding the prince's legs at the knees and feet now. The prince began to shake his head as he awakened from the blow.

"You did well, my brother," Masoud said, his white teeth gleaming. "Just as I knew you would."

The prince moaned. The Russian grabbed a black sack, shook it loose and slipped it over the man's head.

"What is happening?" the prince asked. His voice sounded weak, disoriented.

"We are giving you your first taste of the tyranny

your family has subjected upon our people for decades,"
Mahfuj said. "Now be silent."

He glanced at Abdullah's face. The huge man's jaw
jutted, his eyes glowing with bright ecstasy.

He could see through the windshield of the white
van as it emerged from the underground parking area
and merged into the traffic.

The last phase had begun, Mahfuj thought, as he silently wondered once again if they would emerge from
this as *mujahadeens* or as *fedayeens*.

FBI Field Office, Las Vegas

BOLAN WAS FEELING a bit of frustration as he went over
the information about the pending arms deal, with both
Agent Dylan and Sheriff Dundee looking at the diagram he'd drawn on the dry erase board. He'd expected the FBI to be its usual, cautious self, but he'd
expected more out of Dundee. The man seemed reti-
cent to commit.

"Am I not explaining something clearly enough?"
Bolan asked, looking into their faces. "This arms shipment is coming in tonight at 0400. I'm certain it's coming into the Autry ranch by plane."

"And what's the source of this information?" Dylan
asked.

"You know how it is," Grimaldi replied. "It's classified."

"I'm sorry," Dylan said, "but I'm still having trouble
processing exactly how you obtained this information."

Bolan could hardly tell her that part of it came from
Aaron Kurtzman breaking through several firewalls to
intercept email and cell phone transmissions between

the Russian *mafiya* and the Autry ranch personnel, and the rest was just pure gut instinct. After the big NSA eavesdropping controversy, he knew her first question would be, "Did he have a warrant to intercept those transmissions?"

"Time's running short," Bolan said. "The countdown's already started, and if we're going to hit Camp Freedom, we'll need to get a team together and do some practice drills. That place is well fortified."

"You got that right," Grimaldi added. "It's a regular fortress. But get me a Black Hawk with a couple of miniguns, and I'll do it solo."

"This is southern Nevada, pal," Dundee stated. "Not Afghanistan."

"Supposition is fine," Dylan said, "as far as it goes, but we need something we can take before a judge, in a court of law. Otherwise, we risk getting whatever we do find tossed out on a technicality."

"I can give you a phone number to call to verify its validity," Bolan said, "and to vouch for the veracity of our intel, if you want."

"Another mysterious, ask-me-no-questions phone number?" The now-familiar crease appeared between her eyebrows once again, and she shook her head. "I'm afraid I'm going to have to contact my supervisor about this before we can get authorization to bring any more personnel into this operation." She got up from her chair, took out her cell phone and began to make a call as she walked away.

"That's the FBI for you," Grimaldi said when she was out of earshot. "Always impatient, but afraid to fart without the blessings of their supervisor. It's a wonder they can even go to the bathroom on their own."

"Unfortunately," Dundee said, "as much as I hate to, I'll have to agree with her." He looked directly at Bolan. "Don't think for a minute, if I thought hitting that ranch-turned-base-camp would bring the killers of my two officers to justice, that I wouldn't break down the damn gates myself. But…"

An uneasy silence fell over the room, which was interrupted by the ringing chimes of Dundee's cell phone. He unclipped it from his belt, looked at the screen and pressed a button.

"This is Dundee," he said.

Bolan watched as the big lawman's face tightened and figured that it was not good news. The audible half of the conversation yielded little except that Dundee said he'd be right there. He terminated the call and hooked the phone back on his belt. "There's been a mass shooting over at the Algonquin. In the underground parking area."

The mention of the hotel piqued Bolan's interest. "That's where Prince Amir is staying."

Dundee nodded. "It was his group that was attacked. Seventeen people down, seven of them Secret Service agents. Several either dead or critically wounded."

"Was the prince hurt?" Bolan asked.

Dundee shrugged. "Don't know yet. We're trying to sort things out. I'm told that some of the victims are possibly foreign nationals. I'm heading over there now to check it out."

"Draper?" Grimaldi asked.

Dundee shook his head. "I won't know any more until I get there."

"We'll be going with you," Bolan said.

Algonquin Casino and Hotel

BOLAN WATCHED AS Dundee's car slowed ahead of them. He could see the big lawman giving instructions to the uniformed officer at the entrance to the underground parking area. The officer straightened and waved them through as Dundee's car moved forward into the parking garage. Bolan followed in the Escalade. Grimaldi was uncharacteristically silent in the front passenger seat, and Dylan was equally stoic in the back.

Ahead, by the rear entrance to the hotel, more officers were directing them where to park. The traffic lanes were crammed with vehicles with rotating red-and-blue lights. A blue-and-white ambulance sat idling in the lane, its red, blue and yellow lights flickering. Yellow crime scene tape had been pulled taut, blocking off access to the area. More tape, this strand red, had been strung closer to the interior of the crime scene. Bolan could see the CSI techs taking photographs. Dundee pulled into a parking space, and Bolan pulled in next to him. They all got out of the Escalade.

"Come up this way so we don't disturb anything," Dundee said, motioning toward an adjacent aisle.

The big lawman's expression looked even grimmer as they walked toward the area that was littered with bodies. Dundee motioned for them to stop as he went forward to confer with a group of detectives. Bolan scanned the main area of carnage. Seven bodies lay twisted on the concrete sidewalk. Four appeared to be Secret Service agents; the others were apparently civilians who'd gotten caught in the cross fire. The black Hummer was parked behind the limo, its passenger-side door standing wide open. A man sat in the passenger seat, his torso stretched toward the rear, as if he'd been pulled through the middle section between the two seats. He was wearing the same clothing that Special Agent Draper had on at the Desert Warfare Academy. Another man was slumped forward on to the steering wheel. A crime scene tech leaned over, snapping pictures.

"Oh, my God," Dylan said. She stopped walking and took out her cell phone.

"Don't take any unauthorized pictures with that," a uniformed officer said to her.

She nodded and said, "FBI. I'm just calling my supervisor."

Bolan leaned close to Grimaldi and whispered, "Check out the limo."

The Stony Man pilot nodded and walked carefully toward the limousine while Bolan moved toward the Hummer. As he got closer the tech stopped, looked up and backed away slightly.

"Mind if I take a quick look?" Bolan asked.

The tech looked him over, lowered his camera to his side and took a step back.

The Executioner moved around the vehicle, taking in the scene from all angles. The man in the passenger seat was definitely Special Agent Draper. The other occupant of the Hummer looked vaguely familiar. Bolan recalled seeing him a few times. He felt a twinge of sadness at the death of the agents, especially Draper, but he knew this was the reality of the never-ending war. He pushed all emotional thoughts from his mind and let cold, hard rationality take over.

Both men had obviously been attacked from behind. Their throats had been cut. Bolan reviewed his memory of the departure at the training facility. The prince and four of his entourage had entered the limousine, accompanied by a Secret Service agent. Two more agents were in the front seat compartment of the limo. Draper had gotten into the front passenger seat of the Hummer after they'd shaken hands. Abdullah had gotten into the back seat of the vehicle.

"You thinking what I'm thinking?" Grimaldi asked, walking up next to Bolan. "Didn't Abdullah get into the back of the Hummer?"

Bolan nodded.

"We should've taken that big, Arab son of a bitch when we had the chance," Grimaldi said, his face twisting into a mask of anger. "I got that on my agenda the next time I see him."

"Any of those other bodies look to be Prince Amir?"

Grimaldi shook his head. "The prince doesn't appear to be among the dead. At least as far as I can tell." He shook his head. "Draper was a good guy. I liked him."

Bolan nodded. "This is far from over. I've got the feeling the worst part's yet to come."

CHAPTER SIXTEEN

Highway 51, Approaching Camp Freedom

"There they are," Strogoff said, lifting his hand from the steering wheel of the Jeep as the headlights illuminated the police license plate on the squad car that was parked on the side of the highway about fifty yards from the front gate.

"Forever vigilant," Androkovich said. He was sitting in the passenger seat, and Masoud and Shabahb were seated on the floor in the rear of the vehicle. They had dropped the prince off at the Billman house for safekeeping, but the Russian still had to go back and affix the explosive, plastic shell on the top of the ambulance. Plus, leaving Mahfuj and his hulking new assistant guarding the prisoners gave him an uneasy feeling. What was to stop them from piling everyone into the ambulance and leaving to set the explosion off themselves? The way he'd taken out all those Secret Service agents said a lot about his prowess. The man was efficient. Lethally so.

He reflected on the possibilities and decided he was worried about nothing. First of all, lethal or not, Mahfuj was still a stranger in a strange land and aware of his limitations. He had to know he had neither the knowledge nor the skill to pull off getting the loaded ambulance past the security lines at the marathon.

Plus, the Russian thought, I still have his brother.

"What is it?" Masoud asked.

"Police," Androkovich said. "Nothing to worry about."

"Police?" The Arab was beginning to look very nervous. "Do you wish for us to duck?"

"No. I doubt they will try to stop us. Even if they do, they have no reason to check inside this vehicle."

"But," Masoud said, "it would be awkward if my presence here were discovered, would it not?"

With a questioning look, Strogoff pointed to the gun holstered on his hip.

Androkovich shook his head. "If they had sufficient reason to stop us, they would have done so already. This is merely a surveillance. An ineffective attempt at intimidation."

They rolled by the squad car, and the Russian waved.

He watched the reflection in the side-view mirror to see if the police moved. They did not. He felt vindicated, but also a tad uneasy. It was like juggling meat cleavers. One miscalculation and you could lose a hand.

Strogoff turned on to the main road into Camp Freedom.

If things went as planned, Androkovich mused, this was, most likely, his last trip here. He thought about simply turning around and killing Masoud right now and stealing whatever money he had in his briefcase and taking off. He played that scenario in his mind's eye, imagining the expression of shock and fear on the Arab's face. But this briefcase only held a pittance compared to the huge, final payment they had promised him. And he would get the money transferred to his special account in Switzerland before he dialed the final number to set off the explosion.

He took a deep breath. There was no sense in getting ahead of himself.

"Park by the second barn," Androkovich said. "I want to check on Little Miss Sunshine."

Strogoff grinned as he pulled over and stopped.

"Are we there?" Masoud asked.

"Not at the landing site," Fedor said. "But close enough. Bring your briefcase. We can wait inside."

Masoud smiled and nodded.

Androkovich opened the door and slid out. He heard something just as he opened the rear door for Masoud and Shabahb. Turning, he saw two men approaching wearing cowboy hats. Even in the darkness he knew immediately who they were. Masoud, who was dressed in a light gray suit, froze in place. The Iraqi leaned against the side of the Jeep and said, "Oh, shit."

"What's up, Shane?" the Russian asked, forcing a grin.

Shane licked his lips but didn't reply. Instead, it was Rand Autry who spoke up.

"Andrews, have you seen my daughter?"

Androkovich slowly shook his head. "Can't say that I have. Why?"

"Because she's missing," Rand Autry said. "That's why." The old man's mouth worked like an angry rabbit. "The last time I saw her, she said she had a bone to pick with you."

"When was that?"

"Last night," Rand said. His eyes narrowed as he apparently noticed Shabahb and Masoud for the first time. The old man's head craned forward slightly, and he pointed with his index finger. "Pancho?"

Ibrahim grinned and nodded. "*Sí, Es* me, boss."

Rand shifted his gaze toward Masoud and scrutinized him. "You'd better be a Mexican, too, boy."

Masoud said nothing.

Rand sauntered forward.

"Dad, don't," Shane said.

The old man turned toward him. "Shut your mouth.
I'm investigating something."

He walked around Masoud, then turned and whirled
toward Androkovich. "Who is this guy? He don't smell
like no Mexican. Looks like one of them damn Arabs
to me."

Masoud still said nothing.

Androkovich thought about the ramifications of this
unexpected encounter. Still, perhaps it was a godsend,
a gift. He intended to collect them all eventually. Now
they had come to him.

"You were asking about Eileen," the Russian said.

Rand's head swiveled toward him. "That's right."

"I was going to tell you," Androkovich said. "I think
I found her cell phone out here by the barn last night."

"What?" Rand's lower lip jutted. "Let me see it."

"I don't have it with me. I put it in the barn."

The old man's lips peeled back from his teeth in a
look of utter disgust. "Go get it, then. And show me
where you found it. Hurry up. And I still want to know
about this damn Arab."

Androkovich glanced at the big, .357 Colt Python
revolver that Shane had on his hip. He didn't think that
the younger Autry would have the balls to try to use it,
but he might be tempted if he'd been doing some of his
secret cocaine sniffing.

"Okay," Androkovich said, raising his left hand like
a magician while he unsnapped his SIG Sauer with his

right. He raised his weapon and pointed it at Shane's chest. "Don't move, either of you. Put up your hands." His peripheral vision told him that Strogoff had drawn his weapon, too. Shane raised his hands. His father stood there, arms at his sides, like a defiant bantam rooster. Androkovich stepped around behind Shane and pulled the Python out of its holster.

"Get your hands up, old man," the Russian demanded.

"Andrews, what the hell you think you're doing?" Rand asked.

"Taking you to see your bitch of a daughter," Androkovich said. "Now move toward that side door."

"I ain't doing nothing," Rand said.

"Dad," Shane cautioned.

"Shut up," his father said. He turned back to the Russian. "You get off my property now. You're fired."

Androkovich backhanded the old man with the barrel of the Python, splitting his cheek open and knocking him to the ground.

"Don't hit him," Shane begged. "Please."

"Then pick his ass up and carry him through that door now," the Russian shouted, extending the SIG toward Shane's head. "Or I'll shoot him right now."

The younger Autry squatted next to his father and helped the man to his feet. A stream of blood ran down the side of his face like an errant tributary. Rand said nothing, but his eyes never left his tormentor.

"Put them with the girl," the Russian said, hefting the Python in his left hand. It was a unique weapon. He wouldn't mind keeping it, but that was not in the cards. It was going to be the weapon Shane used to kill his father and sister before committing suicide.

FBI Field Office, Las Vegas

AFTER SIFTING THROUGH the facts and evidence that they had available, Bolan, Grimaldi, Dylan and Dundee all sat huddled around a table in the FBI office building. The frustration was mounting.

"You think that I don't want to take these assholes down?" Dundee frowned. "Hell, if I thought it would help, I'd bust down the damn gates at Camp Freedom myself and lead the troops in."

"The sheriff's right," Dylan added. "We just don't have enough to justify it."

"What about that damn black Jeep your surveillance team saw driving in there?" Grimaldi asked. "That ought to be worth something. And why the hell didn't your guys stop it?"

"The report of that vehicle hasn't been substantiated yet," Dundee said. "It may not be involved in the shooting at all."

"So?" Grimaldi shot back. "Sometimes you have to go with your gut."

Dundee blew out a heavy breath. "You know how many damn black Jeeps we spotted driving around the city? We can't stop them all."

"Seems to me you haven't been stopping any of them," Grimaldi shot back. "That guy Autry's dirty. I can feel it."

Dundee shook his head. "Don't even suggest that this damn situation isn't making me sick, but this is too damn important to risk losing everything on some technicality, if and when it goes to court before some liberal judge."

"I thought all the judges in Nevada were hard-asses," Grimaldi said with a grin.

Dundee snorted. "I don't know how you operate in the Justice Department, but without something solid, like a license plate, we're SOL until we get something that can definitely, and legally, tie Autry and his people to the crimes."

The two men stared at each other.

"Maybe we need to take a break," Bolan said. "At the moment, we're spinning our wheels."

Dundee shifted his huge bulk and got to his feet. "Sounds like a good idea. I need to check in with my detectives on any progress." He took out his cell phone and ambled away.

"I should call in, too," Dylan said, taking out her cell phone as she got up and strolled away, as well.

Bolan and Grimaldi looked at each other across the expanse of tabletop.

"What's our next move?" Grimaldi asked.

Bolan took out his cell phone. "I'm going to call Hal."

Brognola answered Bolan's call on the first ring, as usual.

"Okay, how bad is it?" he asked.

"Bad," Bolan said. "We've lost way too many good men. Park Rangers, armored car guards, police officers and Secret Service agents. And now the prince is missing."

"I know," Brognola said. "I didn't figure it would be good news when the phone rang at midnight, but I didn't expect that the bottom of the garbage bag had fallen out."

Bolan could hear a long exhale.

"Any ideas about the prince?" Brognola finally asked.

"Hard to say at this point," Bolan said. "It looks like a couple of his guards are missing, as well. I'd say at least one of them was quite possibly involved."

"Yeah, but it happened on U.S. soil. Just what we need. Getting caught up in an international incident."

"Whoever did this had a lot of support," Bolan said. "And I'm thinking that Autry was involved, too. The Secret Service agents were wearing soft body armor, and the bullets went right through the Kevlar. I'm guessing that the shooter used the same style of old, Soviet steel-core ammunition as the armored car heist. It's all pointing to Autry."

"You think he's got the prince?" Brognola asked.

"I don't know," Bolan said. "It's like trying to put together a jigsaw puzzle with only half the pieces turned right side up. But if I had to guess, I'd say he or his people could provide a lot of answers."

"Your guesses are pretty much bankable," Brognola said. "What do you want me to do?"

"Any more intel on that arms deal?"

"Aaron's been sifting through a bunch of new transmissions. They keep referring to 'the item,' but nothing other than it's still set for 0400."

Bolan considered that. There were too many coincidences tying everything together for this "item" not to be significant. He had to hit Camp Freedom again, preferably around the same time the arms shipment arrived. That gave him about six hours.

"We're not getting a lot of support from the Bureau or the locals," Bolan said. "What are the chances of you sending Able or Phoenix out here to help us with a little raid?" He was referring to Able Team and Phoenix Force, Stony Man Farm's action teams.

"Slim and none," Brognola said. "And slim left town. They're tied up in missions far, far away. Sorry."

Bolan signed off and looked at Grimaldi.

"We've got to intercept that arms shipment tonight," he said. "I think if we hit Camp Freedom, we'll find a lot of the answers we've been looking for."

"Yeah, but that place is like a fortress and we sure aren't going to get much help here." Grimaldi spun his hand around indicating the surroundings. "We need a strike force."

Bolan reached into his pocket and pulled out the card that St. Alban had given him.

"Maybe I know where we can find one," he said.

Ambulance Storage House

MAHFUJ AND ABDULLAH sat on the floor in the empty living room leaning over a small, uncovered lamp, the only source of light in the room, as they ate figs and drank orange juice.

"But I still do not understand," the big man said. "Will we not face certain execution when we arrive back in our country?"

Mahfuj waved his hand dismissively as he chewed another fig. "Everything has already been set into motion. My father's cohorts in the military have those loyal to him ready to strike in key places." He shrugged. "It will include several assassinations among the ranks of the National Guard, but once the king is dead, and the military has seized power, everything will fall into place."

Even in the dim light Mahfuj could see the lines of worry creasing Abdullah's face. "But the Americans... Will they not intervene?"

Mahfuj smiled. "That is the beauty of what we must do in a few hours. It will assure that they remain pre-occupied with their own tragedy, and then overcome with guilt."

"Guilt," the big man said slowly. "Why?"

"Because the terrorist attack at the marathon will soon be traced back to the bigoted rancher, Randall Autry. It will look as if he plotted to discredit Arabia by recruiting two Muslim students from the Eastern Province—*Shi'ites*—and making it look like they helped kidnap the royal prince to discredit our country and start a civil war."

Mahfuj picked up a fig. "Once the plot has been traced back to the bigot, the American President will be paralyzed. The house of Saud will be out of power, a true leader will be in control of our country, and Arabia will be once again destined for greatness, not slaves to the whims of apostate kings and princes."

He placed the fig into his mouth and chewed, watching Abdullah's face. The lines of concern seemed to be dissipating. "It is all falling into place, just as my father, Mustapha, has planned. At first I was somewhat skeptical of the complexities of such a convoluted venture, but now, it is coming together with the precision of a fine timepiece." He laughed. "Like a Rolex wristwatch. The kind the king is so fond of wearing. I will give you one for helping us."

"And this Russian," Abdullah asked, "do you trust him?"

Mahfuj waited a few seconds before answering. His own nagging doubts about the trustworthiness of the Russian niggled at him, but this was not something he wanted to share with Abdullah. He was big and loyal, but essentially stupid. He needed to be led, like a horse.

"I trust that he will act according to our plan," Mahfuj said. "I have the best assurance of this. He will not be paid until it is complete."

Abdullah's head bobbled up and down in agreement.

Mahfuj knew that he had him now. All doubt had been removed. "The Russian does what he does for money. We do it for our country. And for honor."

Abdullah considered that, took a drink of water, and then nodded. "*Inshallah*."

Mahfuj smiled. Not only had he totally converted this giant to his side, he had allayed Abdullah's concerns. It certainly was a sign that the plan would succeed. He lifted the dish and offered another fig.

Abdullah took it and then looked to the three trussed-up bodies lying a few yards away.

"Should we not feed them?" Abdullah asked.

Mahfuj licked the juice of his last fig off his fingertips and nodded. "Feed them one at a time, and do not untie them. I do not wish to shoot them prematurely."

Abdullah picked up the plate of figs and the bottle of orange juice. As he moved toward the three captives, one of them moaned softly.

"Please, I must go and relieve myself."

Abdullah looked back at Mahfuj, who shook his head.

The big man stepped over to the farthest captive.

The prince stirred, straining against his bonds.

"Are you not comfortable, Your Highness?" Mahfuj asked. The moment was as delicious to him as the figs had been. He had long waited to see this spoiled royal brought to his knees.

"I have been listening to you," the prince said. "Your plot will never succeed. My grandfather will never allow it."

Mahfuj laughed. He couldn't help himself. "Your grandfather is a senile old man. And he will soon be dead."

"Not before he sees you and your traitorous family beheaded in the square."

"My family?" Mahfuj said. "Ironically, your grandfather is in the company of my father as we speak. If he does not go into cardiac arrest when he hears of your abduction, my father has a little concoction that will help stop his ancient heart." He smiled. "It is long overdue for a rest. A permanent one."

The prince squirmed. "The National Guard will never let you overthrow the royal family. You are a fool as well as a traitor."

"*I* am a fool?" Mahfuj laughed.

"You are a member of the royal family?" one of the Shi'ites said. "Please, help me. Tell him to spare us."

"Congratulations," Mahfuj said. "You have bridged the gap between Sunni and Shi'ite." He stood up and walked over to the three bound men. "But do not be concerned. You two Shi'ites will be welcomed as martyrs in paradise. But…" He knelt beside the bound prince and plucked at the knot securing the black hood over the royal's head. His fingers unwound the cloth string, and he pulled the hood off almost gently, holding the prince's head in both his hands. "You, Your Highness, will burn in hell for all eternity for your apostasy."

The prince's face winced. "You have me. Release them."

"Ah, an attempt at being noble." He smiled for an

instant, then drew his mouth into a tight line. "How out of character for you."

"At least untie us so we can pray."

Mahfuj laughed. "You are suddenly concerned about your prayers?" Mahfuj put his mouth close to the prince's ear. "Now, listen to me very carefully. I am neither a fool nor a traitor. *You* are the traitor. You and your family are the traitors. You live a life of luxury, revel in your apostasy, and mock the pillars of Islam."

"Release me at once," the prince said. "And I'll consider recommending leniency for you and your family."

"No."

The prince's eyes flashed. "If you do not release me immediately, I shall see your head roll in the city square of Riyadh."

Mahfuj struck him with an open palm, once, twice, three times. Then he spit into the prince's face and stood up. As the prince started to speak, Mahfuj kicked him in the abdomen.

"Enough of your insolence, apostate. Now learn humility, and the true nature of bravery and sacrifice. Know that your life, and the lives of these two Shi'ites is going to help usher in a glorious, new era for Arabia." He looked down at the prince, whose torn lips leaked a trail of blood from his mouth. "An Arabia devoid of the pernicious autocracy of the House of Saud."

CHAPTER SEVENTEEN

Camp Freedom

Under the dark canopy of the desert sky, the three men stood next to the barn as Androkovich laid the items on the seat of the ATV. He wrapped the three fake paramedic shirts around the two burner cell phones and detonator caps, then tucked the bundle into his backpack. He glanced at his watch. It was 0110. The plane with the Semtex would be arriving in less than three hours, and he had only three hours after that before setting off the blast at the marathon. This was the final push down the field, like a football game. He straightened and looked at Strogoff.

"So you're clear with everything?" he asked.

His partner nodded, motioning toward Masoud, who stood there in his nicely tailored suit with the briefcase full of money. "We meet the plane, do the payoff, and then stash the Semtex in the barn where they'll be sure to find it."

Androkovich nodded. "Then take the Jeep out the back way and wait at the house on Billman. We'll rendezvous there after the bomb goes off."

Masoud exhaled loudly. "Why are you not supervising this last arms payoff yourself? Don't they know you?"

"They know my partner, as well. And don't worry. Despite the Southern drawl of his English, he speaks Russian better than I do."

He looked at Masoud. "You have to trust us to get the rest of the job done."

The other man caught his gaze and waited before speaking. "As you must trust me to make the final payments to your Swiss accounts."

Androkovich held Masoud's stare, and then smiled as he said, "A relationship built on mutual mistrust. The best kind."

He turned to Strogoff. "And you know what to do with the Autrys, right?"

His partner's grin was malevolent as he touched the handle of the Colt Python tucked into the side of his belt. "A murder-suicide. I still have to get Shane to sign the note."

"If he does, fine. If he doesn't, that's all right, too. With his penchant for nose candy, it will be the logical assumption. Just make sure you insert the gun into his mouth at the proper angle."

Strogoff nodded. "And the girl...I'd like to do her last."

He took this to mean that Strogoff wanted to have a little sexual fun with Ms. Eileen Autry. While the idea had occurred to him as well, he didn't want things to get more complicated either. "No, it's too risky. We don't want to upset the applecart at this late date. Keep your eye on the ball."

"Yes," Masoud added. "We do not have time for trifles."

Strogoff flushed. "What about the rest of the men?"

"Leave them here with orders to defend their posts.

Tell them we will be coming back soon. Give them some of the money from the armored car heist. They'll be kept busy counting it. By then the authorities should be all over this place. Those who don't go down can substantiate the overall subterfuge that the Autrys are to blame." He paused and thought about another loose end. "And get rid of Ibrahim, too. That loudmouth will loudly flip to the highest bidder."

His partner nodded but looked a bit troubled by these instructions. Androkovich didn't want Strogoff to know that he was planning to travel to Europe alone. He flashed his widest grin and slapped the man's shoulder. "By then, you and I will be on our way to Mexico."

Strogoff smiled. "To live the rest of our lives as rich men."

Androkovich held his grin as he thought, At least one of us will be.

FBI Field Office, Las Vegas

BOLAN HAD DRAWN the diagram of Camp Freedom in black on the dry erase board and now used a red marker to designate their plan of attack. St. Alban and his three team members sat in the front row of the meeting room. Behind him was Agent Dylan, Sheriff Dundee and the county SWAT Team.

"Okay," the Executioner said, placing the tip of the marker on the lower section of the diagram. "This will be our entry point. We'll move up covertly through here." He drew six *x*'s on the board along with some arrows. "The airstrip is here, and we have to be in position when it lands."

He looked around the room at each of their faces.

"No sweat," one of St. Alban's men said.

"Keep in mind that could be a tall order," Bolan continued. "As I mentioned, they have motion detectors and Claymore mines set up along the ridge here." He indicated the area near the fence where he had previously entered.

"If you're wondering where he's referring to," Grimaldi said, with a grin, "just look for a bashed down or recently repaired section of fence."

Dundee snorted like a Brahma bull in a cage.

"Getting back to the matter at hand," Bolan said, "we'll be dealing with some bad dudes. These militiamen have proven that they're not afraid to shoot, and they've got some pretty heavy weaponry and some sophisticated equipment. In addition to the Claymore mines and motion detectors that we know are on the compound, we believe they are involved in numerous murders, including that armored car heist, which means they also have fully automatic Kalashnikovs and a PTRS antitank weapon."

A hush fell over the room, and somebody let out a low whistle.

"Where did a bigoted, Nevada rancher get stuff like that?" St. Alban asked.

"From what we gathered," Bolan said, "he's in bed with the Russian *mafiya*. Intel says that's who's flying this special shipment in tonight."

"Any idea what this shipment is?" St. Alban asked.

Bolan shook his head and allowed himself a rare smile. "I guess we'll find out in a few hours."

"Yeah," Grimaldi said. "And second place is a bullet. You guys got decent body armor?"

St. Alban's team all had Level 4, as did the county SWAT team.

"Keep in mind it may not stop what they'll be shooting," Grimaldi stated.

The men nodded.

Bolan resumed his briefing. "Once we're in place and the plane is landing, Sheriff Dundee's team will provide a diversion at the front gate."

"What kind of diversion?" St. Alban asked. "I thought the whole purpose of us helping with this was due to them not having enough probable cause to hit the place?"

"They have a legitimate right to go to the front gate and ask for entry to speak with Rand Autry," Bolan said.

"And I can be quite loud and bellicose when I want to be," Dundee added.

"As this is going on," Bolan said, "we'll move in and take the plane, the militia members, and any *mafiya* henchmen here on the airstrip into custody." He paused. "This could be dangerous. I don't expect these guys, especially anybody associated with the *mafiya*, to go down easy."

"We didn't expect a cakewalk," St. Alban said. His guys uttered a couple of "Hoo-rahs."

They're full of bravado and bravery, Bolan thought. He'd seen so many young men in uniform thumping their chests. It was easy going until the rounds started flying. He hoped these guys would be up to the task. They'd performed well in the controlled training scenarios at the Desert Warfare Academy, and they'd all been deployed to war zones. But being outnumbered and quite possibly outgunned with limited support in this kind of firefight was a totally different thing.

"Like I said," the Executioner continued, "I don't expect this will be easy, but once that part's been accomplished, Sheriff Dundee's team will move in from the front gate."

"Once we hear the sound of gunfire," Dundee said, "we'll have what they call exigent circumstances, which, in turn, allows us to gain entry, forcibly if necessary, to investigate." The big lawman's face lost all its mirth. "By any means necessary."

"I've got an FBI SWAT team en route, as well," Dylan added. "We'll be on hand to provide support if and when you need us."

"Looks like we'll need all the help we can get," Grimaldi said. He reached into his satchel and began pulling out portable radios with ear mikes. "These will give us communication up to about a hundred yards, but no farther than that. There aren't any repeater towers tuned to this frequency, so use them sparingly." He gave his last ones to St. Alban, Dundee and Dylan.

"We'll systematically move up to the main buildings," Bolan said, "clearing each one as we go. We're looking for hostages, so be sure of your targets, should you have to shoot." He stopped and picked two magazines off the table. Holding them up side by side, the Executioner pointed to the red mark on the base of one and the green mark on the other.

"Sheriff Dundee has been gracious enough to provide us with two types of ammunition. The red marker indicates the projectiles are frangible and will not overpenetrate the walls inside the buildings. The green markers indicate regular, full-metal-jacketed rounds. Those will go right though the walls. When we're securing the plane and eliminating any residual resistance, we'll be green. When we do our building searches, we switch to red. Green means 'go,' as in go right through you, red means 'stop,' as in stop in the wall."

"Anybody color blind?" Grimaldi asked.

A ripple of nervous laughter emanated from the room.

"We continue with our sweep until we've cleared and searched all the buildings." He dotted the four big barns and the house. "Remember, Prince Amir has been kidnapped, and we have reason to believe that he is possibly being held in one of these buildings. He's a member of the Saudi royal family and a guest of our nation." He paused and looked at each man. "The rescue and safe recovery of the prince is of paramount importance to the United States. Any questions?"

No one said anything.

Bolan figured he'd emphasized the obvious. There was little left to do but paint up, do a final ammo and equipment check, and move out.

CHAPTER EIGHTEEN

Billman Safe House

The whirling sound of the electric screwdriver filled the confines of the spacious garage. Androkovich stood on a stepladder next to the cab of the ambulance and applied more pressure to force the long screw to pierce through the metal frame. Mahfuj and Abdullah held the plastic shell, filled with the shrapnel, over the front part of the box-like tail section.

"Are you certain this will work?" Mahfuj asked. The sweat was rolling down his face.

The Russian nodded and sank in another screw. "I already have the holes drilled for the detonation wires," he said. "It will be the biggest IED ever."

"But will it inflict the maximum casualties?" Mahfuj asked. "The explosion has to be bigger than the one at the Boston Marathon."

"At Boston they used backpacks," Androkovich said. He placed another long screw against the plastic and eased the trigger to start sinking it slowly through the plastic shell. "As long as we back it in, facing the crowd, it will do the job."

"What about the prince and the two Shi'ites? Are we guaranteed that they will perish, as well?"

"I'm putting a Claymore mine inside the ambulance.

It will be connected to the detonator. The authorities will no doubt assume it went off prematurely."

"But will it be fatal?"

Androkovich smiled. This man took hatred to a new level. "Have you ever seen a Claymore go off?" He waited a few seconds. "Seven hundred steel balls blasting outward at twelve hundred meters per second. It has a blast range of fifty meters. Can you imagine what it will do to the three of them in such a confined space?"

Mahfuj's face was impassive. The Russian had just met the man and disliked him intensely. His brother, Masoud, was a bit less driven. This man was all business. Killing business. Not the type to inspire trust.

Finally the screw went in all the way. Androkovich got down.

"When do I get my money transferred?" he asked.

"As we discussed, when the blast goes off. Arrangements have been made to make the wire transfer."

Androkovich inhaled deeply. It was the eleventh hour and time to make the slight adjustment to their arrangement. He looked at his watch. The plane should be landing in about fifteen minutes. They would be leaving here in another hour. He looked back at Mahfuj. The man's eyes were dark and hard, like obsidian.

"Move the ladder to the other side, and we'll finish up."

The Arab did not move for several seconds, then grabbed the ladder as Androkovich picked up the box of screws in one hand and held the electric screwdriver in the other.

"We leave here at 0500," the Russian said. "And I want to verify that the money has been transferred before we leave."

Mahfuj slammed the ladder on the concrete floor. "No. My brother will make the transfer only after the explosives have been detonated. We were very clear on that during our negotiation." He pulled back his BDU shirt, and Androkovich could see the handle of the Beretta extending from the left side of the Arab's belt. A few steps away the big man, now also armed with a .357 SIG Sauer from one of the dead Secret Service agents, released the plastic shell, letting the edge sag downward as he lumbered forward.

"I'm confident that everything will go off without any problems," Androkovich said slowly. After all, English wasn't their primary language. "But in the rare event that something unforeseen does happen to your brother, I want the money transferred now."

Mahfuj glared at him. "Have I not made myself clear?"

Androkovich knew the man was armed and volatile, but the Arab was also dependent on this final phase going through without any complications. He ignored the attempted intimidation, repositioned the ladder, and then said to Abdullah, "Hold that section up so I can secure it with the screws."

The giant didn't move.

He stared at him as he ascended the ladder, then glanced nonchalantly at Mahfuj.

"We don't have time to play games," Androkovich said. "If I have to, I can do this last part alone, but you can't accomplish the plan without me. So may I suggest that you tell your large helper here to hold the shell up so I can finish, while you call your brother and instruct him to make the transfer now. I want to verify it before we leave."

Mahfuj stood there in silence, chewing his upper lip like a recalcitrant schoolboy. Finally, he said something in Arabic to Abdullah and the big man lifted the plastic shell in place. Mahfuj took out his cell phone and began pressing buttons. As he held it to his ear, the Russian addressed him one more time.

"And speak in English," he said. "I want to hear what you're saying."

The Arab's stare was malevolent, but he nodded.

Landing Strip, Camp Freedom

BOLAN AND GRIMALDI lay in the darkness in the shallow arroyo that was about twenty yards from the crushed gravel landing strip. Gaining access to the area had proved easier than their previous visit. There was fencing along this southern section as the Autry ranch melded into the public land that his cattle had grazed on for two decades. Bolan had discovered several motion detectors, five Claymore mines and several trip wires. It would have been a rather unpleasant sojourn for any trespassers in the dark if they didn't have night-vision goggles.

He checked his watch: 0410.

The intercepted message had said four on the nose, but in the dark world of drugs and weapons smuggling, things hardly worked on a dependable timetable.

"Cooper." St. Alban's voice sounded in Bolan's ear mike. "Vehicle approaching."

Bolan saw it, too. An open Jeep, from the looks of it, with a driver and two passengers. The vehicle pulled off to the side of the runway next to a three-foot-high box covered by a tarp. The front seat passenger got out and ran quickly to the covered box and undid some bungee cords. He tore off the tarp, revealing a portable generator.

"He's activating the runway lights," Bolan said softly after keying his mike.

Almost in unison, the droning sound of a small plane's engine became audible.

"Sounds like a Cessna," Grimaldi whispered.

Bolan said nothing. Countless previous firefights had prepared him for what was about to unfold. He knew he could count on Grimaldi, but was concerned about St. Alban and the others on his team. They had performed well in the training scenarios, and they had military experience, but a situation like this with so many unknown variables was like going from junior varsity to the professional leagues.

The generator sputtered to life, and the noise of its percussive cycling filled the cool, night air. Seconds later the driver got out of the Jeep and walked to the area near the generator. He bent and flipped some sort of heavy switch.

Twin rows of lights snapped on, lining each side of the runway. Bolan switched to his alternate frequency and called Dundee.

"The plane's coming in," he said. "Should be landing shortly."

"Ten-four," Dundee said. "One guard at the front gate. I've got the red-and-blue lights on the BearCat ready and my bullhorn in my hand. I got a call from Agent Dylan. The FBI team's prepping at their HQ."

Bolan relayed this information to Grimaldi.

The plane's engine grew louder, and its wing and fuselage lights suddenly became visible. It circled the field once and then came back, slower this time, as it descended for the landing.

The third man had gotten out of the Jeep. Bolan used his night-vision goggles to check each of their faces. One of them was George Duncan. He'd been the first one out. The driver was the guy with red hair that Bolan remembered from the first confrontation on the highway between the authorities and the Autrys. The third man looked Middle Eastern, although he didn't have a full beard. His hair was somewhat long and stylishly waved. He wore a suit and jacket, although his collar was open, and he carried a briefcase.

He's the moneyman, Bolan thought as he switched back to his team frequency. It was strange that none of the Autrys were present. It was their ranch. The guy in the suit could provide a lot of answers to a lot of questions.

The plane's tires struck the crushed gravel runway.

"Get ready," Bolan said, keying his mike. "We move when they get out of the plane, and we see how many we're dealing with."

"Roger that," came St. Alban's muffled reply.

The plane was a light-colored Cessna, just as Grimaldi had predicted. It began coasting toward the three men, the propeller cycling down into slower and slower rotations. As the plane came to a full stop, the pilot angled the fuselage in such a way that the side door was facing the three waiting men. The door opened, and a man's head appeared in the opening.

"*Doh*—" the man in the plane began.

"Please, speak in English for the benefit of my friends," the guy with the red hair interrupted.

The redhead's English had a Southern twang. He obviously had a good command of Russian, as well.

The man in the plane got out with a wide grin. He was short, but barrel-chested and he had cropped brown hair. The butt of a semiautomatic pistol rode the left side of his belt. Two other men stepped out of the plane, both carrying 7.62 mm AK-103 rifles. They pulled the folded stocks back into shoulder-firing position.

The first man sauntered forward, extending his hand and speaking in Russian.

The redhead shook the man's hand, said something else in Russian, and then switched back to English. "Masoud, this is Dimitri."

The dark-skinned man in the suit moved forward, carrying the briefcase in both hands. He nodded and Bolan heard him speak for the first time. His English had a slightly British inflection. Bolan placed it as possibly Saudi.

That would make sense with the prince being somehow involved in this, he thought. It was time for the front gate diversion.

He switched to the alternate frequency, told Dundee to start the ruckus, then switched back.

The two men on the runway exchanged more conversation, and Dimitri told one of his two bodyguards to "Go get it."

The man looked around warily, slung his rifle and moved back to the plane.

"Get ready," Bolan said, keying his mike. "We go on my signal."

The man got two mid-sized cardboard boxes from the plane, walked back to the others and set them on the ground. Dimitri held out his hand.

"There you are," he said. "And now, you show me money, yes?"

The dark-skinned man in the suit began to open the briefcase. Suddenly the redhead's cell phone jingled, and everybody froze as he answered it.

"What do they want?" he asked, then listened and said, "Tell them that you have to contact Rand Autry, but he is sleeping." He waited, then yelled into the phone. "I don't care what they say. Tell them to wait. I'll come up there myself in a few minutes."

He pressed buttons on his cell phone, waited, then said, "Get the rest of the men over to the front gate. There's something going on with the cops." He slipped the cell phone back into its case on his belt.

"What is it?" the dark-skinned man asked.

"Police," the redhead said. "They're demanding to talk to the old man."

Dimitri's head jerked, and he said something in Russian.

"Don't worry," the redhead said. "I'll take care of it. Now let's get this done."

His cell phone rang again. As he reached for it, Bolan snapped his selector switch to auto, keyed his mike and said, "Go!"

He and Grimaldi got up from their prone positions, their weapons at the ready. Both had chosen M-4s over the smaller, lighter MP-5s that they also had. St. Alban's team all had AR-15s and Bolan wanted the ammo to be uniform in case they had to exchange magazines. On the other side of the plane, he could see St. Alban's men advancing. They passed over the bright runway lights, causing a flicker. The men on the tarmac noticed and immediately turned to open fire.

Bolan brought up his M-4 and fired a short burst. One of the Russians from the plane jerked and fell to the ground. Bolan fired another burst at the second man.

St. Alban's team opened fire, as well.

Dimitri pulled out his pistol and began firing wildly as he grabbed for the briefcase. The dark-skinned man wouldn't let go, and the Russian turned and shot him in the chest. He grabbed the briefcase and ran for the plane as the Arab slumped to the ground.

"Don't let them take off," Bolan shouted into his mike. His voice sounded far away due to the transitory deafness brought on by the explosion of the rounds. Grimaldi peppered the nose of the Cessna with his weapon on full-auto. Perforating holes appeared in the shiny metal, but the propeller seemed to accelerate slightly.

Dimitri turned and fired at them. Bolan acquired an immediate sight picture and squeezed the trigger, sending another burst into the barrel-like chest. As the Russian fell, Bolan noticed one man running toward the Jeep. He was set to fire when his peripheral vision caught the muzzle-flashes from two of the remaining assailants and ducked.

The Jeep took off without lights.

George Duncan yelled, "Red, wait!"

The vehicle disappeared into the darkness.

On seeing that, Duncan turned and began running at them, holding his rifle at waist level and firing on full-auto. His face looked maniacal.

Bad form for an instructor, Bolan thought as he sighted in on the man's chest and pulled the trigger.

Duncan jerked slightly, took two more tentative steps and collapsed face-first on to the ground.

Bolan did a quick scan of the area. St. Alban's men

were already hitting the plane. Another rapid burst of gunfire and the pilot slumped. The engine whined, and the propeller immediately began to lose power, each rotation noticeably slower. After thirty seconds, St. Alban turned and gave Bolan the thumbs-up sign that the plane was secure.

Bolan's hearing was gradually coming back. He checked each fallen adversary for signs of life. There were none. Grimaldi, who had been covering Bolan, nodded and went to the boxes on the runway. He used his rifle barrel to push open the flaps of the two boxes and then shone his flashlight inside.

"Semtex and detonator caps," he said. "Luckily, they're not connected yet, but somebody was planning a big party."

Bolan relayed the information to Dundee, advising him that the scene at the airfield was secure.

"We encountered some armed resistance over here," Dundee replied, "but they surrendered pretty quick once we started firing back from our BearCat. We're almost to the main house."

"We'll check these buildings and tag up with you in the middle," Bolan said. He turned to Grimaldi and gave him a sitrep.

His partner grinned. "Looks like Dundee finally found that probable cause he was looking for."

Bolan directed one of St. Alban's team to stay and guard the scene. "The rest of you form up on me. We're going to clear those buildings."

There were four huge barn-like structures in the distance, perhaps a quarter mile away. He caught a flash of brake lights between the buildings that quickly disappeared. It had to be Red in the Jeep, driving without lights. Beyond the cluster of the barns, Bolan could see the oscillating red-and-blue lights of Dundee's police vehicles. He switched to Dundee's frequency and advised him that they were approaching from the south. "You've also got an armed suspect who fled this scene in a Jeep. We're trying to locate him."

"Ten-four," Dundee said. "We're going to hit the main house now."

Bolan and the rest of his team moved forward at a cautious speed, stopping periodically to check the area with the night-vision goggles for hostiles and booby traps. Over by the main house he heard the sound of sporadic gunfire, accompanied by the pinpricks of muzzle-flashes.

They stuck to the gravel road that led back to the main ranch area. It took them the better part of eight minutes to cover the quarter mile or so to the first building. Bolan saw the Jeep parked in front of the closest one. He sent two of St. Alban's team along the right side and one along the left to secure the perimeter. Bolan, Grimaldi and St. Alban moved along the front. The building was the smallest of the four, but it was still wide enough to accommodate a pair of semi-tractor trailers. Besides the two massive folding front doors, there was a smaller, side door to the right.

Bolan reached out and tried the handle. Locked. He stepped back, positioning himself to deliver a kick to the door when he heard the sound of a round going off inside the building.

A woman's scream. Another round, this one sounding a bit muffled.

More screaming. Pleading...

Bolan delivered a hard kick to the door, and it swung

inward, bounced off the wall and rebounded back toward the doorjamb. The Executioner went through first, his M-4 at the ready position. He knew Grimaldi and St. Alban would be right behind him.

The area inside was dimly lit by two rows of partially illuminated overhead, fluorescent lights. The main floor was littered with an assortment of detritus. He saw two lighted rooms on the back wall. The three men spread out, moving toward the two rooms, wading through the sea of discarded junk: empty paint cans, two paint-spraying machines, some kind of dust masks, crushed, plastic soft drink bottles, cardboard stencils and bundles of fast-food wrappers. The tangy smell of spray paint was pervasive.

Bolan saw movement in the room to the left. He pointed to it, and Grimaldi nodded. The soldier then motioned for St. Alban to cover the door of the other room while he and Grimaldi moved to the first one. It looked as if it had been constructed as a storage shed with no regard for aesthetics: solid plywood walls without windows and a crude door. A thin line of light illuminated the space underneath and along the top.

Inside the room a woman screamed again, punctuated by the sound of a slap, hand on flesh, and a gruff male voice telling her to "Shut up."

Bolan kicked open the door and saw a flash of movement. Instead of entering the room, both he and Grimaldi stepped to the side of the opening, using the flimsy walls to obscure as much of their bodies as possible. Bolan knew the thin plywood offered little in the way of cover. With his M-4 securely against his shoulder, he swept the interior of the room.

Eileen Autry stood in the middle of the floor with a

terrified expression etched into her face. The man called Red stood behind her, his left arm hooked around her neck, his right holding a big, chrome revolver to her right temple. He was effectively using her body as a shield, leaving only a small portion of his head visible over her shoulder. The bodies of two men, their hands bound behind their backs, lay about four feet away.

"Stay back," Red ordered, "or I'll kill her."

"Drop your weapon," Bolan said. "You're completely surrounded. There's no hope of escape."

Red's eyes flashed, and his face twisted into a network of creases.

"You're going to give me a car to drive out of here," he said, "or she'll be a corpse."

Tears ran down Eileen's cheeks. "Do what he says. Please. He killed my father and my brother. I don't want to die."

Bolan and Grimaldi had played this same scenario a few times before and knew their roles.

"Nobody has to die," Grimaldi said in an overly loud voice. "At least not if I can help it."

As Red canted his head toward his left to address Grimaldi, Bolan acquired the sight picture he needed and squeezed the trigger of his M-4. As the empty shell casings blew out of the ejection port, Red's head jerked backward as if he'd been poleaxed, his right eye socket a bloody wad. His legs turned to soft rubber, and the hand holding the pistol dropped downward, the gun bouncing off the hard concrete floor. Eileen collapsed, too, but caught herself with her outstretched hands before she hit the floor. Bolan was already moving forward, sweeping the rest of the room. Grimaldi was sweeping, too. He grabbed Eileen and pulled her up and away as

Bolan checked Red. He'd fallen on to his side, a bloody halo surrounding his head.

Eileen began to cry hysterically, and Bolan told Grimaldi to keep her where she was. He immediately moved back to the door and joined St. Alban who said that he'd observed movement in the lighted space under the door to the adjacent room.

The two men moved to that door, and St. Alban tried the knob. It turned easily, and the door swung inward. As he visually swept the room, Bolan saw a man leaning back in a padded easy chair eating a hamburger. A computer and monitor were on the desk behind him. When he saw them, he quickly dumped the burger on the desk and raised both his arms over his head, waggling his hands.

"I surrender," he said. "Don't shoot."

This guy appeared to be Middle Eastern, but Bolan didn't think he looked Saudi. He ordered the man to get facedown on the floor. The guy was pretty obese and had a hard time raising his corpulent body from the chair. As he got on to the floor, he repeated his pronouncement of surrender.

"You're the boss," he said. "Anything you say. Just don't shoot me. I am ready to negotiate."

Bolan told St. Alban to cover the man as he cleared the rest of the room. Finding nothing, he used his radio to brief the others that the first building was secure, then turned back to the prone man.

"Where's Prince Amir?" he asked.

The obese man raised his head. "He is not here. But I'm not saying anything more until we negotiate my deal."

Bolan frowned, moved forward and after searching the prone man, secured his hands behind his back. "Watch him," he said to St. Alban.

He went to the next room and found Grimaldi standing over Eileen. She was sitting on the floor, crying as she held her father's limp form on her lap. Rand Autry had been shot in the right temple. Shane's body lay next to them. He was on his back and had sustained a facial wound.

Grimaldi pointed to the two bodies and shook his head.

After leaving one of St. Alban's men to guard the prisoner and Eileen, they moved quickly to clear the rest of the barn buildings. The search yielded nothing but a barracks full of empty bunk beds and footlockers in one, and a twin engine plane in the other. Bolan figured it was the first plane he'd seen land here two days earlier. It was empty of any cargo. After conferring with Dundee on the alternate frequency, Bolan confirmed that the big lawman had eight militiamen in custody, three more wounded awaiting transport to the hospital and two who were dead.

"Tactically neutralized, as we like to say," the big lawman said.

"We've got a few of those, too," Bolan replied.

"A few of these assholes are flipping already," Dundee said. "They're not patriots, like they claim. They're ex-mercs, mostly. One of them showed us the masks from the armored car robbery. Told us Frank Andrews was the guy who shot those officers. I'm gonna take this town apart, piece by piece, until we find him."

Bolan nodded. The Autry ranch had been secured, but where the hell was the prince?

CHAPTER NINETEEN

Las Vegas Marathon Finish Line

Androkovich sat behind the wheel of the ambulance and watched as the throngs of people walked past him toward the starting point of the race. He checked his side-view mirror and saw the sun rising above the horizon and was glad that he'd taken the time to tape pieces of white cardboard over windows of the rear cab, lest Mahfuj and Abdullah see the sunrise and realized they'd missed their morning prayers. Or perhaps they hadn't and were kneeling inside the cramped quarters of the ambulance section with the prince and the other two Arabs. Fundamentalists were so predictable.

The Russian was surprised at the ease with which he'd been able to move the ambulance up behind the rows of tents and portable toilets to get so close to the finish line. He'd backed it in, positioning the rear of the ambulance, the side with the plastic shell full of explosives and shrapnel, facing the area where the throngs of marathon welcomers would be clustered. The Las Vegas sign was about fifty feet away, and he found himself hoping that the blast didn't damage it too much. He'd always held a slight fascination for the artistic design. Still, it was plastic and temporary, like everything else in Vegas. It could be replaced in a heartbeat and without a second thought, and probably would be once the images of the blast, and the massive casualties lying around it, were forever and indelibly imprinted upon the American psyche by the ubiquitous news stations and internet.

The race would be starting in a few minutes. That left him a comfortable margin of about two hours to verify that the Saudis had transferred the money to his Swiss account before he would arm the device and walk a comfortable distance away with his disposable cell phone.

Dial it, send it and drop it, he thought, and I'll be walking away from the blast a rich man. A very rich man.

He decided to check in with Strogoff. He was supposed to call after the transaction was complete, but he hadn't yet. If all went as planned, Masoud would have paid for the extra Semtex, Strogoff would have planted it in the barn with the rest of the evidence, and then set up the Autry murder-suicide. In his mind's eye he could see the headlines: Rancher's Son Kills Family, Then Self. It would be front-page news, provided his partner set everything up correctly.

But why wouldn't he? He was exceptionally competent, and as far as he knew, his financial future was riding on the success of the Arab's plan, too.

His revelry was broken by the opening of the small window in the door that separated the driver's compartment from the rear, ambulance section. Mahfuj's face appeared there.

"Has your man contacted you?" he asked.

"Not yet."

"I have not been able to contact my brother. Could something have gone wrong?"

Androkovich hoped not. Although they'd been paying him in installments, the final payment was yet to come. Masoud was supposed to have taken care of that earlier.

"I'll give Red a call," Androkovich said. "How are your friends doing back there?"

"This place smells abominable," Mahfuj replied. "They have all soiled themselves."

"*Mit ahs fey*," the Russian said, using some of the Arabic he had picked up.

Mahfuj snorted. "That is how you say you are sorry to a woman. You must say *Mit ahs sif* to a man."

Androkovich smiled and thought about repeating the first phrase again but decided against deliberately antagonizing the Arab butcher. As he punched in Strogoff's cell phone number, the odor from the rear cabin wafted into the driver's compartment. It did smell bad.

The phone rang several times and then went to voice mail. Not a good sign. He wanted to check on the status of the money transfer to his account immediately. Maybe the final implementation of the plan would have to be adjusted slightly.

Maybe the bomb would have to go off sooner, rather than later.

Camp Freedom

AFTER CLEARING ONE of the rooms in the Autry house that wasn't considered a crime scene, Bolan watched as Agent Dylan gave the Arab prisoner a bottle of water. He looked at it with a smug dissatisfaction.

"What, you do not have any soda?" He grinned. "I

learned in New York that is the how you Americans refer to such drinks."

He'd given them little more than his name, Ibrahim al Hussain, aka radical Yemini cleric Ibrahim al Shabahb. Bolan was on the way to getting more information about the prince's whereabouts until Dylan entered the picture with her FBI SWAT team in tow. She immediately informed both Bolan and Dundee that her supervisor advised her that she was to take custody of any foreign nationals and report back to him.

"That's okay with me," Shabahb said. He turned his corpulent face toward Bolan and added, "No offense, boss, but she's a lot better-looking than you."

Bolan wasn't amused, nor did he have time for standard Bureau protocol. He and Grimaldi stood by and watched as Dylan read the man his rights.

When she was finished, he grinned. "I heard that before, on TV, but I like that part about the lawyer. I think it would be best for me to have such representation before I say anything more. I want my new deal in writing."

Dylan looked flustered.

Bolan motioned for her to step outside the room, and they closed the door behind them.

"We're running out of time," the Executioner said in a low voice. "The prince is still missing, and this guy is the key to finding where they've stashed him."

She compressed her lips. "I know. I'm just as frustrated as you are. I've got a call in to my supervisor to see what I can offer him due to the exigency of the circumstances."

Grimaldi, who was leaning against the wall, snorted a laugh.

"Exigency?" he said. "That's a real understatement. Give me five minutes alone with the son of a bitch and I'll get what you need."

"Right," Dylan shot back. "That sounds real good."

Bolan reviewed what they'd found at the massive set of crime scenes so far. The Semtex, the detonator caps, the dead Arab, whose photo they'd sent to Brognola for possible identification, the murder of the Autrys, and the contents of the one barn. Bolan thought back to his unauthorized visit. During the drill, which he was certain had been a rehearsal for the armored car heist, he'd seen a guy stepping out of the barn wearing one of those protective facial masks. The kind men used as breathing protection when doing spray-painting cars. The odor of the empty paint cans and sprayers, white and blue, along with the remnants of some cardboard stencils, told him they been painting something big inside the barn. The stencils had been too damaged to decipher, but Bolan was convinced it all fit together somehow.

"Like I said," he told her, "we need answers fast."

Her smile was wan. "What's that old joke, I'm dancing as fast as I can?"

"Not fast enough," Bolan said. "Go take a walk."

"What? You can't order me around."

"Watch me." He motioned for Grimaldi to enter the room. "Let's take those five minutes."

He pulled open the door and slammed it shut behind him, twisting the locking mechanism in place.

Shabahb had just finished taking a long sip from his water bottle.

"This isn't very cold," he said. "Can you get me some ice?"

Grimaldi and Bolan exchanged glances. They both

knew they had only a few minutes to extract the vital information before the FBI SWAT team descended on them like a sudden hail storm.

The Iraqi raised an eyebrow. "What? You are the tough guys?" He held up the half-empty bottle. "Are you going to water-board me? I do not think you have enough."

Bolan nodded and Grimaldi swung his fist at Shabahb, knocking the plastic bottle from his hand. Although neither one of them subscribed to actual torture, they both knew the implied threat could work better in some instances. Grimaldi pulled out his SIG Sauer and pointed it at the Iraqi's head.

"What?" Shabahb smiled. "Are you going to shoot me? Then you shall never know what I know. Now, may I have some more water, please?"

Bolan nodded at the Stony Man pilot.

Grimaldi pulled out a long custom-made sound suppressor and began threading it on to the barrel of his pistol.

"Oh, yeah," the Iraqi said, his grin widening. "A silencer. I have seen those in the movies. Did I tell you that I used to work for Saddam? Do you really think you two can do anything to frighten me?"

"We aren't here to frighten," Grimaldi said. "Just to get results."

Shabahb shrugged. "Did I mention that I was also a translator for him, and then for your U.S. Army?"

"Nice work if you can get it." Grimaldi pointed the silenced SIG at the man again.

The Arab smirked.

Grimaldi pulled the trigger, firing a round directly

between Ibrahim's open legs. The Iraqi screamed and tried to jerk his legs up on to the chair.

Someone banged on the door and tried to open it. So far, the lock was holding.

"Looks like my aim was a little low," Grimaldi said.

"Probably from the added weight of the sound suppressor," Bolan stated.

Grimaldi nodded. "You know, I got one of those laser-sights on this baby. I'll have to use it." His thumb flicked the lever and the red dot appeared on Shabahb's stomach. The Arab's eyes widened as it traced downward, over his crotch.

"You two are crazy," the Iraqi said, the panic obvious in his voice. "Please, do not shoot me."

"Then tell us what we want to know," Bolan ordered. "I'm running short of time and patience."

"What do you wish to know? I know a lot."

"Where did they take Prince Amir?" Bolan asked.

The banging persisted on the other side of the door. Grimaldi grabbed the knob with his left hand as he moved the pistol's red laser dot over Shabahb's lower extremities with his right.

"They never brought him here. They have a safe house where they took him and the other two."

The other two? Bolan wondered exactly how much they didn't know, and how much time he had to figure it out. Dylan's voice came through the door, demanding they open it.

Bolan knew he had to pick his next words carefully.

"Where's the safe house located?" Bolan asked.

"I do not know the address." A wet spot materialized on the front of Shabahb's pants, seemingly attesting to his veracity. Neither Bolan nor Grimaldi mentioned it.

More banging, this time more substantial, shook the flimsy door in its frame.

"Agent Cooper," Dylan's voice said, sounding much sterner. "I must advise you if you do not open this door immediately, I'll be forced to bring federal charges against both of you."

"Don't you have to call your supervisor first?" Grimaldi yelled. He moved the red dot to the wet spot. "How about it, Ibbie? You want to have a 9 mm vasectomy? Oh, wait a minute." He waggled the red dot in a circle on the front of the man's pants. "You're a Muslim, right? How about a nice circumcision instead?"

He put his hands over his face. "Please, no."

The Executioner didn't like using this method or the ultimatum, but he was at the end of the game, and it was time to throw a Hail Mary pass downfield.

"What's their plan, Ibrahim?" Bolan said. His voice was a growl now. "Last chance."

"The marathon," the Iraqi said, sobbing. "The marathon. They're going to set off a bomb with the prince and two Saudi students. But I had nothing to do with it. Believe me. I had no part in it."

"A bomb," Bolan said, letting the controlled fury ebb into his tone. "Where and how?"

"In the vehicle."

"What vehicle?"

Shabahb shook his head so hard his fat cheeks shook. "The ambulance."

Suddenly everything clicked into place for Bolan: the paint canisters, the spraying machines and stencils…blue and white…the ambulance at the armored car robbery… What other kind of vehicle could get close enough to the race without being noticed? He gestured for Grimaldi to put away his gun and twisted the knob opening the door. Dylan and three FBI SWAT members in full regalia stood there with sour expressions on their faces.

"Did you hear it?" Bolan asked.

"I did," Dylan replied.

"Then let's go."

CHAPTER TWENTY

Las Vegas Marathon Finish Line

After Androkovich had tried his partner's number for the seventh time and was once again diverted to voice mail, he knew something had gone wrong. Strogoff would have either answered or was down for the count. Maybe the police or the Feds had raided the Autry ranch. The Russian decided he had to operate on that assumption. It was time to adjust his plans. He used his satellite phone to check the status of his accounts in Switzerland only to hear that there had been no transactions in the past twenty-four hours. That meant Masoud was most likely down, too.

He flipped the auto-switch that would allow the vehicle to keep running once he removed the keys and pulled them from the ignition. The transmission was also locked, so the vehicle could not be taken out of Park. No one would be moving the ambulance until they got a tow truck and picked up the remains after the blast. As he opened the door and slid out, he heard the side door open. Mahfuj ran around the front of the vehicle and grabbed Androkovich's arm in a grip of steel.

The Russian glared at him but didn't make any obvious move to shake off the other man's hand. Instead, he said in a calm voice, "What are you doing? Release me at once, you fool. Do you want to attract attention?"

Mahfuj's face glistened with sweat, and his blue paramedic shirt showed enormous half-moons of wetness under each arm. When he spoke, his voice was a low growl.

"I cannot reach my brother on the phone. What is happening?"

Androkovich shrugged. "I don't know. I was going to try to find out."

"Going where?"

He didn't answer.

Mahfuj's mouth twisted downward, and he stuck his right hand inside the loosely fitting shirt. "Give me the cell phone. The one for the detonation." His fingers gripped the butt of the pistol.

"Don't be stupid. You'll ruin everything."

"Give it to me now." He started to pull out the Beretta.

Androkovich shook his head and reached into his pocket. He withdrew the cell phone and handed it to the Arab. "Here, but it will do you no good."

Mahfuj flipped it open and pressed the buttons. His eyes narrowed, and a look of fury twisted his face. "What is the number for the detonation code?"

The Russian smiled and tapped his right index finger on his temple. "It is in here. Do you think I'd be naïve enough to leave it on the phone? Now give that back to me."

Mahfuj hesitated.

In the distance, Androkovich could hear sirens. He looked around and saw several of the uniformed police officers moving about, checking various sections where the other paramedics had parked, and telling people to move back.

This was definitely not the time to be standing still arguing. He reached over and plucked the cell phone from Mahfuj's hand.

"They're on to us," he said. "Get the prince and we'll take him as a hostage."

"No, he must die," Mahfuj said. "I have already texted my father that we have him here."

"Don't be a fool. He's our ticket out of here."

"That is the second and the last time you will call me a fool," Mahfuj said. As he reached inside his shirt again, Androkovich lashed out with a clubbing right. His fist collided with the Arab's jaw, and he collapsed, striking his head against the side of the ambulance. The Russian began to walk briskly away. He was assessing his next move when he saw the black Escalade with the dented hood tearing up Las Vegas Boulevard followed by two black sedans, both of which had red lights flashing on their dashboards. A uniformed police officer ran past him. Another one approached and stood in front of him, his hand on his weapon, which was still holstered.

"Hold up a minute, sir," the cop said. "I need to see your ID."

Androkovich stopped, smiled and asked, "Can it wait till I take a leak? I'm about to piss my pants."

Before the officer could respond, the Russian brought up the stiffened fingers of his right hand and sunk them into the area at the base of the cop's neck. He immediately grabbed his throat and began gasping. Catching the man, he quickly lowered him to the ground.

"A little help over here," he called. "I've got an officer down."

Two other cops ran to his side and asked what happened. The gasping officer was unable to talk, and Androkovich told the other cops to lay him out straight.

"He just collapsed. I need to get my medical kit to establish an airway. Keep his feet elevated and his head back like this." He took the one cop's hands and placed them on the fallen officer's head. He stood and said, "Be right back. Stay with him."

He ran off in the opposite direction of his ambulance. Perhaps fifty yards away was the place he sought, the place he'd scouted as an alternate escape route, should things go awry.

Glancing over his shoulder, he saw Mahfuj getting to his feet, his eyes seeming to zero in on the Russian despite the throngs of people.

Off to the left of the ambulance, the three unmarked police cars jerked to a stop. Two men in black BDUs got out of the Hummer. It was the same two from the course, the government agents. The female FBI agent was getting out of the second car, and the big sheriff, Dundee, was getting out of the third. They had to have hit Camp Freedom.

He had perhaps forty more yards to go, and he decided to sprint, taking the cell phone out of his pocket as he ran, punching in the numbers to set off the detonation.

MAHFUJ SAW THE Russian running through the crowd. He was heading for what appeared to be a barren area, but Mahfuj remembered him mentioning a secondary escape route: the drainage tunnels that ran underneath the streets.

He ripped open the rear door of the ambulance and yelled to Abdullah.

"Give me your pistol."

The big Arab looked dumbfounded, then removed the gun from his belt line and handed it over. Mahfuj glanced over his shoulder, keeping an eye on the Russian, and then turned back to Abdullah. "Kill them all," he said. "Use your knife. Then get away from here."

"Where shall I go?" Abdullah asked.

He was like a loyal horse that Mahfuj had taken into the battle. He had no choice but to release him now and hope they would be reunited later.

"Find your way back to the safe house on the street called Billman," Mahfuj said, knowing this would be a near impossible task for Abdullah, whose English was limited to a few phrases. Mahfuj realized now he had failed to make an adequate backup plan, but all was not lost. If the prince was killed, and he could catch the Russian and set off the blast, the plan would move forward. His father, the first desert falcon, would see to it.

"It is the will of God, my brother," he said as he slammed the door and ran off.

"There," Bolan said, pointing to the ambulance. There were several in the area, but only one had a guy running from it. Bolan recognized him. The Arab with the bandaged hand from the prince's security detail. He hurried through the crowd, pushing people out of his way with furious abandon. About fifty yards farther, away from the omnipresent crowd of people, Bolan caught a glimpse of another running man. He was too far away for a positive identification, but the Arab seemed to be chasing him, which meant the running man was most likely Frank Andrews.

Bolan and Grimaldi closed in on the ambulance, with the Stony Man pilot getting there first and reaching for the rear door. He ripped it open and saw Abdullah pulling back the head of a seated man with his left hand, a long knife in his right. Grimaldi yelled and started to acquire his target, but Bolan filled the space next to him in a heartbeat later and pumped three bullets into the huge Arab. The enormous body jerked up and then back. Turning, the giant snarled and lunged forward with the knife. The Executioner shot the man two more times, his last round drilling between the man's eyebrows. Abdullah tumbled forward out of the ambulance and on to the ground. Bolan saw that three men had been handcuffed to metal braces inside the ambulance. Two of them wore black hoods. The last one, the one whose throat Abdullah was about to cut, did not. Bolan recognized the battered face of Prince Amir. A Claymore mine sat facing them and the wires leading from the mine were threaded through the links of the handcuffs.

"We've got to get them out of here," Bolan said. "Have Dundee call his bomb squad."

Dylan arrived next, with Sheriff Dundee huffing and puffing about twenty yards behind.

"Oh, my God," she said. "What'll we do?"

"I got this," Grimaldi said to Bolan. "You go after Andrews and the Arab. Most likely they're planning to set this thing off by cell phone."

"You sure?" Bolan asked.

Grimaldi nodded as he climbed up into the rear of the ambulance. "Go get those sons of bitches."

ANDROKOVICH FELT A round whiz by him with an accompanying gunshot. He glanced over his shoulder and saw Mahfuj about thirty yards behind him, a gun in his right hand. Behind him the Russian could see another figure running toward them: the big American. What was his name? Cooper?

Another shot whizzed by, and this time Androkovich saw Mahfuj's arm jerk with the recoil. He thought about pausing to return fire, about dropping that Arab son of a bitch right there, but that would give Cooper a chance to get closer. Besides, he was almost at the manhole.

The ground dipped slightly, and the Russian dropped to his side, sliding down the angled embankment to the concrete base of the manhole cover. He dropped his cell phone into his pocket and pulled out his knife. It was a KA-BAR that he'd kept strapped to his belt along with a small, high-powered flashlight. The tails of the blue paramedic shirt had concealed it easily. Fitting the blade between the metal rim and the concrete edge of the base, he pried off the cover in seconds. The corrugated, metallic rungs were set into the concrete, providing an easy, ladder-like descent. Androkovich knew from his previous reconnoitering that this hole extended down about ten yards. He had to make the descent quickly, or he'd be caught in a kill zone. No time to punch in the rest of the numbers to detonate the ambulance just yet.

But, he thought as he dropped into the hole and began a hand-over-hand descent with his feet gliding

over the sides of the rungs, a nice, big explosion would
be just the diversion he'd need to get away.

MAHFUJ REGRETTED FIRING the gun. He had little chance
of hitting the Russian. It was too hard to line up a shot
while running, and Mahfuj knew it was too risky to
fire again. Additionally, he had actually been aiming
for the Russian's legs, to incapacitate rather than kill.
He needed the Russian to dial the proper number to
set off the blast, and had no doubt he could persuade
him to do just that with a bit of emphasis on placing
bullets in painful, yet nonlethal parts of the Russian's
body. He had watched the National Guard torturers
do it many times. The trick was to start low, aiming
at the feet first. The toes, actually. An injured digit
caused a lot of pain and did not necessarily send the
victim into shock.

Mahfuj increased his pace. He was used to running
short distances with bursts of speed playing football, but
this prolonged dash had winded him. His lungs burned,
but he dared not falter. Not with the faith of his father
and brothers, the fate of his nation, riding on his shoulders. He had to catch him.

And the Russian had dropped out of sight.

What was this?

Mahfuj ran harder, then did a quick glance behind
him. The big American, the one who had been watching
him from the desert warfare school, was about thirty
meters behind him. Mahfuj was effectively caught between two foes. As he continued running, he stuck the
Secret Service man's pistol under his left arm, pointing
behind him, and fired off the remaining rounds. He kept
firing until the slide locked back, then he dropped it.

He had no ammunition to reload it. Mahfuj had no idea if he'd hit the trailing American or merely slowed the man's progress, nor did it matter. He ran up the slight incline in the Russian's footsteps and saw the dip in the ground and the open manhole cover.

The Russian had gone underground, and Mahfuj knew what he had to do. He took three long strides to stop himself as he pulled the Beretta out of his belt.

He would continue after the Russian, but first he would kill the troublesome American.

BOLAN HAD BEEN closing the distance between him and the Arab when the man began shooting wildly behind him. The Executioner saw that the man wasn't aiming, and the shots were fanning out to the left. Angling to the right, Bolan took out his Berretta 93-R. He held off firing. Shooting on the run was seldom accurate, and he was cognizant that he only had three magazines total. He knew from experience that ammunition could be used up very quickly in a firefight, and he had no backup personnel on this one.

The Arab had suddenly disappeared in what appeared to be a dip in the ground. Bolan knew the area had slight arroyos. It also had an underground network of storm drains. Were Andrews and the Arab heading for one of them?

Bolan had seen the Arab firing at Andrews as they both ran. That meant that their relationship had to have soured in some way. Perhaps Andrews lacked the zealotry to complete what now had to be a failed mission. Or perhaps it was something else. Maybe Andrews had the cell phone, and the Arab wanted to detonate it sooner rather than later.

Bolan angled to the right as he approached the area where the Arab had disappeared. The embankment elevated with a slight incline, and Bolan threw himself forward and rolled twice as he neared the edge, not wanting to silhouette himself on top of the ridge. As he peered over the edge, he saw the Arab at the bottom of the downgrade with a blue steel semiautomatic pistol in his hand. It appeared to be a Beretta.

The Arab saw him at the same instant and straightened his arm to fire, but he was a split second too late. The 3-round burst from Bolan's 93-R rippled across the Arab's chest. He hunched forward, staggered for two steps, and raised his gun again. Bolan squeezed off another quick burst, and the Arab grunted and fell forward, the gun falling from his hand. The Executioner rolled his body over the edge of the slope, got to his feet and ran down to the bottom. The Arab was seriously wounded, judging from the sucking sound he made taking each breath, but he still grabbed for his dropped weapon. Bolan stepped on the man's arm and picked up the Beretta himself. It was the same caliber as his own gun. Now he had additional ammo.

Bolan patted down the wounded man for other weapons and any cell phones. He found two, one of which appeared to be a satellite phone. The soldier pocketed the items and looked at the man's wounds. The blood leaking through the right side of the light blue shirt was dark. Bolan's bullets had hit the Arab's liver, no doubt. His face already had taken on the graying cast of someone near death.

"You're too late, American," the Arab said. "You cannot stop us. Arabia will be free of the yoke of Saud tyranny."

He coughed up blood, smiled beatifically, then shook with a dying spasm.

Bolan touched the barrel of his Beretta to the dead man's open, sightless eye.

No involuntary flicker of response, no sign of life.

Bolan moved to the open manhole cover and took a quick peek downward. A series of metal rungs imbedded in the concrete wall formed a ladder that went down about thirty feet. No doubt Andrews, who'd been ahead of both of them, was down there now, but was he running through the tunnels or lying in wait for one of them to follow?

Bolan's hearing had been slightly impinged by the fired rounds, but he was confident that if the ambulance bomb had gone off, he would have heard it. That meant that the people at the site were still in danger. And Andrews most likely had the cell phone that could set off the blast. Being underground could block the transmission, so that meant he had to be found before he got to a place where he could climb out of the underground network. Bolan moved to the edge of the circular concrete hole and looked down, holding his Beretta. The ladder descended into darkness. Bolan felt for the flashlight in a pouch on his belt. It was there. He started to pull it out, then stopped. Instead, he holstered his Beretta and grabbed the dead Arab.

Going down into the dark unknown was always better if you had a friend, he thought, as he dragged the dead man to the edge of the manhole, looped his feet over the edge and positioned himself over the opening. Bracing his back against the side opposite the rungs, Bolan lowered the dead body feet first. He gripped the rung with his left hand and the collar of the dead man's shirt with his right. Pressing his own body against the opposing wall for leverage, he was able to keep lowering the corpse downward. After about fifteen feet the darkness seemed to expand, and Bolan could feel the vertical tunnel widening. The wall he'd been pressing his back against was ending.

Suddenly a series of shots sounded from below. Bolan dropped the body and grabbed his Beretta. The selector switch was set on 3-round burst, and he held the weapon under the concrete ceiling and sent a burst of shots in a semicircular arc as he simultaneously dropped the rest of the way down.

He landed on flat concrete, the impact sending a jolt of pain up his feet and into his absorbing leg muscles. Instead of remaining upright, Bolan used the momentum to continue all the way down, flattening out next to the corpse. Three muzzle-flashes lit up the darkness about twenty yards away from him in a black expanse. The rounds made a squishing sound as they pierced the dead body next to him. Bolan returned fire into the abyss as he reached for his mini flashlight. By the time he got it out and shone it in the direction of the muzzle-flashes, he could see the silhouette of a man running.

Bolan took aim and fired.

The silhouette kept going, zigzagging now. The Executioner assumed he had missed.

Getting to his feet, he raced in the same direction, periodically fanning his flashlight beam over the area in front of him. It widened to a long tunnel with an arched ceiling of smooth concrete. The air smelled cool with a hint of dampness, but lacked the stench that he expected. Bolan did a quick survey of the pathway before him and shut off his flashlight. Despite a slight cant to the floor, to allow for storm water drainage, the path was basically flat and unobstructed. He stayed to the left, assuming that Andrews was most probably right-handed and any rounds he fired while running would likely stray right. Unless he stopped and turned around, in which case it would be a toss-up.

Bolan quickened his pace, zigzagging to the center and then right.

A bright flash appeared ahead in the darkness, accompanied a second later by a thunderous clap and the whiz of a bullet that zipped by to the immediate right of Bolan's head.

He brought up his Beretta and stitched a quick, 3-round burst across the expanse ahead, the muzzle-flashes from his own weapon looking like split-second igniting flares. Bolan flattened to the ground and waited. No more rounds came. His adversary was either waiting or running.

Either way, he's a target, Bolan thought, and fired another burst.

He rolled twice to the right and held his flashlight next to his weapon. Pressing the button on its end, Bolan swept the beam in an arc through the inky blackness.

Nothing. Andrews was on the run again.

Bolan wondered if the man knew where he was going, or if he'd just happened upon this route through sheer luck. If it were the former, he had a definite advantage. He knew the twists and turns and how to get where he wanted.

Bolan knew one thing for sure: he couldn't let Andrews reach the open sky. That would free up the cell phone transmission and allow him to detonate the ambulance bomb.

He pushed himself to his feet and began to run.

It was all or nothing at this point. Everything to gain and everything to lose. A gambler's roll of the dice. But this was Vegas, after all.

ANDROKOVICH FELT THE pain in his right side with each step. One of the American's bullets had hit him, but it felt like a graze, or perhaps a through-and-through. His breath was coming in ragged bursts. This man chasing him was indomitable. He felt like stopping, resting, but knew he couldn't. At the last second he sensed the passageway narrowing, the ceiling slanting downward. He kicked something, and he jerked until he realized it was only an empty bottle. It skidded across the floor. His feet dragged through more discarded junk. Suddenly, he knew where he was, and it renewed him. The tunnel angled left, then right as it emerged to the storm drain plate in the deep arroyo. The place where the homeless vagabonds lived underneath the hot days and bright lights.

The pain in his side lessened as he turned the corner. He knew he had only perhaps fifty more yards to go. He switched on his flashlight and saw an old man wrapped in a blanket, his bleary eyes blinking at the sudden brightness.

"Who're you?" the old man asked. His bare arms were so skinny they looked like the tendrils of a plant.

"Get up," the Russian ordered, moving forward and pulling the old guy away from his blanket. He shoved the man into the center of the tunnel, back toward the advancing American, and said, "Keep moving that way."

"Hey, mister, I ain't done nothing to you," the old man said. "Lemme alone."

"Move, you old piece of shit," Androkovich yelled and fired a round in the old man's direction, close enough to scare him. The man took off running, yelling, "Don't hurt me, don't hurt me."

The Russian looked in the other direction and saw the rectangular opening with the sunlight shining down. He had twenty-five yards to freedom.

And to detonation.

DESPITE THE LOUD reverberations of sound from the rounds going off in the tunnel, Bolan's hearing was coming back. He put it down to adrenaline and strained to listen as he ran. The persistent ringing aside, he was sure he'd heard voices, someone yelling.

The corridor narrowed. The wall ahead was solid, and the tunnel angled sharply to the left. He positioned himself at the right-angle turn, and using the corner to shield most of his body, he leaned outward, searching the immediate area with the Beretta in his right hand, his left hand underneath holding the flashlight. Someone was running toward him—someone yelling.

Had Andrews gone off the deep end?

Bolan pressed the button of the flashlight and illuminated the passageway. A thin bearded man in tattered clothes and with a terrified expression was approaching.

"Don't hurt me, don't hurt me, don't, don't don't—"

Bolan grabbed the man and brought him to the ground. "Where is he?" Bolan asked.

"Don't hurt, don't hurt me," the man said. He buried his face in his hands.

Bolan told the man to stay there and got to his feet. Holding the Beretta at combat-ready, he sprinted forward, figuring that Andrews had used the old man as a diversion to gain more ground. He switched on his flashlight and swept the area ahead with a quick motion.

The beam caught several dark drops on the concrete.

Blood.

Bolan didn't see this as an advantage. It might slow Andrews, but it could also make him more dangerous.

The most dangerous opponent is one who has nothing to lose, Bolan thought.

Bad odds, even for Vegas.

ANDROKOVICH COULD SEE the lighted passageway that led to the arroyo. It was only about five yards ahead now. His side ached as he moved, and he could feel the blood pumping out of his body with each step. Perhaps the bullet had done more damage than he'd thought.

Three yards now.

Noise behind him.

He turned, saw the American and raised his weapon, firing off three more rounds.

How many did he have left?

He didn't know, but the slide wasn't locked back, so he knew the SIG Sauer was not empty. No time to drop the magazine.

Only one yard to go.

Something stung his upper back. Another damn bullet?

He turned and fired the remaining rounds in the American's direction, his fingers fumbling with the cell phone as he continued to walk. The brightness was only a short distance away now. The sunshine looked bright on the dry, reddish tan earth. Two more steps. The slide had locked back on the SIG, so he dropped it, concentrating on punching in the final numbers and then pressing Send as he worked his body through the enlarged gap between the wire mesh of the dilapidated metal screen and the concrete wall. He felt the wonderful, hot, burning rays of the sun on his face.

It would be a big bang. A really big bang.

BOLAN HAD CROUCHED to avoid the final series of wild shots from Andrews. The man had dropped his gun and scrambled out of the drainage tunnel through what looked like a space between the drain filter and the wall. The soldier ran as fast as he could to the opening. He leaned out and saw a pair of legs working furiously to ascend the embankment. It was Andrews, and he was holding a cell phone.

The Executioner leaned through the opening and squeezed off three rounds, each one striking Andrews in the upper back. He jerked with the impacts, arching his back, and tumbled over, flopping down and sliding to a stop at the bottom of the arroyo. Bolan managed to fit through the tight opening and ran to the fallen man. His hand still clutched the cell phone. A could of dust hung in the air like wispy smoke.

Bolan strained to listen.

No loud booms.

Perhaps Andrews hadn't had time to send the call.

Something buzzed near Bolan's ear. He reached up and found his ear mike hanging next to his neck. He reinserted it and heard Grimaldi's voice sounding far away.

"Sarge, are you there?"

"I am," Bolan said.

"Did you get them?"

"I did."

"Good. Everything's great here, too. I managed to disarm this puppy all by my lonesome."

"Roger that, Jack."

It looked as if this one would end with a whimper instead of a bang.

CHAPTER TWENTY-ONE

Saudi Arabian Embassy, Washington, D.C.

Mustapha readied the special tea for the king. The old monarch's Rolex watch sat on the solid gold tray next to the cup. Word had come down hours ago that the king's grandson had been abducted, and the American authorities assured them that every measure was being taken to assure his quick rescue.

This, of course, was no surprise to Mustapha, who had gotten an earlier text from Mahfuj saying, We have him.

Mustapha had thought the old man would keel over at the news, but he did not. He did, however, grasp his chest and sit down immediately. The king's personal physician, who had traveled with them from Riyadh, gave the old king some medicine and advised that he rest.

"How can I rest at a time like this?" the king bellowed.

An hour had passed since the news, and Mustapha assumed that they would be waiting by the phone and watching the American news channels for any updates.

It was time for him to return the king's Rolex, along with some tea to bolster the monarch's spirits…and stop his already overtaxed heart.

Mustapha had mixed in the special pills that the Russian had given him, guaranteed to stop a healthy heart and leave no trace, much less the weakened one of an old man.

The king was in the next room. The phone had rung a few minutes earlier. News, no doubt of Prince Amir's untimely demise. It was a time of sorrow, a time for commiseration, a time for the warming numbness of the special tea.

As he picked up the tray, Mustapha felt his cell phone vibrate with an incoming text.

That would be Mahfuj telling him that the deed was no doubt done.

Only a few more pieces needed to be assembled. The four desert falcons were soaring now, zooming in on their prey.

But wait. Mustapha reached into the long pocket of his *thobe* and took out the vibrating phone. It was his satellite phone, the one for international calls. This message was from Mamum, back in Riyadh. Mustapha's eyes widened in disbelief as he read it.

All is lost. They have discovered us. They are here.

This cannot be, Mustapha thought. The plan had been foolproof, like a chess game, each move so well thought out in advance.

Suddenly he heard voices in the adjacent room. The king's room. Loud voices, gruff, but joyous. Mustapha turned and saw the king's bodyguards framed in the doorway, their faces emblematic of doom. The largest one, Hamid, pulled his *thobe* aside, and his hand closed over his *jambiya*, his eyes burning in his brutish face with unbridled fury.

Mustapha set the cell phone on the table and stared at the long, shiny blade as Hamid drew it from its sheath.

The four desert falcons have fallen from the sky, Mustapha thought. But I shall leave this Earth on my own terms.

Picking up the teacup, he brought it to his lips and drained it in one long delicious drink. He felt only a slight burning as it went down, smiling as he set the cup back on the tray.

"*Inshallah*," he said, as the first burst of pain came quickly, followed by the enveloping darkness.

EPILOGUE

Bolan, Grimaldi, Dundee and Dylan sat at the big table in the FBI office conference room sipping coffee from paper cups.

"Well, I can't say I'll be sorry to see you two leave town," Dundee said, accompanied by a low chuckle. "I haven't seen so many bodies dropping since I don't know when. I'm just glad we got those SOBs and prevented another marathon bombing."

"Damn straight," Grimaldi stated.

Bolan nodded in agreement.

Dundee took another swig from his cup and gave Bolan a sideways glance. "So tell me the truth, you guys aren't DOJ, are you?"

Bolan said nothing.

"Hey," Grimaldi said, leaning forward. "Haven't you figured out who we are yet?" He cocked his thumb toward Bolan and lowered his voice. "He's the Lone Ranger."

Dylan laughed. "You aren't so bad yourself, *Tonto*. If you hadn't disarmed that IED, we'd all have gone up in smoke, along with the prince and a lot of innocent bystanders."

"How's the prince doing?" Bolan asked.

"He should be released from the hospital shortly," Dylan said, standing up. "I'm sure he'll have quite a reception waiting for him in Washington when he gets there."

Bolan had already been briefed by Brognola that the Saudis had taken quick steps to end the planned coup as soon as they were notified of the plot. The identification of the dead Arab on the landing strip at Camp Freedom had told them where to look. Apparently, two of the dead Arabs here were related to the other plotters in Saudi Arabia.

"Suffice it to say, there'll be a lot of heads rolling in the square in Riyadh," Brognola had said.

"I wonder if His Royal Highness learned anything at the desert warfare school?" Grimaldi said, getting to his feet.

"Actually," Dylan said, "he was rather humbled by the whole thing. He even apologized to me for his quote, 'thoughtless, ignorant remarks' before, and thanked me for saving his life."

"What?" Grimaldi said.

"The man who could be king," Bolan stated. "Maybe the experience broadened his horizons for the better. That happens sometimes when you look death in the face."

"He wanted me to convey his appreciation to the two of you, as well," Dylan added.

"Hell," Grimaldi said, "I feel all choked up hearing that."

"I really do think he was sincere," Dylan said. "I'd better go to the hospital and check on him."

"Check on *him*?" Grimaldi said. "How about I take you to this great restaurant I know of in the Venetian, and afterward we can go for one of those gondola rides in the hotel."

Dylan smiled. "I'm very flattered to be asked, but I really can't. As soon as the prince is released, I have to escort him back to D.C. to meet the king. He specifically asked for me."

Grimaldi took a deep breath. "Yeah, well, maybe some other time, then?"

She started to go, then stopped and leaned forward to give him a hug. "Maybe next time. I'll tell one of the other agents to show you out."

Bolan, Grimaldi and Dundee watched her walk down the hallway.

Grimaldi sighed. "Man, I usually don't strike out. I don't feel like eating Italian tonight, anyway. How about I take you two over to the Peppermill and treat you guys to a couple of steaks?"

Bolan grinned. Grimaldi's ego seldom took a beating, so maybe it would do them both some good to unwind a bit before heading back to the Farm. He knew another crisis would be waiting for him. There always was.

* * * * *